Bitter

Business

*to Eileen!
hope things go
well with Joel's
surgery. we will be
praying.
Ann
Cobb*

ANN COBB

706 872 6183

Cover Art by Mary Reynolds

Book Design & Production by WatersDesigns.com

ISBN: 978-0-9883279-8-6

First Edition: February 2015

Please visit the author's web site at: www.AnnCobb.net

Printed in the USA

I dedicate Bitter Business to my readers. Without their words of encouragement the writing process would be more difficult and much less rewarding. I thank each and every one of my readers for your kind words. It makes all the difference.

Acknowledgments

To Margaret Newberry who keeps on reading.

To Sharon Fleming who has the extraordinary ability to master the English language.

To Sandra Ray who can spot a misspelled word a mile away.

To Shari Waters who continues to impress me with her technical abilities.

To Mary Reynolds who brings color and charm to the book cover with her beautiful painting.

Without these people *Bitter Business* would never be more than a document on my computer.

Also by Ann Cobb

Bee's Business
Back to Business

CHAPTER ONE

L et's do it," my older sister Bess announced with
that familiar gleam in her eyes that she always
gets when she is up to something. "We are certainly
capable of hosting a family reunion. All it'll take is
some thought and a little organized work to back it
up. It would be just wonderful to see all the cousins.
We should entertain now that we've completely
finished remodeling the house. Why don't we ask
some of our old friends to come, too, and have a
grand ole time? Come on now, think about it, Bee. I
can just see it. Lots of good food and plenty of time
to sit around and reminisce about old times."

And that's how it all got started. A big family
and friends' reunion. Little did we know that we
were laying out the groundwork for a murder. And
I mean a murder right here on the farm. It makes me
shudder as I think about it now. I should have

1

known better than to listen to my older, but not always wiser, sister. We should have settled for long distance telephone calls to our family members, but no-o, we went all the way and planned a cousins' weekend right here on the farm. Looking back now, I realize I should never have fallen for the idea, but Bess, as usual, caught me at a weak moment.

It was an early spring day. Looking for Bess's glasses had become our every morning ritual. She claimed this particular morning that someone had mysteriously removed them from the shelf over the washing machine. By the way, there was nobody else around the house this morning besides her and me. "There's no way on God's green earth that I've misplaced them again," she adamantly declared with her hands perched on her now ample hips. "I went out to feed the chickens, and when I returned, they had simply vanished into thin air."

I'm really not one hundred percent sure of that. Even though Bess and I had cracked two murders in the past two years and had helped our pitifully inept Sheriff Ledbetter solve several mysteries around the county, we continually misplaced things around the house. Is that a sign of senility? I sincerely hope not.

I believe I had truly instilled the makings of a good private eye in Bess. Even though it was a late-in-life endeavor, we were good at detective work. We had named our business enterprise the B and B Investigative Service and were in high demand around town from anybody who needed a mystery solved.

Why, just last month Bess discovered who the culprit was who was stealing our good friend Mildred's new underwear from her clothesline. It turned out to be Mrs. Ricketson who lived right down the street from Mildred. Bess noticed Mrs. Ricketson wearing a new slip with a Sears and Roebuck tag while they were both getting permanent waves over at Thelma's Cut and Curl. Thelma had asked that they both remove their dresses and put on dusters that she provided for her customers while she applied the toxic mixture to their hair. Bess, a very observant detective, noticed right away that Mrs. Ricketson had on an exact replica of a slip Mildred had described in her police report as being stolen. Discreetly, Bess mentioned right there in the beauty parlor that Sheriff Ledbetter was hot on the trail of the underwear thief in town and that when he caught up with the bandit he, or she, would wind up on the chain gang for at least twenty years, with no parole for good behavior. That very slip and the rest of the unmentionables were found hanging on Mildred's clothesline the very next morning with an unsigned note of apology clamped under a clothespin. Mrs. Ricketson has a tendency to be a kleptomaniac and had narrowly missed that bullet.

Even though Bess was good at undercover detective work, she would never admit to absentmindedness, or doing anything incorrectly, for that matter. In her way of thinking she certainly would never be so distracted as to leave her glasses over the washing machine, of all places. I kept telling her that we're both getting on in years, and forgetfulness is just a natural part of aging. She claims that's all malarkey. She's sixty-two now, older than me by one year, and I'm very absentminded myself.

"You'll find them directly," I insisted, as I rinsed the eggs before putting them in our new refrigerator. "Bess, I don't know how you knew we'd enjoy this icebox so much, but you were absolutely right on target."

"Bee, it's not an icebox; it's a refrigerator, and it is a wonderful convenience, isn't it?" She gushed as she continued, "I just love the shape of our ice cubes. Those metal ice trays with that little lever on top is such a wonderful invention. The other night while we were entertaining the girls over here for our monthly missionary meeting, I overheard Mildred talking about how refreshing our tea tasted with those little ice cubes floating around. I refrained and didn't say a word about us having a new refrigerator. I didn't want to sound as if I was boasting or anything. You know Mildred would have been so jealous of us since her ancient icebox is on its last leg. The last time she entertained the missionary society at her house, I noticed she had a big metal pan slid under her icebox to catch all that rusty water draining from somewhere underneath the monstrosity."

"Bess, that's why you're an excellent detective; you notice absolutely everything. And I really hate to bring it up...but that program Mildred gave about those missionaries in Brazil was one we've heard before, I'm sure. I swear she absolutely cannot put two sentences together without it coming out bor-ing with a capital B."

"I know what you mean, Bee. I believe she read that same old program the last time she was in charge of the meeting. I imagine those missionaries she was talking about are at least a hundred and fifty years old by now and dead and buried somewhere. Oh, and Bee, absolutely nobody can come close to topping the delicious refreshments we served at the meeting here. I swear every crumb of our pies was eaten. Three people even asked for the recipe."

"Bess, you didn't give it out, did you? Mama didn't want every Tom, Dick, or Harry fooling around with that recipe. She meant for us to take it to our graves." I anxiously held my breath until Bess answered.

"I didn't blab. I told everyone I couldn't remember all the ingredients right then. You know good and well I wouldn't give away top secret information like that. Nobody can cook that pie like Mama always could anyway, except maybe me...or maybe...you. I can just imagine Vera will probably serve some old dry pound cake next month. You do remember the next meeting's at her house, don't you? At least we won't have to do a thing...just show up over there and try to wash down her petrified cake with her weak tea."

"Thank heavens for that. You know, Bess, I think everybody did notice how wonderful the house looked. Mildred pretended to go to the bathroom right before we served the refreshments just to get a good gander at the rest of the house. She can really be so nosy. We did put our best foot forward, though. Thank you for everything, Bess. Now that you're living at the farm with me, I feel as if the old house has come to life again. Did anybody at the meeting mention to you how elegant the house looked?"

"Not a single solitary soul. I think everybody's just plain out jealous," Bess answered indignantly. "I thought surely somebody would say something about our new living room drapes. After all the effort I put into sewing those things, and then not a word was muttered!"

"We've had the entire house painted," I added. "Had the floors refinished, even added a new bathroom, and not one person commented on how nice everything looked. You'd think they were all blind or something. Well, I'm not saying a word to Vera the next time we're over at her house about that new living room settee of hers. I don't know if I mentioned it to you or not, but Tillman finally turned a little money loose and allowed Vera to buy the thing. I had to endure her bragging about it a good fifteen minutes over the telephone the other day, but I haven't actually seen it. I finally told her I had to see who was at the door just to get off the telephone with her. She won't enjoy it, though. All she'll think about is keeping it clean. I doubt Tillman will ever be allowed to even sit on it. I imagine she's already covered it with a big ole piece of vinyl to keep the dust off. Oh well, Vera deserves that new settee after everything Tillman's put her through lately. You know, that man's really getting senile."

"What on earth makes you say that, Bee?"

I gave the counter one last swipe and folded the dishcloth over the back of the chair. "Bess, didn't you notice him the last time we were over there helping Vera cut those squares for the missionary quilt? Tillman walked into the house from the barn and asked Vera where his clean handkerchiefs were. For goodness' sake, you'd think the man would know where he keeps his handkerchiefs after all these years. I mean, she had to tell the man at least four times where they were kept. You know good and well she puts them in the same drawer she's put them in for at least the last hundred years. I thought it was downright pitiful. Tillman's always been so active and on top of everything, but I'm afraid he's really beginning to slip. How poor Vera, as high-strung as she is, will be able to handle it is beyond me."

"Bee, I did notice that, but I haven't thought much about it. Gracious, what would Vera do if something happened to that man? She'd go plumb crazy if she didn't have Tillman to boss around."

Vera and her husband Tillman are our closest neighbors and live right up the road from us toward town. She and Tillman stayed on and cared for her parents until her parents' deaths several years before, much the same way Will and I had cared for Bess's and my parents.

"Well, the same thing could strike us. You know as well as I do Mama had an aunt who couldn't remember her own name or address. What was her name, anyway? It seems to have left me momentarily. I'm sure you remember her, Bess. She died when I was about six or seven. I distinctly remember she died the day after the barn caught fire and Daddy lost his prize milk cow in the blaze. It was something like Etta or Retta or something that ended with an 'etta.' Lordy, I hope the affliction isn't hereditary. We could acquire it, too."

"Humph. Speak for yourself," Bess quickly answered as she picked up the broom and began sweeping the kitchen floor with as much determination as if she were attacking the Nazis. Bess doesn't know how to do anything halfway or calmly.

My mind began to wander as I glanced about the room, and I thought how wonderful the house looked. Bess had recently moved lock, stock, and barrel from her neat little house in town out to the farm to live with me. We're both widowed now, and it seemed to be the practical solution for both of us. I had toed the line earlier when Bess and I started the house remodel and hadn't allowed Bess to totally remodel the kitchen, but we did purchase a new refrigerator. We had splurged more than we should have on the house since both of us need to keep a close watch on our finances. You can only stretch a dollar bill so far, you know.

Bess and I were raised right here in this very home by loving and devoted parents. The farm has been my home throughout my entire life. Will, my late husband, and I had purchased the place from my parents and stayed on after we married many years before. We lovingly cared for Mama and Daddy as Will farmed and nurtured the land. We raised our daughter, Margaret, into a fine young woman. She's teaching school over in the next county now but plans to marry a wonderful man, Dr. Walter Jackson, next year. Walter practices medicine right here in Jefferson County. Bess and I have plenty of time to plan a nice wedding, I hope.

Bess stopped sweeping long enough to glance out of the kitchen window. In a fleeting melancholy moment, she sighed. "I do love living here with you, Bee. We absolutely make a great team. It's a great comfort to me that you welcomed me into your home, now my home." But then with more resolve, she declared, "Now I have got to find my glasses. Notice around for them. I'll check the porch when I finish the sweeping. Maybe I overlooked them."

I found Bess's glasses lying on the kitchen table under the pattern directions for the church dress she intended to cut out that afternoon. As I handed them over to her, she sheepishly smiled and

ANN COBB

halfheartedly admitted she must have left them there
after all. Bess has a hard time coming down from her
self-constructed ivory tower.

Bess reached for the dustpan. "Bee, we can't
let the grass grow under our feet. We've got so
much to do to get ready for the reunion. We should
plan it for the last weekend of this month, and we're
already running out of time." Before leaning over to
sweep the dirt and dust into the dustpan, Bess
glanced at the calendar from the Jeffersontown Bank
and Trust Company hanging on the wall by the back
door. "Today is April five, 1948. In a matter of a few
weeks, we must have this house and yard absolutely
spotless. This is our chance to show the whole place
off to our kin. I'm so excited. Let's start with the
windows. I'll wash the insides, and you wash the
outsides. That way we can knock that little chore out
in no time flat."

"Why do I have to do the outsides? You
could do the outsides, and I can do the insides."

"You know you like to be outside better than I
do. Now, it's settled. By the way, we need to get a
good head count of everybody we should invite."
Bess laid the broom and dustpan down and reached
for a pencil and a piece of notepaper.

"You know, since Mama and Daddy died, it
doesn't seem as important to everybody to have a
get-together. I just don't know what the problem is.
You and I'll have to do all the hard work. Nobody
else will have to do a darn thing…except show up
with a covered dish."

10

"They better bring more than one dish," Bess emphatically answered. "You and I absolutely cannot provide all the food for a two-day period."

"Bess, let's be optimistic. I'm sure most will bring several things. Do you think Cousin Doretha and Cousin Cooper will even attempt to come? She telephoned a few days ago and mentioned that she's been troubled with the gout recently and is practically confined to home right now. You know with Cooper getting on in years, it's really hard for them to go anywhere. I think Cooper and Doretha are really the sweetest, most gentle people I know. They were always Mama's favorites of all her kin people."

"I know, Bee. All my growing up years, I always thought they were a married couple. I never dreamed they were brother and sister until I was about twelve and began to wonder why they never had any children. Mama just hollered with laughter when she explained to me that neither had ever married, and they were always content to live together. I sure do hope they can come!"

"Surely they can come. After all, it's only ten miles over to their place. We could have Vonion pick them up in the mornings and get them back home safely later in the day. Vonion won't mind a bit," I answered, as I began to realize how much Bess and I would have to rely on Vonion and Ora Lee for help as we began to plan the reunion.

Vonion and his faithful wife Ora Lee are my farm caretakers and have lived here on the farm almost as long as I have. Vonion had come by the farm soon after he and Ora Lee married and asked Daddy for a job. He was hired on the spot and never left. He and Ora Lee raised their family in the small frame house down the lane from our big house. Vonion worked right alongside Daddy on the farm, and Ora Lee helped in the house and yard. Bess and I had answered to Ora Lee in our youth, same as we did to Mama. I still do. Ora Lee never could tolerate laziness or slothfulness in children, and I had periodically been both. I never feared her, but I respected her authority, knowing she was the one with the switch, and she did use it frequently on Bess and me, as well as her own children.

As the years progressed, a new and different admiration for her replaced my earlier feelings. Will and I relied on Vonion and Ora Lee just as Mama and Daddy always did. It never occurred to me until a few years ago that they were gradually aging. Moving a little slower now, but with the same authority they always wielded, they continued to help manage the place. Even though I rented all my acreage out to Tom Wilson, a neighboring farmer, my need of and devotion to Vonion and Ora Lee had stood the test of time. They remained on the farm, hopefully for the duration of their days left here on Earth.

"Oh, he's gonna feel needed all right," Bess readily replied. "I've got so much work for Vonion to do in the next few weeks, it's gonna make his head swim. I just wish I could figure out a way to make that hog pen smell a little less pungent before the reunion."

"Bess, go easy on Vonion. He's not as young as he used to be, you know. And try to keep your attention on things you and I can control and not things we can't do a thing about. A hog pen is a hog pen, and there's no changing the odor. Just try to remember how good that bacon smells sizzling on top of the stove. Now let's get back to reunion business. We should go ahead and call Cousin Edwina, too."

"Oh, come hell or high water, Edwina will make her presence known this year of all years. She wouldn't miss an opportunity to brag about that free-loading son of hers and Richard's for all the gold in Fort Knox. You know precious Dickie is supposed to graduate from law school soon, and Edwina's gonna be harping about that boy and all his accomplishments the whole time she and Richard are here."

"How well I know. I just dread hearing about that boy over and over and over again. Maybe when we tell her about Margaret's engagement to a medical doctor, she'll shut up. After all, having a doctor in the family is a far cry better than having a lawyer in the family any ole day of the week," I replied with a smirk across my face.

"Oh, and of course Cousin Myrtle will make it. She mentioned in her last letter that she wants to come for a visit soon and that she had already purchased a round-trip ticket from South Carolina to

Georgia on the Greyhound bus for that very weekend. She's probably already laid out her entire wardrobe for the trip. Bless her heart."

"More than likely. It'll be so good to see that old soul. She's lasted a lot longer than I ever thought she would. Why, I believe she's had more ailments than anybody I've ever known. Do you remember in one of her last letters she mentioned she had just gotten over a bout with the swan flu? I've never even heard of that condition, have you?"

"Never. She probably just had a cold and wanted to make it sound a little more dramatic. She can get carried away at times. Bless her heart."

"How many times do you plan to bless her heart, Bess?"

"As many as she needs it. Bee, what do you think about us inviting a few of our friends, too? Most of our friends know the cousins, and I'm sure they'd love to be included. What do you think?" Bess asked. I knew she had already made up her mind.

"Sure we can."

"It's gonna take some planning. We definitely need to limit the number of people we invite. We can't feed everybody in Jefferson County. And everything doesn't have to be perfect, you know. A family and friends' reunion, all on the same weekend. It'll be easy!" Famous last words!

I'm glad my persnickety sister says that everything doesn't have to be perfect. But that'll be the day. The word imperfection is not even in her dictionary, and anything less than impeccable is downright unchristian-like in her opinion.

CHAPTER TWO

A few telephone calls later, we had our invitations completely taken care of. It seemed everybody was eager for a get-together. All Bess and I had to do was get the house and yard ready and prepare food.

In a matter of days, Bess was on a roll, and Vonion and I were hanging on for dear life by a very thin thread. Bess had plenty of orders for everyone. Even Ora Lee wasn't exempt from chores. Bess put her to work starching every doily and curtain on the place and dusting lampshades. That is, after Ora Lee was told to wipe every lightbulb in the house and clean the mirrors and all the picture frames. By the way, who has ever heard of cleaning lightbulbs?

I had been appointed to wipe down every wall and clean the baseboards, window ledges, and molding. Vonion was told to sweep down the screens on the porch and trim the hedges. Afterwards, he was to wash down the sides of the house with the garden hose. I was just hoping and praying we'd all survive this newly self-appointed dictator without a prison outbreak or an attempt to overthrow the out-of-control tyrant.

The previous night, after I had finally retired to my bed with my body lathered in Ben Gay and with strong feelings that the only way out of this prison camp was to flee, I started praying that maybe Bess would let up and be a little more compassionate the next day. I soon realized that wasn't about to happen. As soon as the sun broke over the horizon, Bess resumed her position, and my day of torment began all over again. This time, "give it a little more elbow grease," I was told after Bess inspected my labor from the day before. I could hear Vonion out in the yard muttering something to himself about committing hari-kari. All I could truthfully say about that was he'd better wait to speed up his demise until this reunion business was over, or Bess would eradicate him all over again.

It wasn't quite midday yet, but after several hours of cleaning baseboards, I was exhausted. Every five minutes or so I had to get off my knees to stand and stretch just to get the feeling back into my aching legs. I had been told that every piece of furniture had to be moved out from the wall as I went along. Bess insisted that the backs of the furniture had to be wiped down and the floor underneath scrubbed. I thought that was going a little too far since nobody would ever in a million years know if there is a little dust back there; nevertheless, I was performing the chore just as Bess had instructed. And it was torment!

I was standing in a daze staring down into my bucket, trying to make the executive decision of whether to go ahead and change the dirty water now or wait until I wiped the next window ledge (or maybe just kick the bucket out of the window and go on strike) when I heard the honk from the mail carrier's car as it pulled into the yard. Maybe Mr. Johnny Mack, our mail carrier, was alerting us that the new, top-of-the-line, goose-down pillows we ordered a few days earlier from Sears and Roebuck had arrived in the mail. Bess and I both agreed that we could not dare ask any of our reunion guests to lay their heads on the old pillows Mama and I had made from cotton samples years and years before since they were beginning to smell a bit musky. Excitedly, I dropped my cleaning rag into the bucket, causing dirty water to splash onto our new floral rug, and hurried out the door and down the porch steps. Hopefully, Bess wouldn't notice the rug was slightly damp.

I cringed as I reached the bottom step and stopped short. Mr. Johnny Mack's car was nowhere in sight, but of all the people on this earth, out by the mailbox, Earnest Lee Black was sitting in the driver's seat of his old car with a grin on his face that Ajax couldn't come close to scrubbing off. U.S.MAIL was printed in bold letters on the side of his dusty black

Chevrolet coup. I had heard earlier in the year that Mr. Johnny Mack would soon retire, but never in my wildest dreams had I imagined that Earnest Lee would be his replacement. Maybe it wasn't permanent; maybe Earnest Lee was just filling in for the day.

Earnest Lee Black had been Bess's mailman in town and had persistently tried to drive her insane. Earnest Lee would not tolerate Bess's shenanigans. He pictured himself as a representative of the federal government and would never give Bess any slack concerning the postal laws; he certainly would never bend the law concerning inadequate postage or illegal use of a mailbox. Bess couldn't tolerate Earnest Lee either. He occasionally misplaced Bess's mail and left it in other people's boxes. Once Earnest Lee mistakenly left a wedding invitation meant for the mayor and his wife in Bess's mailbox. Bess never received an engraved invitation to "the wedding of the year" in Jeffersontown and felt devastated. She was never really positive whether she was included in the exclusive list of highfalutin people. She always maintained that Earnest Lee carelessly left her invitation in somebody else's box, accidently on purpose, of course. Naturally, she withdrew from sight the day of the wedding and did not attend the social event of the season.

A war continually brewed between the two of them, and several skirmishes broke out before Bess left her house in town to move out to the farm with me, leaving hard feelings and a few battle scars. Bess always did consider herself above the law. I'm just relieved Bess restrained herself and never committed murder. Murdering an ordinary person would have been bad enough, but murdering a federal employee...I imagine she would have gotten the death penalty for that. There are some things in life you can't control and who delivers your mail is one of them.

I guess I've drug my feet long enough and not informed my readers. It was Earnest Lee who tried to court me last year but to no avail. I let him know right off the bat that while he was a welcomed guest in my house, courting (ugh) was absolutely out of the question. The very idea of me going out with the likes of him! He was far too puny and short, almost sickly looking, and not my type at all. And besides that, if Bess had any idea that I was romantically interested in Earnest Lee Black, she would have permanently flown the coop.

Bess suddenly appeared from around the corner of the house where she had been weeding the iris bed and hurried over to the mailbox. She stopped short and gasped at the sight of Earnest Lee, sitting in the mail car as if he was perched on a king's throne. With a big smirk on his face, Earnest Lee opened the car door as soon as he was sure Bess wasn't brandishing a weapon and triumphantly stepped out. A stunned Bess, with her dirty hands over her opened mouth, took a backward step, as Earnest Lee jauntily walked around his car where he removed two large packages from the back seat and laid them on the ground beside the mailbox.

I'm certain I saw hot, burning flames shoot from Bess's eyes right before she exploded. "Don't you even think about leaving our packages on the ground, Earnest Lee...that is, if you know what's good for you! Give those packages to me right now!"

Earnest Lee promptly picked the packages up from the ground, handed them to a furious Bess, and quickly jumped back into the car before Bess could take aim and throw them back at him.

Juggling the packages in her arms, Bess barked at Earnest Lee through the opened window of the car. "And don't be driving over our grass! I've been sprigging grass out here for over a month, and you're driving right over it! You're purposely trying to ruin our lawn!" Bess motioned to me to come over, and she quickly heaved the bulky packages at me as if deadly germs from a contagious disease Earnest Lee had contracted were falling all over the wrapping paper.

Earnest Lee grinned as a mouthful of chewing tobacco propelled from his puckered cheek through the car window, narrowly missing Bess, and proudly replied, "Ms. Bess, you know I wouldn't intentionally mess up your grass. I swear you get meaner and meaner. I know you'll be tickled to know I'm the new mailman out here. I've had a big promotion. Now I get to ride in an automobile and deliver the mail. I don't have to rely on my old worn-out feet and legs anymore. My walking days are finally over. Now don't get yourself all worked up over nothin'. I was gonna hand them packages over to you, but you was too busy being furious."

Earnest Lee grinned a little wider as he deposited a bundle of letters into the mailbox and victoriously pulled off after a hasty salute. I really don't believe he meant to, but his back wheels spun out of control and the car backfired, giving Bess a face full of hot, dusty air. And Bess surely didn't need any more hot air.

I was stunned as I stood there, balancing the packages, and watched as Bess angrily stomped her feet and then kicked the mailbox with all her might. Revenge was written all over her dusty, dirty face. Earnest Lee had gotten the best of Bess today, but there would be more days coming, you can bet money on that. I suppose you might argue with a federal government employee, but you'd never win. At least life on the prison farm wasn't dull today.

Lunch time gave us a short reprieve on "The Hard Labor Farm." I set the table with Mama's everyday china and was slicing loaf bread for ham sandwiches when Bess came dragging in from the iris bed. What a pitiful picture she made—stained, ripped dress, hair that hadn't seen a comb since early morning, and a frown covering her dirt-smudged face. Bess despondently closed the screen door. "Bee, are we making any progress? There's so much to be done. We haven't even planned the food for the reunion yet."

"I've been thinking about that, Bess. Let's invite Tom Wilson and see if he'll help Vonion barbecue one of Vonion's old goats. Everybody loves barbecued goat. That could be lunch for Saturday, along with our Brunswick stew. Fish for Saturday night supper. I'm quite sure Tillman would see about catching a string of red bellies from the river and frying them up. You and I can take care of all the extras. Sunday, we'll have all the leftovers and maybe make some homemade ice cream. What do you think?"

"Why, Bee, I think you are right on target again. We'll just have to catch up with those men and twist their arms if need be, but I'll bet they'll be agreeable. We need to make a grocery list and do everything ahead of time. Hey, lunch looks good. I could eat a horse."

"Bess, why don't you check with Tom after lunch? I believe I heard the tractor go by this morning. He's already begun to break land out back of the house. I'm sure you can persuade him to help out even though I know he doesn't have much free time right now with planting time upon him. I swear, Tom's such a good man. It's a pity he never married or had any children. He would have made a fine husband and father."

"Bee, he is a fine man. I've always thought of him more as a brother than anything else, so don't start matchmaking. As soon as we finish lunch, I'm gonna hunt that man down. Why don't you check things out with Tillman this afternoon? Maybe

Vera'll help out too. By the way, I brought the mail in."

Bess reached into her dress pocket and brought out a packet of letters. "I'm so mad about our federal government replacing Mr. Johnny Mack with the sorry likes of Earnest Lee that I could chew a nail right in two. Can you believe that jackass got the job? He probably wanted this route just to drive me closer and closer to my breaking point. I'm gonna fill his tires with buckshot the next time he drives over our grass. That'll teach him a lesson he won't soon forget."

"Bess, you better watch your mouth. Give the poor man a break. He's just doing what he was hired to do."

"I'm gonna give him a break all right. But it might be the kind that requires a cast."

I laughed out loud. "Let's finish our lunch and get on with this reunion business. Mercy! And, Bess, remember you said yourself, 'Everything doesn't have to be perfect.'"

"Did I say that?" Bess sheepishly asked as she looked through the small pile of mail. "A bill from the power company, a flyer from Pearly's department store, and, oh, a letter from Cousin Edwina."

"Open it, Bess. It's high time we heard from the Queen of Sheba."

Bess quickly tore into the envelope, pulled out a sheet of scented stationary, and began to read out loud. "'We'll arrive on Saturday morning, and we plan to stay until Sunday afternoon. Since I've been under the care of a doctor lately for advanced arthritis, I won't be physically able to prepare food, but I would be glad to help out with expenses.'" Bess rolled her eyes as she muttered, "Oh, brother," reached farther into the envelope and pulled out a folded check. "She's enclosed a check for two measly dollars." Bess quickly tore it to shreds. "Have you in all your life heard of anybody being so stingy and downright rude? A check of all things. What does she think two dollars will buy anyway? I wouldn't care if she left her superior self at home this year. Why, I've never been so insulted in all my entire life. She doesn't have any more arthritis in her bones than the rest of us. "

"Go on, read the rest, Bess."

"'Dickie plans to attend the reunion also. He will meet us on Saturday afternoon. He's coming from college and will stay the night. Dickie will graduate from law school in a few months, and then we will have an important lawyer in the family.'" Bess wadded the note in her fist and said, "Pooh! She's already started rubbing it in, and she hasn't even arrived yet."

"So it would seem; but Bess, be kind. Mama wouldn't want us to be thoughtless of her kin people."

The familiar clickety-clack from Will's old lawnmower drifted through the open window. "Vonion's back to work, so I guess we better finish eating and get our afternoon started."

As I was washing the last of the lunch dishes and Bess was wiping the last crumbs from the table, Ora Lee trudged through the kitchen with her arms full of starched kitchen café curtains, fresh from the line and ready to be pressed. I could tell by the way her feet were dragging and the tired expression across her face that it was just a matter of time before Ora Lee would resign her position as slave and overthrow Bess, our powerful dictator. As soon as she spotted Bess, she muttered, "A clean house is good, but this here is re-dic-u-lus."

CHAPTER THREE

I proudly report we survived the week. The farm was looking better, but I'm afraid we were all pretty wilted. The weekend had finally arrived—the weekend before the Big Weekend, that is. We had cleaned everything that didn't move and some things that did. Bess couldn't stand to think that some of our guests might detect an odor coming from the pigpen. She figured that Vonion could scrub the hogs down with a wire brush, and amazingly, he actually did perform the disgusting task, but only under much duress. After Vonion scrubbed the hogs down and let them out into the pasture, he and Bess shoveled piles and piles of manure out of the pen onto the bed of his pickup truck to be hauled away from the house and yard. Later it would be spread under the pecan trees for fertilizer. I don't really know what Bess was thinking about because miracles don't just happen overnight. Even after three big loads, all Bess's idea had accomplished was a big hole in the middle of the pen where those shiny, disinfected hogs could wallow just a little deeper in the mud and muck. Bess even sprayed the pen down with some kind of fragrant disinfectant, but it didn't work either. An hour after she had finished with her perfumed overhaul of the pen, it didn't smell a bit better. You might say it smelled worse. Imagine cleaning deodorizer mixed with "you know what." The only thing Bess's effort accomplished was that she finally realized that there are some things uncleanable, and one of those things is a hog pen. Vonion kept insisting throughout the whole process that the effort was useless, but Bess turned a deaf ear to him and kept shoveling with a vengeance. I'd bet she'd listen now. Not only had they not cleared the air out at the barn, but Bess had also wrenched her back while doing all that heavy shoveling.

With most of the cleaning out of the way, we could devote the next few days to other chores: grocery shopping, ironing tablecloths, setting up tables and chairs in the yard, and cooking. Vonion and Tom Wilson had readily agreed to barbecue a big goat, and Tillman had graciously stepped up to the plate and said he'd take care of a fish fry. Vonion instructed us not to distract him whilst he was barbecuin' 'cause he "had to focus on it and nothin' else." He had already built the pit and begun gathering oak wood for the fire. He said he dreaded picking out the prize candidate for barbecuing from his small herd since each and every one of them was particularly special to him in one way or another. Oh brother! Ora Lee was to make the barbecue sauce under Vonion's strict orders not to tell a single soul what really went into it, but Ora Lee did mention to Bess and me that Vonion had given his recipe to Roscoe so that the goat barbecuing tradition wouldn't die completely when he went on to the great beyond.

Bess endured the entire weekend in throbbing pain. Sunday school, church, or an afternoon drive through the countryside was totally out of the question for her. She kept trying to get me to commiserate with her, but I was so aggravated I never sympathized with her once. The very idea of cleaning a hog pen! With her hand pressed against her aching back, she hobbled out to the porch after a full day of seclusion in her bedroom. I pretended not to notice her obvious discomfort as I glanced over the list of guests jotted down on my Blue Horse tablet. I never glanced her way as she groaned and painfully lowered herself into the rocker right next to mine. Instead, I jotted down another entry: Old Man Peterson.

"I just don't see how we can entertain without including Old Man Peterson. He'd be hurt if we didn't invite him. Let's add him to the list."

Bess leaned forward in her chair and with a strained, pitiful voice, muttered, "I guess we can, but if we invite him, we can't leave Earl out, and this thing is getting totally out of hand." She groaned again, this time louder, and rubbed her shoulder. "We've already invited Foy Jackson, so we might as well go all the way and invite all the neighbors. But you know yourself, those old men won't provide any food. None of them can cook a lick, and we wouldn't want to serve anything they concocted if they did bring it." She reached down and rubbed her knee, and I continued to pretend not to notice.

"Bess, we're going to have to stop somewhere. Now let's invite those old geezers, and that's absolutely it. How many does that make, anyway? Vonion might have to barbecue two goats, and he's gonna fling a fit when we tell him. You'd think those old goats out in the pasture were his playmates, for goodness' sake."

"Okay, let's review. You write and I'll dictate." Bess started rubbing her neck. "First, there's you and me. Then add Vonion, Ora Lee and Roscoe. Next, Tom Wilson, Vera and Tillman, Old Man Peterson (a crusty old widower who lives down the road and has a twinkle in his eyes that's directed straight at Bee), Foy Jackson (Walter's father, another old widower who lives across the branch from us. He has had to resort to spending his days in a wheelchair since arthritis has set up in his crippled body), and Earl (another bachelor neighbor). And if we ask Earl, we absolutely have to include Mildred. (Mildred is Earl's sister and one of our dearest friends. She is a widow woman who lives in town.) Of course Sam (Bess's younger, unmarried son) and

Freddy (Bess's older son, his wife, Jean, and their two young sons) are definitely included as well as Margaret and her Walter.   Now let's add Cousin Myrtle, Cousin Edwina and Richard, and, of course, the new lawyer in the family, Dickie.   And last, but not least, Cousin Doretha and Cousin Cooper. Now we absolutely are not going to add another name. Come hell or high water, that is it...Oh, Bee!   We can't leave out Eve Waters and her children. (Eve Waters is a poor, young, neighbor lady who continues to believe that her wayward husband will magically reappear at her doorstep any day, after he left her to fend for herself and their children going on three years now.   She cares for her home and family and scrapes by with a few odd jobs she picks up around the community and with a little charity from us and many of our neighbors.)   Eve would be so hurt if she thought we didn't consider her to be one of our special friends."

"Bess, can we handle all those people?   That's a whole lot of mouths to feed."

"We can and we will.   We've got lots of help. Tillman said it wasn't a problem at all to catch the fish and fry them up. Vonion's got the goat situation totally under control.   Now let's finish our grocery list and get some rest.   Tomorrow is a big day. Do you think Ora Lee will iron those tablecloths while we finish the cleaning tomorrow?"

"Finish cleaning?   We're through with the cleaning.   I'm not picking up another mop or dust rag. You're going to have to be satisfied with things just as they are right now. Bess, this whole place is spotless. Mercy! Now, let's get something to eat and go on to bed. The Queen of England isn't making an appearance here, you know. And even if she was, I'm not cleaning another thing!"

"I guess you're right, but let's try not to mess up anything this week. Oh, Bee, what about a lemon cheese cake for Saturday and maybe a big, chocolate sheet cake for Sunday? Do you think we should bake a batch of teacakes and a couple of coconut cream pies, too? That's probably enough sweet stuff. Oh, maybe we need a few pecan pies. I think definitely I'll make pecan pies and some chewy cake like Mama used to make. The children will love my chewy cake. I don't know if I can sleep a wink with all this cooking going through my head and this throbbing pain in my body."

"Bess, you might not be able to sleep, but I can. I'm going in to fix us a bite or two for supper, and then I'm hitting the hay. I need to start tomorrow fresh and that requires sleep. Now quit thinking so hard."

"What about Brunswick stew? We should start chopping onions and boiling a couple of hens tomorrow," Bess hesitantly added.

"Let's don't attempt Brunswick stew, Bess. Nobody will miss it. Now don't say another word about it. It's too much trouble."

"If you say so, but I really think we—"

"No. Now, I told you to quit thinking so hard."

The stick hitting the side of the bucket woke me from my peaceful night's sleep. I always thought of that noise as my alarm clock, and most of the time I was glad to hear it. It reminded me that I was alive and had a whole new day to look forward to. Bess, on the other hand, hated "that racket," as she called it. "Vonion could call up those hogs quietly if he wanted to," she complained. "Daddy always did. He poured the slops in the trough, and the hogs 'bout ran over him to get to it. Daddy didn't have to make a ruckus to get their attention. The only thing he had to worry about was getting out of the way before the hungry creatures trampled him to death to get at it." I agreed that Vonion probably could, but I knew he never would.

That noise from the barnyard always gave me the reassurance that everything was as it should be here on the farm. It alerted me that Ora Lee had stirred around, giving Vonion peace about leaving their little home down the lane. I knew that all the livestock were safe, and no predator had silently come in during the night; and I knew absolutely that Vonion was alive and kicking, and in control out in his barnyard domain.

I lay there thinking how glad I was to have Bess in the next room. She, too, was probably waking up about now and assessing the day. I'd better hurry and say my morning prayer before she knocked on my door, advising me that we were already behind with our extra chores. We were to check in with Tillman and Vonion today and get a list of items they needed for their assigned meals. I was to contact Tillman, and Bess was to contact Vonion. I expect Vonion would have preferred to have me to assist him, but he can't always have his way. As soon as breakfast was over, I planned to run over to Tillman and Vera's with my Blue Horse notebook and make a list of everything he needed for the fish fry. Bess was to do the same with Vonion. We planned to make the rounds in town this afternoon, picking up all the supplies, if Bess was able. Poor thing. Hopefully, after today, we could check those two meals off the list of things to see about. Then on to the next list.

My mind continued to wander. I know sometimes I create problems with my mind, but suppose Tillman forgot about the fish fry all together? He was really not capable of remembering everything he has to do anymore. I wondered if I needed to touch base with Vera privately and see how she felt about that touchy situation. Now that Tillman was becoming a tad senile, he was probably way in over his head trying to see about catching fish, cleaning fish, and frying fish. What was I thinking, asking that forgetful old man to organize a fish fry for us? Oh, Lord, I better get on over there right now and talk with Vera! Then I had another fleeting thought…I might just have to grab Will's old fishing pole, dig worms, and head down to the river myself! How many red bellies would I need to catch to feed a big crowd of people? I decided to add a footnote to my morning prayers and ask God to make sure Tillman was able to fish and also to make sure the fish were bitin'. Lordy, what kind of predicament had I gotten myself into this time?

Bess was already stirring about as I walked into the kitchen. Even with that same pained expression across her face, I could tell she was really geared for action this morning. I had already started in about the dilemma of Tillman handling the fish fry when she stopped me dead in my tracks. "Bee, I've got enough to worry about just getting Vonion propped up to do the barbecuing without worrying about Tillman. Get on over there and talk with Vera. Make sure she stays behind that absentminded old man, too. You know she'll see about everything; we can always count on her. Now, I can't be worrying about the fish fry; I've got too many other things on my mind." As if a sharp pain suddenly hit her, she moaned and grabbed her back.

"I'm on my way, and heaven help me if Tillman can't catch those fish. I'm good at a lot of things, but fishin' isn't one of them."

Bess grimaced in pain but nodded her head.

I soon discovered that my anxieties were groundless. Tillman was not at home that morning, but at the river...fishing. He had already scrubbed the cast-iron wash pot he used for frying fish until it shined. I knew it would take a good bit of firewood to keep that washtub full of hog lard hot enough to fry the fish, but as soon as Vera showed me the mountain of firewood Tillman had chopped and stacked, my concerns completely disappeared.

"Bee, don't worry about a thing," Vera said. "You know good and well that I'm gonna stay behind that forgetful old man. Just as soon as he gets the fish cleaned, I'm gonna keep them fresh by sticking them down in my deep freezer. That way they won't spoil. Friday, I'll start thawing them all out and personally go over them again with a knife just to make sure they're clean. We'll get the pot and all the firewood over to your place by Friday morning at the latest. Old Man Peterson is helping us out by providing the lard. All we have to do is pick it up over at his place. I'd ask you to go over and get it, but I know you don't have time to avoid his romantic advances today."

I rolled my eyes at Vera and thanked her. "I don't know what I'm gonna do about that frisky old man. I've told him time and again, I'm not interested in him, but he just won't listen."

"He's still got fire under his kettle, that's for sure."

"Well, he better douse that fire soon, or I'm gonna have to completely avoid him from now on."

"Bee, you should be flattered."

"Flattered that an eighty-five-year-old man wants to court me? Vera, please."

"All right, all right. Enough said about that topic. But one day you'll be sorry."

"Vera, enough IS enough. I'm not interested in keeping company with any man, especially the likes of Old Man Peterson. Now back to the fish fry."

"Everything is completely under control. Now, go on home and worry about something else."

"Well, that certainly takes a load off of my mind, Vera. I guess I'm just a little jumpy this week. I want everything to be perfect for the weekend. Oh, I hope it doesn't rain. Vera, what am I gonna do if it rains? Where would I put all those people? And Vera, we could have a terrible spring storm. You know I remember in years past we've had some really bad wind this time of the year."

"All right now, Bee, you're letting your imagination run wild. We're having beautiful weather this spring. Go on home and relax, for goodness' sake, and if I need you for anything, I'll call."

I knew Vera was right, and I did let up on my worrying somewhat after her pep talk. I rushed home to give Bess a full report. We didn't need to worry about the fish fry, only enjoy it. Vera and Tillman didn't need our help; they had thought of everything. I couldn't wait to tell Bess we were one step closer to having a perfect weekend with friends and family!

As I pulled the car into the yard, I could hear Bess out under the barn having a heated discussion with Vonion. From the pitch of her voice, I detected she wasn't faring as well with Vonion as I had with Vera. I decided not to interfere in their warfare and went on into the house. I knew it was likely I'd hear both sides of the controversy sooner or later, anyway.

I was laying out Mama's white damask tablecloth and napkins on the kitchen table when Bess walked in. We didn't want Edwina to think we couldn't properly set a table, and Bess and I had agreed we'd have a dessert table set up in the dining room and use our fine linens and Mama's best china. I had already mixed the starch with water in my largest enamel dishpan and was ready to dip the linens into the mixture. Ora Lee would do the ironing, but her strength was limited, and I knew she wasn't able to dip and wring out a heavy tablecloth.

"Bess, there's a teeny, tiny tear in the corner of the tablecloth, but otherwise it looks perfect. I hope Ora Lee can hold out to press it this afternoon. She already ironed all the sheets and pillowcases this morning and left them in the guest bedroom. She told me to tell you not to touch a thing in there; she'll make the bed this afternoon. I'd better hurry and get these linens on the line to dry."

"Good ole Ora Lee. I don't know how she does it. She is just amazing. Even at her age, she still wants to keep doing her part. I wish I could say the same for ornery ole Vonion. He says that one goat is absolutely enough and for us to not even think twice about butchering more than one of his prize animals. What's he raising those goats for anyway, if we can't eat them? That's what I want to know."

"Well, Bess, I hate to say it, but you're up against a brick wall with that man. There are some men in this world that can be swayed, but the Vonion Washington that we know is definitely not one of them."

"Bee, I just hate that we have to depend on men. I never could depend on Fred to do a thing around the house, and now we have to depend on the likes of Vonion Washington. We're really scraping the bottom of the barrel in the men department."

CHAPTER FOUR

In my way of thinking, and my daddy always said so, too, hard work pays off. This time it really had. By late Friday afternoon the place just sparkled. No layer of dust could be detected on a thing, and I mean anything. The barn was sanitized, the chicken coop raked, and the flower beds were clean as whistles. Bess's eagle eyes had seen every unwanted intruding weed, and she had unmercifully plucked each invader up by the root. The yard was swept and the grass mowed. The windows in the house glistened in the sunlight. Sitting atop the newly mowed grass in the side yard like a crown of glory was a brand new picnic table. Bess had purchased it from the furniture store in town Tuesday morning and had it delivered yesterday in a big truck to the house as a surprise for me. Vonion had pulled the hay wagon from the barn into the yard for us to use as a substitute serving table. Bess had threatened Vonion that it had better be clean; after all, we were to use it to serve food. Vonion, trying his level best to stay in Bess's good graces, had scoured it down with lye soap and then squirted the whole thing down with the garden hose. He proudly informed Bess that there weren't notin' on or between those wood planks but air, and hit were clean air.

We were all dead tired, but we had almost made it. The goats were roasting over the spit in the edge of the woods near Vonion's backyard. (And I did say goats.) Reluctantly, Vonion had relented and butchered two of his biggest, finest goats. From a distance I could see Tom Wilson and Roscoe reared back in straight chairs around the fire as a satisfied Vonion threw another limb on top of the embers. They would probably make a night of it. That was a man's world down there, and I knew to stay far away. Drinking a little moonshine whiskey, swapping stories, and watching meat sizzle on a spit were the true makings of a satisfying night. All I had to say about that situation was they better not let that meat burn, or they'd have me and the warden—oh, I mean Bess—to answer to .

As I lingered by my kitchen window, I could also make out Ora Lee, busy sweeping the front porch of their little, unpainted home. Ora Lee still had her pride. She would want her house to pass inspection right along with the big house. She said she was almost certain the cousins would come calling on her sometime during the weekend, and she wanted her place to look its best. Ora Lee's standard of cleanliness was slightly less than mine, just as mine was considerably lower than Sister Bess's, but Ora Lee was still a particular old woman.

Bess and I had spent the better part of the last few days in the kitchen preparing everything we thought we could cook ahead of time. With the sideboard loaded down with cakes and cookies, salads and vegetables chilling in the refrigerator, and bread and rolls kneaded and rising, we cleaned the last of the flour and cinnamon from the countertops in the kitchen. I sighed heavily. "I'm ready to hit the hay. We've got a big day tomorrow, and I want to feel spry in the morning. We can finish the rolls in the morning while we heat the vegetables. I think we've done everything we can do ahead of time. "

"I think you're right. Now, Bee, don't sleep too hard on your hairdo, and remember to put your sleeping cap on."

"I will, but you know how hard it is to sleep with your head in one position. I don't know why I was completely left out in the hair department. Bess, I swear I don't know where your good hair came from." I wearily untied the apron from my waist and placed it on the kitchen table beside the jars of pickles and preserves we had laid out to be opened in the morning.

"I just spend a little time on it, that's all. I have to coax it in place the same as you. You just don't have any patience with yours. Just keep remembering Cousin Edwina will ride up here tomorrow with her hair looking as if she just stepped out of a Hollywood beauty parlor. That should give you a little incentive to work a little harder on yours in the morning."

"Oh, Bess, please don't put any more pressure on me."

"I'm just saying the truth, Bee, and you know it good and well. And I imagine she'll be wearing the latest fashion too. More than likely, Queen Edwina had Richard buy a new automobile just to show it off this weekend. But Bee, we can't let them intimidate us. They've got their problems just like we do. I especially feel sorry for poor old Richard. That man waits on Edwina hand and foot. How would you like to do all of Edwina's fetchin' and totin' all the time and then listen to her complain about what you didn't do? He doesn't have a bit of backbone, but he must have the patience of Job. I wonder how he's ever made enough money to keep up with Edwina's high standard of living all these years. You know yourself that Edwina can spend money like there's absolutely no tomorrow looming ahead."

"Well, he must have made a fine living selling all that insurance. They certainly seem to live high enough on the hog. Sometimes I wonder if we're even kin to Edwina. Maybe she was adopted or something. Mama always said Edwina's disposition was different from the rest of the family. I don't really know what she was getting at, but she might have known something she never told us. You know

Mama never would gossip about anybody, especially kinfolk."

"You can forget all that. Edwina looks and acts just like Mama's dead sister, Pearl, and we've all got the same blood. We just need to watch it and make sure that streak doesn't come out in one of us."

I thought it might be too late for Bess.

"Well, how do I look?" I asked Bess, as I walked into the kitchen bright and early the next morning. "Does my hair look at least passable, and how about this dress?" Bess, looking very smart, but practical, was already dressed for the day in a pale yellow blouse and navy skirt; a starched, bright yellow apron was tied around her waist. In my opinion Bess had added a few pounds since her move to the farm, but regardless, she still carried herself very well. "Maybe I should change into my beige skirt and white blouse," I said as I smoothed the box pleats of my dress down over my hips. "This floral dress makes me look fat, and with an apron over it, I'll look even fatter. I think I'll change right quick. Give me a few minutes and I'll be ready for the day."

"Bee, you don't have time to change. You look fine. You've done the best you can do with what you have. Now tie on an apron and let's get started with the last minute cooking. There's no time to waste. We'll have people driving up sooner than we expected, and we're not ready by a long shot. I just wish I knew where Mama's Fostoria cake plate is hiding. I've looked high and low for the thing and can't find it anywhere. We need it on the dessert table for the lemon cheese cake."

"It'll turn up sooner or later," I answered, as I hastily tied my apron on and mentally reminded myself to quit worrying about my appearance. That's always easier said than done, I thought, as I remembered where I had left the cake plate. No time to fetch it now.

Neighbors began arriving just as I took the last of the rolls from the oven. Vonion delivered Cousin Doretha and Cousin Cooper about the middle of the morning. They were sure a sight for sore eyes. Excitement beamed from their tired, old faces as a flustered Vonion helped them down from his truck. "I wouldn't a' missed this day for all the gold in Fort Knox," Cooper exclaimed, as he hobbled over to one of the recently cleaned yard chairs. "I can just taste that barbecued goat right now. When are we gonna eat, girls?"

"Soon, Cousin Cooper, but let's wait for everybody to arrive. We'll spread all the food out directly," Bess laughingly replied. "I hope you have a big appetite because we plan to feed you well."

I soon spotted Margaret's little Chevrolet coupe as it scooted down the lane followed by Walter in his daddy's pickup truck. His daddy's wheelchair was too cumbersome to be brought over in a car so Walter had volunteered to bring it over in the bed of Foy's pickup truck. In a thick cloud of dust, an unfamiliar dark sedan brought up the rear.

Margaret and Walter parked side by side along the pasture fence. Walter quickly jumped out and lugged his father's wheelchair from the truck over to the sedan. He gently and carefully helped the unfamiliar nurse place his father's withered, frail body into the rolling chair. I had not met this particular nurse before; however, I had been informed by Margaret a few days earlier that Ms. Hilda Hawkins had recently been hired after the previous nurse had been excused because of her uncontrollable temper and urges to curse and use offensive language. Carrying her bad disposition and unsettling nature along with her, the previous caretaker had been given her walking papers after only a month. Walter had found this particular nurse after noticing a classified ad in the newspaper. She had described herself as gentle and reliable with a real love for old people. So far so good, I was told.

Vera, Tillman, and most of the neighbors had arrived earlier in the morning. Earl and Tillman were busy moving chairs from the porch to the yard while Vera arranged a few flowers from her garden in a big vase to be placed in the center of the food on the wagon. Earl had picked up Cousin Myrtle from the bus station earlier in his pickup truck, and she was already busy smiling and rocking as she watched all the activity.

As soon as Doretha and Cooper were settled in, sounds of more car doors closing echoed through the yard. Queen Edwina and her entourage had finally arrived. And then there she was, standing beside the car with a parasol in one hand and a brown leather pocketbook clutched under her other arm. Bess and I hurried over to greet her as she haughtily directed Richard to open the car trunk and remove their luggage. A stern command to Richard, then a forced smile toward us, and she had made her grand appearance.

Cousin Richard was always humble and obedient. In contrast, Edwina began putting on airs as soon as she spotted us. "Girls, you both look so good...for your ages, I mean. Oh, Bess, this farm life must be agreeing with you . You look so healthy and plump. And you've acquired a farmer's tan, I believe. I know I look pale as a ghost, but there's simply no need for me to expose my sensitive skin to the sunshine. The harsh sunlight really spells disaster to your skin, girls. Bess, you'll soon find out, I suspect."

"Edwina, you do look wonderful," I lied, as I gave her a welcoming hug. "How was the trip? Was there much traffic on the highway this morning?"

"Oh, there was hardly any traffic at all. Richard has no sense of direction, though, and he lost the way. We ended up in a hay field somewhere over on the other side of Jeffersontown, but we finally made it. I just don't know how you two can abide living out in the middle of nowhere. I'm so used to town I doubt I could ever get accustomed to all this...farm life." Edwina waved her arms in the air just as one of Bess's active grandsons tore right into her rear end, knocking some of the hot wind clear out of her. The child never slowed down but kept on running as Edwina awkwardly tried to regain her balance and grabbed for poor Richard. Her weight must have been a little more than he could support, and both collapsed into the nandina bushes Mama had planted more than half a century before. So much for her grand appearance. Inwardly I was tickled, but I didn't dare crack a smile.

The yard was overflowing with cars and trucks. Bess's grandsons, becoming more and more excited and rambunctious, darted around the yard in between the vehicles, playing with their new cap guns. Chaos really prevailed when the mischievous youngsters opened the gate to the chicken pen and raced in. An avalanche of frightened chickens flew out in an attempt to avoid the two lively children with the noisy toy guns. An irritated Vonion, trying his best to capture the chickens and return them to the pen, scrambled about, but with an army of two active little boys stirring up the chickens, it was a lost cause.

The yard was brimming with excitement and feathers as Ora Lee waved her walking stick in the air in an attempt to keep the old rooster from landing on top of her head. Bess, completely out of character, realized she had lost control of the situation at hand, gave in to the comedy, and threw back her head in hearty laughter. That's what broke the ice. Between gales of laughter and gaiety, everyone herded chickens back to the pen. The morning was off to a good start.

CHAPTER FIVE

The noontime meal must have cast a spell on everybody—everybody that is except Bess and me and, of course, the children. The lunch had been delicious and so filling that the entire bunch of guests were nodding off out under the big oak tree. Cooper had declared without a doubt that the barbecued goat was the best he had ever put a tooth into. "If we had only had a little Brunswick stew to go along with it," he sluggishly said as he began to doze.

Eve Waters' children had invited Bess's grandsons to a game of baseball over in the field behind their house where they had fashioned a baseball diamond. They raced off excitedly as soon as we excused them. Bess was a little concerned that the children might get into mischief, but Eve assured her that there was not a thing to worry about.

Freddy and Jean were so glad to get the little fellers out of their hair for a while they didn't put up a fuss at all about their little darlings going off unattended. Satisfied sighs and snores filled the air until the sound of the horn from the mail car sharply interrupted the tranquil atmosphere.

"That's got to be Earnest Lee with the mail," Bess complained, as we began gathering plates, silverware, and glasses to carry back into the house. "He better put that mail in the box and keep on going. We don't have time to mess with the sorry likes of him today. And he's getting later and later with the mail every day. I might have to report him to the postmaster again. He does everything in his ability to infuriate me."

"Bess, you can be so coldhearted. It's Saturday, and you know the man has two routes on Saturday. Ours happens to be the last in the line. Let's signal Earnest Lee to stop and have a bite to eat. We've got plenty." I quickly signaled for Earnest Lee to pull the car over to the side of the yard before Bess could stop me. "Being neighborly never hurt a single soul," I reminded Bess.

Earnest Lee abruptly slammed on brakes when he saw me motion. The engine ground to a halt, and he quickly jumped from the car and sprang toward the house on his wiry, spindly legs. He dramatically gave Bess and me a deep bow. "Ladies, nice day. How's the party going so far? Looks about as dead as a graveyard 'round here to me. Want me to liven things up? I just happen to have my fiddle in the car. I could play my rendition of 'This Old House' or 'I'll be Coming Round the Mountain.' They's both favorites of mine."

"We couldn't possibly impose upon you, Earnest Lee," Bess firmly replied. "The mail has to be delivered on time, so you better hightail it on out of here. Hail or high water isn't supposed to stop you from your sworn duties. I've heard you say that many times."

"Oh, Earnest Lee, take a few minutes and grab a plate," I quickly interjected. "We've got plenty of barbecue and all the trimmings. You're welcome to stay and eat all you can hold." Bess grimaced. I knew she was aggravated with me, but she'd eventually get over it. "Everybody's resting right now so those tunes will have to wait until another time."

"There won't be another time for you, Earnest Lee. Hurry up and eat and be on your way," Bess quickly responded, more determined than ever to get rid of her adversary.

Bess's irritation never seemed to have any effect on Earnest Lee. He always seemed to ignore it. "Your generosity overwhelms me, ladies. It has been a while since breakfast, and everything does look especially good. Maybe just a bite or two. I haven't had barbecue since last Fourth of July. That wouldn't be barbecued goat by any chance?"

Earnest Lee didn't have a shy bone in his body, especially about his eating. Truck side bodies would have come in quite handy to hold the mountain of food he piled on his plate...and he ate every bite before climbing back into his car and speeding off.

Bess seethed with irritation.

"Well, Bee, we've done it again," Bess proudly proclaimed after we carried the last of the empty platters and bowls back into the kitchen. "I've never seen people put away so much food. You'd think they were all starving to death. I bet Richard hasn't had a square meal since last Christmas when they visited. Remember he ate both turkey legs and half the fruit cake. He wolfed down that barbecue today as if it was gonna be his last meal. Edwina probably never puts a decent meal on the table for that man. She might accidently chip a painted fingernail on the stove."

"We did have a good spread, all right. Your string beans were flavored just right, and my sweet potatoes were as creamy as could be. And did you see how everyone devoured the cake? I'd say our first meal of the weekend was a huge success," I smugly replied, as I covered the remains of the barbecue with one of our nicest tea towels. "Bess, everybody else is nodding off. Why don't we rest a few minutes, too? You know, we need to let our lunch settle a bit. I think I'll sit down right here at the kitchen table for a few minutes and rest my eyes. Why don't you go on to the bedroom and lie down across the bedspread for a spell? Everybody is relaxing right now, so let's do the same."

"All right, if you insist. I know you're exhausted and I do feel a bit weary. Let's take a few minutes off before everybody gets revved up again."

An hour later I was feeling refreshed as I walked out to rejoin the group. A lively conversation about politics and how this country was going to the dogs if we kept the same sorry scalawags in office could be heard clear down to Vonion's house, I suspect. Each one was trying to outtalk the other. Tom Wilson and Cooper were whittling with pocket knives as they puffed away on their pipes. I could always detect the wonderful aroma of Sir Walter Raleigh pipe tobacco when I was near either of them. It had been Will's brand and just to catch a whiff always gave me a nostalgic feeling.

Richard was vigorously chewing on a cigar and nervously jiggling change in his pocket as if he had something pressing on his mind. He absentmindedly pulled his lucky rabbit's foot from his pocket and examined it before carelessly dropping it, along with several coins, into the dust around his feet. He quickly bent over, picked it all up, dusted the rabbit's foot off, and dropped it all back into his pocket to nervously jiggle some more. I wondered if he still considered the rabbit's foot lucky.

Tillman was busy rolling another cigarette. Vonion, Roscoe, and Earl were leaning against the farm wagon, chewing tobacco, careful to spit behind the nandina bushes. Foy was still sound asleep, and his nurse was sitting nearby, reading a paperback book.

Most of the women were clustered together under the shade of the big oak tree. Margaret glanced my way as I walked up. She said that Walter had excused himself, explaining that he had patients waiting to be seen, but would be back as soon as he could. I knew he might be tied up for the rest of the day. Margaret was in love for the first time in her life, but she was beginning to realize that the life of a doctor's wife would be difficult and lonely.

Children and grandchildren were the main topics of conversation. Margaret began to tell the group about one of the devilish little boys in the third grade class she was teaching this year over in Bert County. Everybody laughed as she described how the little fellow continually tried to sneak his old dog into the classroom. "I'd overlook the dog and let him in once in a while, but the critter smells just awful. All I need is for some parent to criticize me to the principal about their precious little child returning home smelling like a polecat."

I hesitantly pulled up a wooden straight chair beside Edwina and quickly regretted it. Before I could take a breath, she began filling me in on all of the amazing endeavors of her one and only child, Dickie. Dickie had his first tooth at three months, walked at the early age of eight months, and talked at ten months. He had acquired more Boy Scout badges than any other boy in his den and, single-handedly, had won every basketball game during his entire high school career. With a superior I.Q., the young man had easily made straight A's all the way through high school and college.

"Now that Dickie's almost finished with law school, he'll soon make a big name for himself. I'm sure he'll want to practice law in Atlanta or some other big city where he can really make big money. I declare, we are so proud of that boy. Bee, I can hardly wait to see him. He called on the telephone last night and said he'd arrive some time during the middle of the afternoon and that he has a big surprise for Richard and me. I just can't imagine what that boy has gone and done. He probably went out and bought us a gift and wants to present it to us in front of the whole family. That would be just like the darling boy. I've been hinting to Dickie for a while that I would just love a new set of fine china. Do you think that could be it? Or do you think he might have even gone so far as purchasing a nice piece of jewelry for me? That would be more fitting, you know, as a way of saying how much he appreciates everything Richard and I have sacrificed so that he could attain such a fine education. Whatever it is, I'll bet it's expensive. " And on and on…

Edwina never shut her mouth long enough for me to get one word in edgewise. I was dying to tell her all about Margaret's engagement to Walter, THE MEDICAL DOCTOR, but it wasn't to happen. Just as Edwina began praising Richard, of all people, and bragging about how considerate to her that he had always been and how he'd never asked her to tote a thing around, except maybe a handkerchief, we heard the sound of a motor.

"He's here," Edwina exclaimed, as her eyes sparkled in anticipation. "My precious boy has made it." Edwina excitedly stood and waved her handkerchief in the direction of Dickie's sports car as it came to a sudden halt next to Earl's old pickup truck.

That darling boy had finally arrived!

CHAPTER SIX

Y ou would have thought that the long-awaited
Santa Claus had arrived Christmas morning
from Edwina's reaction as she spotted Dickie
motoring down the lane. She sprang to her feet like
a woman half her age in training for the Olympics in
sprinting. Waving her handkerchief as if she were
trying to stop a runaway train headed straight
toward her, she let out a yell that resembled a high
school cheerleader at a football game. Everybody
immediately hushed and gawked as Edwina rushed
right by a stunned Richard on her way to hug her
boy.

Dickie quickly jumped from the car, waved
and called, "Hey everybody," and then grabbed his
excited mama. Lingering in her son's embrace a little
longer than necessary, Edwina glanced toward me

and gave me a smug smile. Her precious boy was here at last!

I could quickly see that Dickie had changed little since last Christmas. He was still the sawed-off, younger replica of his father. Richard's gray hair was thin and fine; Dickie's darker hair was wispy and finer. Richard had a huge nose with nose hair protruding at the end; Dickie also had an enormous nose. Richard's voice had a high pitch; Dickie's was higher. Edwina always criticized Richard about his poor posture; Dickie carried himself much the same as Richard, but Edwina considered her precious boy perfect, always excusing his poor posture as a manly gait. Well, you get the picture. There was a strong resemblance, and neither could ever pass himself off as Clark Gable, even in the darkness of night.

Richard eventually stood and slowly ambled toward the car. It was clear that Richard knew his place, and it was second in line in the greetings department and, more than likely, in every other department. As soon as Edwina released her death grip on her boy, Richard and Dickie affectionately shook hands. Edwina grabbed Dickie and began pulling him in our direction. Dickie whispered something in his mama's ear, and Edwina shrieked with pleasure. "Dickie wants to give me his surprise right now," an excited Edwina called.

Dickie smiled broadly and walked around to the passenger side of the car with Richard and Edwina following close behind. "I think I'll close my eyes until Dickie gets it from the car," Edwina announced as she rounded the corner of the car. It was obvious she could hardly contain her emotions, as she stopped and pressed her hands over her eyes. She soon began to wiggle and squirm in anticipation of her wonderful and mysterious gift. With Edwina's eyes closed but Richard's gaze firmly fixed on the car door, the surprise stepped out. A dark-haired creature with the grace of an exotic dancer extended her long, bejeweled arm toward Richard. Poor Edwina was about to meet her match!

"Mama and Daddy, I'd like to introduce my wife, Mrs. Richard Perkins, the second. Mavis, dear, this is Mama and Daddy, Mr. and Mrs. Richard Perkins. Mama, you can open your eyes now and meet your surprise. I'm a married man and this is the love of my life."

Mavis looked at Dickie in shock. "Dickie, I thought we were on our way to the beach for the weekend, and this was a quick stop to meet an old friend. I didn't know we were about to meet your...whole family. I would have fixed myself up a little more."

"It's a surprise for you, too, dear. I just couldn't wait for you to meet the family, and I thought that today on our way to the beach would be the perfect time."

Mavis reluctantly smiled toward Richard and Edwina through layers of heavy makeup, lowered her dark eyes in Dickie's direction, wiggled a little closer to her husband, and encircled Dickie with her long, slender arms into a seductive embrace. "How thoughtful of you, dear. I really had no idea, and I'm not at all prepared to meet the family."

Dickie smiled at his new wife and gave her a sudden, impulsive kiss on her cheek. "You're just wonderful. Mama and Daddy will love you."

Mavis grinned directly toward Edwina before turning her head toward her new husband to give him a big, wet kiss smack on the lips. Mavis released Dickie, and the new groom turned toward the crowd with a big grin on his face and a bright strip of red lipstick smeared across his perfectly dentist-straightened white teeth.

There are absolutely no words to adequately describe Edwina's expression. She grabbed at Richard for support as her face crumpled and her body collapsed. Richard again found himself in the position of holding up all two hundred pounds of Edwina's limp body as her legs buckled under her bulky frame. As a loud, pitiful moan filled the air, trusty Vonion raced over to be of assistance to the newly proclaimed father of the groom.

"My smelling salts! My smelling salts! Richard, get my smelling salts!" Edwina managed to command between another moan and her anticipated fainting spell.

A bewildered Richard maneuvered Edwina's large frame over to one arm and reached into his pants pocket for a small bottle. I immediately realized this was to be one of Edwina's famous spells and raced over with one of the yard chairs. Richard and Vonion gladly deposited all of the grief-stricken dead weight into the chair.

Bess, hearing all the commotion from the porch, rushed over with a folded newspaper, shouting, "Move back everyone. Give her room to breathe," and began fanning Edwina with a vengeance.

Vonion quickly stepped backward and proclaimed, "We's got a real situation here. Call Doc Walter. We's in need of med-i-cal help."

"She's just fainted," I said to Vonion, as Edwina began to come around. "She'll be all right as soon as she gets over the shock."

Amidst all the commotion, I noticed Mavis pull away from Dickie and, with an aggravated gasp and a roll of the eyes, lean against the car. I can only imagine what that poor girl must have been thinking. Poor Dickie was looking from one significant woman to the other, frantically questioning himself as to which one needed his immediate attention. I had a sudden premonition, right then and there, that the pitiful fellow would spend the rest of his life in the same precarious situation in which he found himself right this very moment.

Edwina nodded, opened one eye and then the other. Without even a gesture toward the strange new light in Dickie's life, she commanded Richard to get her into the house and to a bed before she had a heart attack right out here in the yard...for pity's sake. Vonion and Richard, along with extra help from Tom Wilson, maneuvered a heartbroken Edwina up the porch steps and into the house.

Before excusing ourselves to attend to Edwina, Bess reached over and gave Mavis a quick hug. "Edwina has a tendency to overreact. We're glad to meet you, Mavis. We're Dickie's cousins, twice removed, on his mama's side. This is my sister, Bee."

Naturally, Dickie's wife would be welcomed by me. I nodded and extended my hand toward the shocked young woman and gave her a second hug. "We're honored to have you here at our home. Edwina will come around shortly, you'll see. Let's just give her a few minutes to collect herself. Make yourself at home. Now, Dickie, you introduce everyone, and there's plenty of food in the kitchen. Bess and I will be back out in a few minutes after we look in on your mama."

Dickie nodded, as if he was used to his mama having this kind of emotional outburst, and made no move to leave his bride's side. He began making the rounds to introduce Mavis to everyone. Bess and I headed up the steps. Just as Bess opened the screen door, we overheard loud, angry voices coming from the direction of the bedroom. I gently closed the door behind us and Bess put her finger to her mouth. Knowing full well it was a sin to listen in on a conversation not meant for our ears, we stood silently and listened as Edwina preached to poor Richard.

"Richard, you better get out there right now and talk some sense into that boy. That hussy isn't anything but a gold-digger if I ever saw one, and I can spot one a mile away."

"Edwina, lower your voice. For once in my life, I fully agree with you. That boy's done gone and made a fool of himself. He ain't nearly through getting his high-priced education, don't have a job, and ain't got a pot to pee in or a window to throw it out of. If he thinks I'm gonna keep supporting him, he's got another think coming. I've done all I can do. It's hard enough feeding his mouth, much less two mouths. It's high time for him to wake up and smell the roses. I'm not giving him another red cent, and you can put a stamp on that and mail it! That boy needs to grow up and start supporting himself. I ain't doing it no longer, and that's my last word on the subject."

"Now Richard." Edwina seemed to be mellowing. "I'm sure the boy will realize he's made a mistake, and we can annul the whole thing. All you have to do is to talk some sense into him. Oh, Richard, the very idea of Dickie bringing that...that floozy here, and right in front of my entire family, embarrassing me like that! I thought you had taught him better. Why, Bee Martin and Bess Johnson will never, ever let me hear the end of this. Richard, get my smelling salts out again and hurry up. I believe I'm going to really faint this time and maybe even throw up."

ANN COBB

"Don't you dare throw up! If you do, you can clean up the whole thing. Now get a hold of yourself, Edwina."

"Oh, Richard, my baby can't be a married man. He's hardly out of knee pants."

"Oh, your baby is old enough all right, and he's definitely been out of his pants. He's just not ready for that kind of decision. People don't get married until they can support themselves, and Dickie's a far cry short of that. Why, that boy has to ask me for every penny he spends. I don't even know where he found the money to get a marriage license. It'll be over my dead body that he gets another penny from me...and I mean it this time."

"Richard, that is a bit harsh, don't you think?" Edwina was really beginning to whine now. "You can give the boy a little more money until he finishes his education. After all, he's not cut out for manual labor. He's extremely delicate. He takes after me, you know. Oh, Richard, we can't turn our back on the boy. Maybe we can tolerate a wife if we have to, even though she does look like a hussy. Whatever does Dickie see in her?"

Richard hopelessly shouted, "She's a looker, Edwina, for Pete's sake! What she sees in your baby is what I really want to know." Richard stomped out of the room, hurried right past us without so much as a nod, and was out the door.

Bess and I had heard enough. Edwina was sobbing into one of Richard's monogrammed

68

handkerchiefs as we rushed into the bedroom. Bess patted Edwina and tenderly said, "Edwina, you have got to get yourself together. There's a perfectly nice girl outside just waiting to meet you. Now, why did you make such a scene? Dickie made the decision to get married, and now you and Richard need to be cordial to the girl. You don't know a thing about her. She's probably from a nice family, maybe the daughter of a doctor or a senator or something like that, for all we know."

"Yes, now, Edwina, I'll get you some water, and you lie down here and rest a bit. Then you should greet your new daughter-in-law like the dignified lady that you were trained to be. You know our granny taught all of us to be kind to everyone, including new daughters-in-law. Granny's probably looking down at you right now from heaven and watching you behave like somebody with her head and heart completely out of joint. She's ashamed of you...and we are too." *I just had to add that.*

"But...Dickie is my only child. I've never had to share him with anyone...except Richard, and that doesn't really count. I can never accept anyone else in my precious Dickie's life...but...I do want Granny to be proud of me. Oh, dear me, what should I do?" Edwina wiped away fresh tears.

"You can straighten up and march out there and greet that poor girl...and then apologize, of course," I said, as I gave Edwina a stern stare before walking out to get her water.

Telling Edwina that Granny was disappointed in her had been the key. Our granny didn't stand for her children or her grandchildren mistreating any of God's creatures, and she would beat us to a pulp with a hickory stick if we disobeyed her.

CHAPTER SEVEN

The wonderful aroma of frying fish drifted into the opened windows of my kitchen later that afternoon. I was busy making tea and chopping lemons for our feast when I heard a knock at the door. Bess heard the knock from the dining room and beat me to the door.

"It's me, ladies...Sheriff Ledbetter."

"Come on in, Sheriff," I called back, wiping my hands with a dishcloth as I hurried to the door. Sheriff Ledbetter wiped his shoes on the floor mat (he knew better than not to) and walked in with his hat in his hands and a frown on his sunburned face. Bess greeted him with another frown.

"Afternoon, ladies. Seems y'all got a party goin' on out there. I heard 'bout the reunion from Earl the other day whil'st he was in town. I hope I'm not intrudin' too much, but it's my duty to let you know about the escaped convict."

"Escaped convict?" Bess repeated, as if she was stunned. "Around here?"

"Yes'um, 'fraid so. The state guys asked me to alert everybody in the area. Seems the state prisoners were workin' on the old steel bridge over on River Road when one of 'um wrestled the guard to the ground and got clean away. Happened 'bout two hours ago. They finally got the dogs out on the trail but ain't had no luck yet."

"Oh dear me," Bess answered, as the news set in. "Shouldn't we get everybody in and lock the doors? We've already had an exciting afternoon, and an escaped convict is just about the last thing we need about now."

"I don't think that's really necessary," our pudgy Sheriff Ledbetter answered with authority and clamped down a little tighter on the cigar stub between his stained teeth. "I've already talked to Vonion and Tom Wilson. Tom said he'd alert the other men, but he'd keep the news from the ladies since he and Vonion couldn't handle any more hysterical women right now. Just be careful and watch closely for anything unusual. Don't take any chances, and keep everybody close around the house."

"We're like sitting ducks. He can smell that frying fish for miles around," I replied as the bad news gradually seeped into my mind. "I'm gonna get the shotgun out from behind the door and make sure it's loaded. I can use it if need be."

Sheriff Ledbetter tugged at his suspenders and rolled his eyes back in his head, both nervous habits he had acquired since he had been elected sheriff. "Keep it handy, but ladies, don't overreact. Just use the good sense the good Lord gave you and you'll be all right."

"Sheriff." Bess began to wring her hands. "What does this escaped convict look like?"

"He's a Pink. Eddie Pink. All them Pinks look alike. Got pale skin and white hair. Skinny, chicken chested. He's one of Peg Pink's boys. Been on the chain gang goin' on a year now. He was convicted of stealin' hogs from a farmer over on the other end of Bert County. That boy's been in trouble from the day he was born. I've arrested him myself fer speedin' around in his daddy's old beat-up pickup truck and boozin' it up at the same time. That boy grew up thievin', just like his daddy. You know the apple doesn't fall far from the tree. He ain't smart, but he's swamp wise. He knows them swamps, and he knows the river. We'll eventually apprehend him, though. He's got to come out sooner or later. Hit might take a day or so, but we'll catch up with him."

"I remember that boy," I thoughtfully replied. "Those Pink boys came to my Sunday school class years and years ago. We were giving out candy and goodies for Christmas when he and his brother showed up wearing raggedy overalls and no coats. I felt sorry for them and gave them each an extra bag of candy and later took shirts, coats, and a few pairs of pants out to him and his brother. Those children didn't stand a chance. What happened to his brother?"

"They were actually three of them boys. One didn't ever grow up. Fell in his ma's wash water and drowned when he were just a baby. Hit were a tragedy; that woman never did get over it. The oldest one was killed in action in the Big War, and the mother died from pneumonia soon after. Old man Pink left home right after she died, and I haven't heard a word from him since. Probably took up with another old woman somewheres else."

"Is Eddie Pink dangerous, Sheriff?" I asked.

"No ma'am, I don't believe him to be dangerous, that is, unless he were bein' threatened. Ladies, I'm just sayin', don't take no chances. Anything unusual, let me know. Now, I got other people to see. I wouldn't mind a barbecue sandwich a'fore I left, that is, if you'ns got plenty."

"We've got plenty, Sheriff. Let me fix you up," I answered quickly before Bess turned him down. She only tolerated the sheriff when she absolutely had to, which wasn't often. I, on the other hand, was forced to admit he had his good points. They were few, but he had come through a few times in the past when Bess and I needed him, such as the time we were tied and gagged by a murdering preacher and his girlfriend, and about to be thrown in a river.

The fish fry went off without a hitch. Bess and I kept a watchful eye out the whole time but never saw anything unusual...except maybe when Old Man Peterson gave Mildred the eye. I was a little hurt because up to now I believed that I was the only target of his affection. Oh well, he's not my type, but it's always good to have somebody's attention. I can't believe I said that.

As Tillman and Tom Wilson began the cleanup, Vonion wrestled Cousin Cooper and Cousin Doretha back into the cab of his truck for the ride home. Bess and I herded Cousin Myrtle into the house for an early bedtime. Foy and his nurse had left earlier with Walter and Margaret's assistance. Bess's grandsons, along with Eve Waters's children, were roasting marshmallows over the dying embers of the fire.

The warm sun had dropped into the horizon, leaving a chill in the evening air. Conversations were waning, and a few heads were bobbing. Peace had settled in, and Dickie and Mavis had walked off, hand in hand, into the moonlit evening.

Much later that night, after everyone had retired or left for home, I walked into the kitchen to start another and the final cleanup of the day. I had insisted that Bess go on to bed since the nagging pain in her back had suddenly flared up. The dirty dishes had mounted again, and I knew better than to leave them until morning. I sighed as I filled the sink with hot, soapy water.

Bess and I had done a great job today. With the exception of Edwina's surprise and the sheriff's visit, the day had been a total success. The barbecue had been exceptional, the fish fry outstanding, conversations lively, and laughter frequent. Friendship and fellowship at its best! Soon a good night's sleep and I'd be ready for tomorrow.

Dishes were done one more time. The house was quiet as I folded the damp dish towel over the back of the kitchen chair and walked over to the back window. The bright moonlight spilled in all around me. Throwing Sheriff Ledbetter's caution completely to the wind, I decided to walk out to the back porch and sit a spell in the shadows. I was wound up from the day's activities and wasn't quite ready for bed. My mind was still on the day and the fun and enjoyment everybody had experienced, especially Cousin Doretha and Cousin Cooper...oh, and of course, Cousin Myrtle. Just to see those old people as their spirits rose with joy was pure satisfaction.

I carefully leaned back in one of the wooden straight chairs and propped my feet on the overturned washtub Bess and I used to wash vegetables from the garden. Peace and quiet— nothing like it after a hectic day. I glanced down the lane toward Vonion and Ora Lee's house just as the last light flickered off at their window. After such a busy day, Vonion and Ora Lee would sleep well tonight, I hoped. I'd sleep well, too, if I ever made it to the bed. I'd just sit a spell and rest my eyes, I thought, as I felt myself drifting away.

That's when I heard voices. I quickly opened one eye but didn't dare move. Angry male voices were coming from the direction of the barn.

"I'm not made out of money. Son, your days of living off me are finally over. If you can take a wife, you can support a wife. I'm not giving you another red cent." Was that Richard? I didn't dare take a breath. "Boy, you've been made a fool of. That girl thinks you're loaded, but she's gonna find out you ain't got nothin' except an expensive education." Still listening and not daring to move a muscle, I took a silent breath. I should get up and go into the house, I thought...but I didn't dare move.

"Dad...dy, you can't do this to me. What do you think I came out here to the boondocks for? It wasn't to see all these country hicks. I need money, and I need it now. Mavis and I haven't even been on a honeymoon yet. She thinks we're gonna take a cruise or something expensive like that. I can't disappoint her. Dad...dy, please. Can't you see I'm in trouble? I need money for gas just to get to the beach, and then I need money for a motel and for food."

"Son, you made your own damn trouble, and now you're barking up the wrong tree. And don't go to your mother. She depends completely on me for every mouthful of food she puts into her greedy mouth. She can't give you what she ain't got."

"You don't care a hoot about my happiness, but Mama does. She'll come through, I'll bet. She can sell some of that expensive jewelry she has or cash in some insurance policies. There's got to be a way." Dickie was whining pitifully now and sounded as if he was almost in tears. Sinning again...listening in on a conversation not meant for my ears.

"Get a job. That's the only way. Have you thought about that? Just get a damn job. Plenty of people go to school and work at the same time."

"I can't get a job. I go to school in the daytime, and Mavis wants me at home with her at night. I'd have to quit school, and Mama would have a conniption fit."

"She'll get over it. Just leave me be right now. I've got other things on my mind right now," Richard replied before he angrily stomped off into the night.

I heard Dickie's deep sobs and saw the flicker of his cigarette as I quietly tiptoed back into the house.

And that was the last time I was ever to hear Richard Perkins's voice.

CHAPTER EIGHT

A s soon as the back door closed behind me, the distressing thought that I would be sleeping with Bess—in her bedroom, in the same bed—hit me like a bomb. Memories of the last time that she and I had been forced to sleep together have haunted me ever since, and a few actual bruises remain. Bess was not a good sleep mate. She snored, kicked, and rolled over every few minutes. I had been very noble when Bess and I realized we had more guests than bedrooms, and I had, therefore, relinquished my bedroom to Edwina and Richard for the night. Cousin Myrtle had taken up residence in Margaret's room, and that left me with the distinct pleasure of enduring the entire night watching Bess's chest rise and fall with each snore.

Dickie and his beloved had taken over the front room for the night. The lovebirds could sleep together on the narrow seat of the settee or on the floor; either way it was not a good plan for newlyweds. Bess and I had not had the time or inclination to accommodate this unexpected pair with a better sleeping arrangement.

It was very late that evening when I wearily pulled the covers back after a soothing bath and climbed into bed beside a peacefully sleeping Bess. I prayed that the rest of the night would be tranquil as I lay awake, listening to every sound of the creaking house along with Bess's soft snore and snort. Memories of a young Eddie Pink clouded my thoughts as I heard the back door softly close. That was a heartbroken Dickie coming to bed, or perhaps it was Richard. He might have walked his frustrations out by now and returned to the house at last.

Youngsters such as Eddie usually grow up to be amazingly similar to their parents. They retain their bad characteristics and repeat many of the same mistakes. I remember Mrs. Pink as being stern and standoffish the one and only time I had ever come in contact with her. She had accepted the clothes I carried out to the children as if it didn't matter one way or the other to her if the boys had anything decent to wear at all. I remember a distant expression on her wrinkled, sunburned face as I offered to pick up her children the next weekend for Sunday school and church and return them home. I explained to her that her children were welcome in my Sunday school class, and I would take total responsibility for them while they were with me. She had offered no real answer to me other than to say she'd let me know. She never did and I never ventured out that way again.

I remember asking Margaret about the Pink boys once, and she had said they were backward and indifferent. They had missed a good bit of school on account of their daddy needing them on the farm, and that caused them to fail grade after grade. They had both left school as soon as the law allowed, and she had not thought of them since.

I'm ashamed to say that after my visit with their ma, I had made no other attempt to reach out to the family. I should have followed through with those boys, I scolded myself as I began to doze.

I slept amazingly well during the night, even with the thoughts that an escaped convict could be at large and possibly nearby. Bess and I had been extremely tired, and evidently we had both conked out and slept like babies all night long. It was early morning now, and I was lying awake listening to the crows in the yard when I heard the bucket alarm go off. The sound of the stick hitting the bucket usually woke me from my sleep, leaving me with that wonderful feeling of being at peace with the world; however, this morning I had beaten it to the draw and awakened early, but I was not ready to face the day.

I felt Bess stir and heard her yawn before she muttered, "For Pete's sake, will that man never learn? I've asked him time and again not to do that."

I knew he never would and now that he knew that it aggravated Bess, he would get more pleasure from it than ever before. "I know you're awake, Bee. Let's get on up and stir around a little. Everybody will be up and wanting coffee and breakfast soon. At least the meat is already fried. That's one thing we won't have to do this morning."

"That was a good idea of yours to go ahead and fry the ham and sausage last night, Bess, so now all we have to do is heat it up. Can't we lie here a little longer and rest, please? It'll do us both good." I knew she wouldn't go for that.

"No, we've got a million other things to do. Now rise and shine like Mama used to tell us. Oh, and why don't you call Sheriff Ledbetter and see if they've caught that escaped convict. It would sure rest my mind if he was back in the jailhouse with all the other criminals and not roaming around God only knows where."

That's when the shrieking, bloodcurdling scream reverberated through the house. "RICHARD! RICHARD! Where are you? OH! RICHARD!"

I instantly sat straight up in bed and looked at Bess. "That was Cousin Edwina, Bess. Something terrible has happened to—" I frantically jumped from the bed before I could finish my sentence and grabbed my robe. Bess was right behind me as we dashed down the hall toward my bedroom.

A closed bedroom door only slowed us down. I quickly jerked it open without knocking, and we became the firsthand eyewitnesses to a disheveled Cousin Edwina sitting up in a half-made bed, hollering and squalling. She must have realized she had an audience because she suddenly and dramatically collapsed backward and fell right off the side of the bed before we could make it across the room to her. Another two hundred pounds of dead weight on the floor. Bess reached our anguished cousin first. She reached down and gently patted her face to see if she was still breathing before giving her a gentle shake. "Whatever is wrong with you, Edwina? Are you hurt anywhere?"

Edwina's head bobbed back and forth as Bess shook her. "Bess, stop that shaking and give her time to breathe. Something terrible has frightened her...and where in the dickens is Richard? He didn't sleep in here last night...I don't think. His side of the bed hasn't been slept in."

"Edwina, where...is...Richard?" Bess sternly demanded, as she gave a hysterical Edwina another brisk shake. "Where is Richard? And are you hurt?" By this time Dickie and Mavis had come rushing in with robes hanging wide open and gawking expressions across their startled faces. Mavis might as well get used to Edwina's dramatic behavior. She might have been having second thoughts about her new marriage by now!

Bess looked up toward Dickie as she realized that Edwina was in shock. "Dickie, see if you can get anything out of your mother. Try to find out where your father is."

Dickie leaned over his mother and tenderly patted her cheek. "Mama, what's going on in here? Are you hurt anywhere? And where is Daddy?" I glanced at Bess and she sadly shook her head.

Edwina opened her eyes as big tears began to flow down her pale, puffy cheeks. "Oh, Dickie, (sob, sob) thank goodness you're here. I...I think your father has (sob) left me." Edwina grabbed at Dickie's hand and clutched it to her ample breast. "He...he didn't sleep in here with me last night. I don't even remember him coming into the room last night. He's gone, gone off somewhere and left me."

"Mama, that's just plain foolishness," Dickie tenderly answered.

Edwina pitifully whimpered again as she clutched his hand more tightly to her breast. "He's...he's run off somewhere. He always said he would leave me, and now he has. He wanted to embarrass me before all my kin."

"Ma-ma, you know Daddy hasn't left you, for goodness' sake. He probably just slept somewhere else in the house last night to keep from disturbing you. You were probably already asleep when he came in, and he didn't want to wake you by getting into the bed. Now, let's get you back into this bed, and I'll go looking for him. I'm sure he's dozing out on the porch or maybe even asleep in the barn." Bess gave me another knowing glance that said that wasn't at all possible; the alarm clock had already gone off—you know, the stick hitting the side of the bucket.

Dickie gently helped Edwina back into bed and placed her head on one of our new goose-down pillows. "Mama, you rest, and I'll be back as quickly as I can. Now don't let your imagination run wild. I'll find Daddy." Dickie gave his mama a weak smile and kissed her damp cheek as to say everything would be all right. He reached out to his new bride and gave her a tender touch before rushing out of the bedroom door.

"Yes, now Edwina, just rest," Bess added. "We'll get coffee. Mavis, will you please sit in here and keep your mother-in-law calm for a few minutes while we get the coffee?" Mavis shot Bess a skeptical, horrified glance.

"Please hurry," Mavis desperately answered, as she reluctantly moved closer to the bed.

"Bee, why don't you get a damp cloth for Edwina's face while I get the coffee?" I knew we had a situation on our hands here. What else could happen?

Just as we managed to settle Edwina back down a bit, a downhearted Dickie walked back into the bedroom with a wild-eyed Vonion at his heels. Edwina was propped up on our new pillows and now had Mavis fanning her with the latest issue of *The Progressive Farmer* magazine. A swooning Edwina seemed to have calmed a bit, but she was not braced for Dickie's bad news.

"Mama," a reluctant Dickie said, as he leaned over and stroked Edwina's arm to keep her calm.

"Daddy doesn't seem to be close around anywhere. The car's out there, but... Daddy seems to be gone — vanished." Edwina swooned again, and this time much more dramatically.

I feared the answer before I asked, "Dickie, did you check out the barn and the orchard? He could have even walked down to the pond."

"We done checked all the way 'round the pond. We even went so fer as to go up to the hard road and round back through the pasture. He just ain't nowheres near the house," an overly excited Vonion interrupted. "I seen Tom Wilson go by in his pickup, and we stopped him. He said he ain't seen him nowhere, either, but he'd ride up and down the road a piece and have a look-see. I 'speck he'll question Mr. Tillman and Ms. Vera if they's seen hide or hair of him. If he around here, we'll find him. Don't you worry none 'bout that, Ms. Edwina."

I dared not look directly into Edwina's frightened eyes now in fear that I'd break down too. Instead, I looked straight at Vonion's red, bloodshot eyes and said, "Vonion, you and Dickie head back out and scout around back of your house and around the edge of the woods. Ask Roscoe if he'll help with the search, and tell Ora Lee she's needed up here at the big house as soon as she can get here. Richard's got to be around here somewhere. People don't just vanish into thin air."

That's when it occurred to me, just as I was finishing my instructions to everybody; we should call Sheriff Ledbetter. Suddenly, my imagination went wild. Sheriff Ledbetter was probably still out scouting around for an escaped prisoner, an escaped prisoner who might have Richard chained to a tree or knocked unconscious with a big rock or, even worse, stabbed in the heart with a butcher knife. He could have even slit his throat...or thrown him into the river for the fish to devour for lunch!   I had completely forgotten about Eddie Pink. Dear Lord! Was there a connection? Had Richard and Eddie Pink run into each other somewhere back of the house last night? I'd better get in touch with Sheriff Ledbetter right now, but I couldn't breathe a word of what I was thinking to anybody, especially not Edwina.

"Mr. Richard can't a'got fer. He ain't no young man, you know. He ain't got no stamina or strength in his old..." I heard Vonion saying, and I realized my mind had wandered far, far away. I glared directly at Vonion, hoping my expression would quieten him. Vonion abruptly closed his mouth and didn't finish his thought.

"Bee, I'll get breakfast," Bess announced and started for the door.

"Now, everybody stay calm, and Mavis, keep fanning," I steadfastly demanded, as I followed Bess out the door.

I'm gonna kill Richard when we find him, I thought. That is, if he isn't already dead.

CHAPTER NINE

I could hear Bess rattling pots and pans in the kitchen as I picked up the telephone to call Sheriff Ledbetter. "Good morning, Nellie. Hope you're having a wonderful day," I calmly and cheerfully said to our nosy telephone operator, hoping not to alarm her that anything might be wrong. Five years of having Nellie as my telephone operator had taught me to butter the woman up. It paid to stay in Nellie's good graces; after all, she was totally in charge of all my telephone communications to the outside world.

"Well, so far my day hasn't been so good. My arthritis is acting up something terrible this morning, and my neighbor, Mr. Lawson, is cooking collard greens again. I can smell them clear across the road, and it's making me pure nauseous."

"At least it's collard greens you're smelling this morning and not another dead body. That's something to be thankful for." Mr. Lawson, our local mortician, usually left his windows open twelve months out of the year, and Nellie constantly complained about the strange odors rising from his residence. I thought she imagined things, but I'd be the last person to tell her. "Please ring the sheriff's office, if you don't mind."

"Bee, you know it's mighty early to catch the sheriff in the office. You're probably not aware of it, but there's an escaped convict running loose out there somewhere. The sheriff's more than likely out tracking him down."

"Nellie, just place the call if you don't mind." My patience with Nellie was always short, and I was trying my best to keep from losing my temper or letting on that anything was wrong. "I'll talk to Deputy Vernon if he answers the telephone."

"All right, if you say so. But he's probably asleep. I'll have to let the telephone ring a dozen times to wake that sorry man up."

"Just do it, Nellie," I answered, this time with a little more tension in my voice.

"Ms. Bee, since you and Ms. Bess started that detective business, y'all are becoming more and more temperamental."

I didn't answer but gripped the telephone a little tighter.

Sure enough, it took fourteen rings before a sleepy-sounding Vernon answered the telephone. "Sheriff's office, Deputy Vernon speaking."

"Deputy, is Sheriff Ledbetter in?" I asked.

"No'um, he's still out on a case, Ms. Bee." Since Bess and I have such a close working relationship with the law enforcers of the county, the deputy and the sheriff now know us by our voices.

"Has the escaped convict been captured, Vernon?"

"No'um, he's still at large. Eddie Pink's a pretty slick character, but they'll catch up with him eventually."

"Do they have any idea of his location, Vernon?"

"Sheriff Ledbetter ain't really give me any details this morning. Just told me to say they was working as hard as they possibly could to apprehend that scoundrel. That's about all I can truthfully tell you at the present time."

"Listen, Vernon. Radio the sheriff right now and tell him to call me at once. We've got a situation over here at the farm. Now, do you understand, Vernon? Tell him to call me as soon as he possibly can."

"Yes'um, I understand. I'll call right now. Ten-four, over and out." I heard the telephone receiver drop.

"What's going on out there, Bee?" Nellie quickly asked before I could lay the receiver down.

"We're about to eat breakfast, Nellie, and we're out of eggs. We think we've got an egg thief running around loose. Have a nice day."

Bess was standing in front of the hot stove with a large spoon in one hand and fiddling with one of the stove knobs with her other hand as I walked into the kitchen. "Bee, see if you can slice a few more pieces of ham. Seems as if we had a hungry rat in the kitchen again last night. We had ten pieces of ham fried up and now there's only eight. Somebody must have ventured into the kitchen during the night and made himself a big ham sandwich. Milk's missing too. Bread crumbs were scattered all over the counter, and a dirty drinking glass was left in the sink. If people get hungry in the middle of the night, it seems as if they could clean up after themselves, for goodness' sake."

"You know very well how men are, Bess. Dickie probably got hungry during the night and made himself a snack. Don't say anything about it to him; he's so upset about his daddy and all, but I'm sure he's our culprit."

"Okay, but he could have at least cleaned up after himself. That boy can eat. He put away six or seven fish and a dozen corn dodgers last night, along with everything else we put out. He must have a hollow leg," Bess answered, as she put the spoon down and moved a skillet across the top of the stove.

I whispered, "Bess, that boy probably never gets anything decent to eat. I can't see Mavis doing much cooking, can you?"

Bess quietly giggled. "Not really, but I'm quite sure she has many other hidden talents."

Breakfast was served and eaten. The dishes were washed, and we still had no word from the sheriff. Edwina actually left her bed and came to the table, along with Mavis and Cousin Myrtle. Edwina complained as she ate that her digestive tract was sluggish, and she didn't need to eat but just a bite or two to keep her strength up. She managed to wash down several slices of ham, two fried eggs, a big helping of cheese grits, and two buttered biscuits with cane syrup, along with three cups of black coffee, no sugar. She explained that she never used sugar in her coffee because she had to watch her figure. Who believed that? Not a one of us who had heaved her from one place to another for the last day or so.

Earlier that morning I had called Cousin Cooper on the telephone. Not wanting to upset him any sooner than need be and knowing that Nellie would overhear every word I said, I asked him not to look for Vonion to pick them up this morning. I didn't offer an elaborate explanation other than to say we were all pretty tired, and we had canceled our lunch plans. I told him I'd get back to him soon, and maybe we could come up with another date for a quick get-together.

Cousin Myrtle was now dozing on the porch, and Mavis had made herself scarce in the bathroom. Margaret was still over at Foy's. Not wanting to alert Nellie about our dilemma any sooner than need be, I had asked Roscoe to deliver a note from me to Margaret earlier that morning, explaining our predicament. I instructed her not to overreact and to keep Foy and his nurse calm. I asked Margaret to stay put for the time being and to keep a close watch for anything unusual over there since the convict was still on the loose. Foy and his nurse could use somebody with a level head now, and I knew I could count on Margaret.

I was beginning to fear the worst. Richard had either impulsively walked away and left his wife of over forty years or followed through with a planned, grand departure. If it was planned, he intended to embarrass Edwina in front of the people she most wanted to impress. The only other explanation for Richard's departure was that he had been abducted or detained in some way or (and I hate to say the word) murdered.

Where was that confounded sheriff, anyway? He could have been here an hour ago if he wanted to. There was no excuse for his behavior.

Word spreads swiftly when there's a crisis in the community. More and more volunteers were beginning to show up at the house to join in the search. Vonion had called on his fellow deacons at the East African Eden Baptist Church for assistance along with our two-man volunteer fire department. The telephone had begun to ring off the hook. Willing to stop what they were doing, people were volunteering to join the search. Everyone in the county seemed to be learning about our calamity except our illustrious sheriff.

Dickie and Vonion had set up a temporary headquarters under the oak tree in the side yard along with Tillman, Roscoe, and Tom Wilson. I could hear them from the porch as they organized another search party, this time deeper into the woods and farther down River Road.

Tom Wilson was the unappointed leader. I watched as he scratched his head and began making scribbling lines on the pages of a Blue Horse tablet. The men were being divided into pairs, and each pair was handed a page torn from the notebook to use as a map of the territory they were to cover. They would have their work cut out. Most of the men were carrying canes or hoe handles, tools needed to poke and prod. With the warm days, along with gentle spring rains, tall grass and weeds had shot up all along the roads and in the fields and woods, leaving very poor visibility for anything that might be under the dense foliage.

"Bee, I wish Walter would give Edwina something to calm her nerves. She's getting more and more antsy, and she's making me nervous. I could just kill Richard for doing this to her," Bess whispered, after she slipped up behind me. "It makes no sense at all. Why would he just disappear? There's got to be an explanation."

"Bess, I've got my own ideas," I answered in another whisper. "I haven't shared everything I know with you. Richard took a walk last night after everybody went to bed. That is, everybody was in bed with the exception of Dickie and myself. I was tired and a little on edge last night, so I went out to the back porch to settle down a bit before going to bed. I overheard Dickie and Richard having a heated argument out by the barn about money—or, I should say, Dickie's lack of money. Richard told Dickie that it would be over his dead body that he got another red cent from him, and poor Dickie was devastated. An argument erupted, and Richard stomped off toward Vonion's house, leaving Dickie standing there alone and crying. I crept back into the house quietly, took a bath, and went on to bed. I heard the back door open and close just before going to sleep maybe an hour later, and I thought it was Richard coming in from his walk, but it could have been Dickie. I've got an idea now that Richard never returned to the house. Bess, I'm not saying anything, but Dickie was really out of control. I've tried to remember if I heard the door open and close another time before going off to sleep, and the more that I think about it, I'm sure I didn't. However, I was in the bathroom for a while, and I probably wouldn't have heard the door with the water running."

"What are you trying to say, Bee? Do you think Dickie could be responsible for Richard's disappearance?"

"I don't know, but it's possible. Let's listen carefully to anything we might overhear Dickie say to his mother or Mavis. I hate to think it, but Dickie could have been so desperate for money that he'd do his father in, if you know what I'm saying."

"Bee, I can hardly believe Dickie would do something so terrible as to murder his own father... for money."

"Bess, he was desperate, and desperate people do desperate things. You and I know that. We've seen it before. If he did do it, and I'm not saying he did, he would have done the dirty deed not far from the house; after all, somebody returned to the house within an hour or so after Richard walked off."

"That's true, but if Dickie did kill Richard, wouldn't somebody have found the body by now? Let's don't jump to judgment just yet. Let's give Dickie the benefit of a doubt and don't say a word of this to anybody yet. After all, no body has been found yet."

"Just what I was thinking, Bess. Now, we better get busy. We're gonna have to feed that army of hungry men in a while. I've already asked Ora Lee to mix up plenty of cornbread. Let's fry up more ham."

"I'm right behind you," Bess answered, as she tightened her apron around her waist. "Who would have ever thought we'd be feeding a search party this morning."

Having another frightful thought, I quickly turned and held out my arm to stop Bess. I whispered, "Bess, have you stopped to think that we might have the pleasure of Edwina's and Dickie's and Mavis's company here at the house until Richard is found...dead or alive?"

Bess looked horrified and quickly answered in a louder whisper, "Somebody better crack the whip and get this investigation into high gear."

CHAPTER TEN

Sheriff Ledbetter finally showed up three hours later that morning and three hours too late. With his siren blasting, his sheriff patrol car rolled into the yard. Dust from the lane filled the air as he stepped from the automobile, appearing to be exhausted. His bloodshot eyes sank into his unshaven face, revealing worry and frustration. His feet were dragging. Pond dirt was caked to his clothes, and his left pants leg was ripped and flapping.

"What in blue blazes is all that commotion?" asked Cousin Myrtle, as she suddenly awoke from her third nap of the morning. "Have the Nazis landed in the U.S.A.? Where's my gun?" she sharply demanded, as she tapped her cane against the porch floor with all her diminished strength. "I'd like to teach those heathens a lesson once and for all."

"Now, Cousin Myrtle. It's the sheriff, not the Nazis. And we need his help, so be kind to him."

Cousin Myrtle nodded and closed her eyes again. "Make sure y'all wake me before dinnertime, girls. Barbecued goat...fish, it makes no difference to me. It's all good."

"We will, Cousin Myrtle. Just rest up a little bit now," Bess tenderly answered, as she glanced toward me. "We'll make sure you don't miss a thing."

"That's right, Cousin Myrtle. Just settle back down now."

Bess sidled closer toward me. "Bee, what in tarnation is Sheriff Ledbetter trying to prove with all that noise? It is positively unnecessary."

"Well, I guess we're about to find out," I answered, as I walked over to the screen door to let the weary sheriff in. "Come on in, Sheriff. We've been expecting you for quite a while now."

"Knock some of that dirt off your boots before you come in, Sheriff," Bess quickly demanded. "You know you weren't raised in a barn. And what's the idea behind that siren? You're gonna clabber Hortence's milk and scare the hens right off the nest with all that racket."

"Had to use it to get those darn cows out of the road a mile or so back toward town," the sheriff responded, as he scraped his boots against the side of the steps before brushing the dried mud from his pants legs with his hands. "It sounded so good that I decided to let her go and leave it on for a while. I haven't had the occasion to use it since I sped all the way to Savannah to save y'all's hides from that so-called preacher a year or so back. Y'all were glad to hear it then, as I recall."

"You're right about that, Sheriff," I answered with a smile. "You got to that fancy hotel in the nick of time. We'll always be indebted to you."

"That's what the taxpayers pay me fer, Ms. Bee."

I waved for the sheriff to take a seat in one of the porch rockers. He lumbered sluggishly across the porch and slowly lowered his heavy body into the chair.

"Now what in tarnation's goin' on here? All I really know is what Nellie told me while'st I was tryin' to talk to Mama over the telephone earlier this morning." He tilted his mud-spattered hat farther back on his head and reached into his pocket for his handkerchief to wipe his brow. "I made a call to Mama to tell her to catch another ride to preachin' this morning since I was still tied up with the dad-blasted manhunt. Nellie interrupted our conversation to tell me that I was needed out here because there was a manhunt goin' on. I told her I knew all about the missin' man; we'd been tracking the son of a b...Oh! Oh, excuse me, ladies. That came out all wrong...all night long."

"We understand, Sheriff," I quickly blurted before Bess had a chance to reprimand our high sheriff about his limited vocabulary.

"Nellie informed me that there's another man missin'. This is all so confusin', Ms. Bee."

"Didn't Vernon radio you earlier this morning and tell you about our missing man catastrophe?" Bess sternly asked.

"No'um, I ain't heard a word from that scoundrel. He probably ain't woke up properly yet. Sometimes I think I need to let him go. The doctor done told me that he had some sort of sleeping disorder, and hit ain't really his fault that he falls asleep all the time. I reckon I need to take that into account and keep the fool on. He's good at what he can do...when he's awake, that is."

"And what would that be, Sheriff?" Bess abruptly asked, as her patience was obviously declining.

"Oh, he's got his good points. He can peel an apple all the way 'round without breakin' the skin, and he can brew a fairly decent cup of coffee." The sheriff smiled...and we smiled, too. "Now as I was saying, Nellie relayed to me that she overheard Earl talkin' with his sister, Mildred, over the telephone this morning about a manhunt that was goin' on out here. Nellie said that Earl had called Mildred to tell her that he was joinin' in on the hunt, and he really didn't need the clean Sunday-go-to-meeting overalls she was hurrying to iron. Mildred told him she was sorry she didn't get through with her washin', but she didn't get started early enough on account that she was out here at your farm until late Saturday evening. Nellie said she really didn't get that much from the conversation except that a man had disappeared out this way, and Mildred hadn't finished Earl's laundry." And with a mischievous twinkle in his tired eyes, he smiled and went on. "Nellie said Mildred told Earl she had mistakenly put his underwear into the same wash water as her new red bedspread, and now all his drawers are stained pink. Earl told her hit didn't make no difference to him what color his drawers were, 'they'd wear just the same,' and Mildred said 'thank goodness for that.' Mildred told Earl his underwear and overalls were still on the clothesline since they were still damp, but she'd have them off before the Methodist preacher drove by the house on his way to the church."

We chuckled, and it broke the tension a bit between our favorite lawman and us.

"Mildred is a Baptist, and we Baptists don't need to give the Methodist preacher fuel for his sermons, that's for sure," Bess laughingly replied. I absolutely knew persnickety Bess did, indeed, consider it a sin to have clothes on the line on Sunday. Is it a sin?

"Well, that's about all the information I got from Nellie this time. That Nellie, she usually don't miss a beat. She's 'bout my best source of information...other than, of course, Ms. Bee...and, ah, you too, Ms. Bess." What a relief...We were still in first place. "Now tell me exactly what's goin' on out here."

With mounting concern I had to quickly ask, "Before we get into all that, Sheriff, has that escaped convict been captured yet?"

"I wish to goodness I could say yes, but I can't. That scalawag ain't nowhere to be found. We've been up and down the river, through the woods with the dogs, questioned ever'body we can think of, and still not one clue. His trail has done grown cold, and the dogs are pretty worthless now. He could be in Timbuktu by now, fer all we know. He'll have to come up for air sooner or later, and we'll eventually get our man. I just don't rightly know when or where." The sheriff shook his head despondently before pulling his hat off and wiping the sweat from his forehead and balding head with his stained handkerchief.

I quickly explained our problem.

"I need to question Richard's family, Ms. Bee. First, his wife. Then his children."

"He only has one son. And now he has a daughter-in-law since his son recently married. Richard and Edwina, that's Richard's wife's name, met their new daughter-in-law just yesterday for the first time, and it was a total surprise to them that their son had taken a wife. Dickie introduced his bride to her in-laws right after they arrived here for the family reunion."

"I see."

"I'll get Edwina, but she might not be up to your questions. She's very fragile right now."

"I'll take that into consideration as I question her."

"Why don't you use the dining room for your interrogations, Sheriff?   It's private, and there's dessert laid out on the sideboard.   Feel free to indulge, and I'll get coffee."

"Thank you, ma'am. I might just take you up on that. You know I've got a sweet tooth." Hardly a secret. Sheriff Ledbetter's protruding belly covered his belt buckle, and his grin exposed toothless gums. The exhausted sheriff slowly pulled himself from the overloaded chair. "Just show me the way and I'll wait fer the wife. Oh, by the way, ladies, I'd like fer both of you to stay in the room with me while'st I question Ms. Edwina."

"Certainly, Sheriff, if you really think that it's necessary."

"I do. And remember you and Ms. Bess have been deputized before, and I hereby deputize the both of you again. Now let's get down to business. I want you both to listen carefully to ever'thin' that's said. I need all the ears I can get."

Sheriff Ledbetter carefully placed his coffee cup in the matching saucer and stood as a flustered and anxious Edwina entered the room.   She nervously tugged at her handkerchief as she sat down at the opposite end of the dining table from the sheriff. Sheriff Ledbetter introduced himself and asked Edwina to relax.

"How on earth do you think I can relax, Sheriff? My faithful husband of over forty years has disappeared. He was my whole life. I...I don't think I can go on without him." Edwina sniffed into her handkerchief, and Bess rolled her eyes.

"There now, Ms. Edwina, we'll eventually find him. Nobody just disappears from the face of the earth. If he ran off, he'll eventually make a mistake, and somebody will report seeing him, especially if you post a reward. If, God forbid, he's dead, there's a body out there somewhere. Sorry to put it so bluntly, but by now, I'm sure you've thought the worst."

Edwina tearfully nodded. "Sheriff, (sniff-sniff) something tragic happened to my Richard. I just know it. He would never leave me on his own accord. He loved me too...too much." Pitifully, Edwina wept again into her soggy handkerchief. Bess glanced at me with "the look," and I returned it. Edwina wiped her nose and muttered, "He was totally devoted to me...and to our son."

"I'm sure of it, ma'am. Now tell me, when was the last time you saw your husband? Please be precise with your answer. Everything you say can be very important to the investigation."

"Well, er, he and I were in the bedroom back there in the house last night. I was preparing for bed. It was after dark. I'm not sure what time it was, but not late. He said he needed some air and thought he's go outside for a smoke. I don't like for him to smoke in the bedroom before we go to bed; you know it leaves an awful odor in the air. He said he wouldn't be late and walked out. It had been a trying day and I was exhausted, so I went on to bed and fell asleep. When I awoke this morning, I immediately realized Richard hadn't slept in the bed with me."

"Did the two of you have a quarrel or have a disagreement last evening or recently?"

"Well, er, we did have a slight disagreement yesterday. But nothing dramatic."

"And what was the disagreement about, Ms. Edwina?"

"Dickie, our son, was in need of some extra money, and Richard was not in the mood to give it to him. It was nothing, really."

"And was the disagreement settled before you went to sleep?"

"No, not really. Richard can be very stubborn at times, but I'm sure we could have ironed the whole thing out if we had been given the time."

"I see. Now tell me, Ms. Edwina, has anything unusual or different happened between your husband and yourself recently other than the incident over money fer your son?"

"No, I can't think of anything. We did, of course, meet our son's new wife for the first time yesterday, and that was very stressful. We didn't really quarrel about it...we were just... surprised. It caused some tension between us, but nothing major."

"When you and your husband would...er...quarrel or have a disagreement, what would it usually be concernin', other than your son's need for more money?"

"Well, we didn't quarrel very often, but, um, let me think. We did have a slight disagreement over the directions to the farm yesterday. And Richard was very unpleasant when he realized my bridge club was to meet at our house last week. I don't know why; we didn't bother him. He stayed in the bedroom the whole time while we played cards in the living room. Oh, and Richard wanted to listen to the ball game on the radio night before last, and I wanted to listen to Serenades After Twilight. You see, that's my favorite program on the radio, and Richard knows it. Anyway, he stomped out of the living room and went out to the porch to smoke instead of staying with me and listening to the soothing music. A-n-d, now let me see. Recently, I had new drapes for the dining room custom-made, and Richard thought it was totally frivolous and expensive. He fumed the whole time he was hanging them. A-n-d...I like to go to church on Sunday nights, and Richard usually fusses all the way to the service. Oh, and he absolutely will not cut the grass until I worry him to death about it. That always brings out the worst in him. Now, let me see..."

"I think I get the picture, Ms. Edwina. Now, has your husband ever had an affair with another woman?"

"Why, Sheriff, I am appalled that you would even ask such a thing! Never!"

"Never looked at another woman?"

"Never...unless you consider the church pianist we had year before last. She didn't have any more musical ability than a potted plant. She'd hike up her dress over her knees and let her dress tail fly while she banged away. And I do mean bang. Every man's eyeballs in the entire church had to be glued back in place after every hymn. I quickly nipped that situation in the bud, though, when I changed our seating arrangement to the other side of the sanctuary, second pew from the back. All we could see from back there was her head bobbing up and down like she was riding on a galloping horse. I don't really consider Richard to be a pervert, though. Now that lustful preacher, that was another story. He gawked at the piano player so badly that he couldn't keep his mind on the scriptures or his sorry sermons. We finally had to let him go, but that didn't help matters much. The next preacher was worse. We finally figured out that we should get rid of the piano player and not the preacher."

"Now that's very interestin', but...what about money matters? Did you and Richard argue over finances?"

"Oh, no. We hardly ever quarreled about money. Well...maybe once in a while. Last week, I thought it was necessary to brighten up our bathroom with a new towel ensemble. After I purchased it, Richard had the audacity to make me carry it back to the store for a refund. Mr. McAfee at the Cash and Carry took it back even though I had pulled the tags off, under penalty of law. I know you're a lawman, Sheriff, but I'll bet you don't know that it's a crime to pull the labels off of linens? Well, I didn't at the time either, but now I do, and I promised Mr. McAfee I'd never do it again. And I won't, Sheriff. I promise you, I won't."

And so on and on it went...

Sheriff Ledbetter finally excused Edwina after she complained that she was totally exhausted. Bess escorted her down the hall to take refuge in the bedroom. Obvious by the slump of the sheriff's shoulders and the grim expression on his face, the sheriff was exhausted also.

"Sheriff Ledbetter, did you learn anything at all from your interrogation of Edwina?" I asked, as I lingered in the dining room with him.

"Richard probably committed suicide."

I nodded in agreement.

CHAPTER ELEVEN

Sheriff, you're not really serious, are you? Richard's not the kind of person to commit suicide."

The sheriff frowned. "What kind of person do you think commits suicide?"

"Well, you know, not any of my kin people. We don't do things like that. Why, there hasn't been a scandal in our family since Will's third cousin ran off with the shoe clerk over at Pearly's Department Store years and years ago. And certainly nothing like that would ever happen here on the farm, of all places."

"Why not? It's a possible explanation, maybe even a probable one. Stranger things happen every day. I know that woman's kin to you, but livin' with the likes of her would have been enough to put most men over the edge years ago."

"Well, Richard's had over forty long years to get used to Edwina. I don't see why he'd wait this long to kill himself."

"We can't eliminate anything at this point. And there's always the thought that he might have met up with Eddie Pink out there in the dark."

"I've thought of that, Sheriff. Several things could have resulted from a confrontation with a dangerous criminal on the run."

"Yeah, Eddie might have kidnapped him. Richard could be tied up out there somewhere in them there woods and nobody's come across him yet. Or there's always the outside chance that they're on the run together. That's a possibility." The sheriff hesitated as he pulled his hat off and scratched his sweaty head. "I hate to say it, but an escaped prisoner on the run like Eddie Pink is even capable of murderin' Richard."

"Oh, Sheriff, I hope not!"

"I hope not, too, but Eddie might have thought he had to murder Richard to keep him from talkin'. We can't overlook any possibility."

"I know you're right. I just cannot accept the idea that Richard would have walked away on his own accord. I've always thought him to be a decent and caring man. His nature is not to hurt anybody."

"Depressed people do disturbin' things. Ms. Bee, I don't want to sound rude, but Richard has probably put up with a whole lot in his lifetime, and he might have finally decided to leave it all behind. People disappear every day. They just walk away from responsibility and the people that they're supposed to love and care for. They think they can start a whole new life somewhere where nobody knows them, but most of the time the challenge is too great, and they eventually come back home."

"You're quite the philosopher, Sheriff."

"Shucks, Ms. Bee, I ain't no philosopher, just an observer of people. That's my job, you know. I guess you better get that new daughter-in-law in here. Remember, I want you to stay in the room while I question her. Don't worry about botherin' Ms. Bess. I imagine she's busy."

"I'll round Mavis up for you, Sheriff, but remember, she didn't even know Richard before yesterday."

"There's always an off chance she might have picked up on something. Would it be too presumptuous if I had another piece of pie while'st I wait fer you to get her in here? It ain't often I get accommodations like these."

I smiled inwardly and answered, "Help yourself, Sheriff."

"Oh, by the way, Ms. Bee, where do Edwina and Richard live at the present and what's their last name?"

"Perkins. Richard and Edwina Perkins. Their home is Swainsville. Richard actually grew up there, and he has lived in Swainsville his entire life. His company sells insurance, Perkins Protection, and he's obviously made a good living."

"Umm."

I found Mavis nervously pacing back and forth from the mailbox to the porch, puffing on a cigarette. She protested when I told her the sheriff wanted to question her.

"I hardly knew that old man. I don't see how I would be of any help at all. Tell the sheriff to talk to somebody else, somebody who knows something." She inhaled deeply on her cigarette before tapping the end of it on the mailbox.

"Mavis, dear, you must cooperate with the sheriff. You really don't have much of a choice. Now, I'm sorry you got caught up in this matter, but since we can't change things, just answer the questions the sheriff asks. And by the way, thank you for dealing with Edwina. I know she can be a hard pill to swallow, but she is your mother-in-law now, and she adores her son...er, your husband."

"Please don't remind me." Mavis spit the words out as she threw her cigarette butt into the nandina bushes. "Now, where's that sheriff? I might as well get this over with. I don't know what he thinks I could possibly know about a man I just met yesterday."

"He's in the dining room. And if I were you, I'd pick that up if you want to stay in Bess's good graces. She'll spot that cigarette butt the second she walks out of the door."

"Oh, brother." Mavis gave me a disgruntled glare before reluctantly reaching down.

Mavis stomped up the steps just as Vonion rounded the corner of the house carrying the milk bucket. "There you is, Ms. Bee. I been a' lookin' ever'where fer you." He dropped the bucket to the ground and wearily leaned against the mailbox. "I'm pure gave out. All that walkin' and huntin'; hit's downright frustratin'. Mr. Richard ain't nowhere round here, but if'n he is, he's plum invisible. And them crazy chickens and hogs is jittery as lit firecrackers this morning. Somethin' bad disturbin' the peace out there. Notin' I could do would settle them antsy hogs down. They wants to fight and that just ain't in their nature. Hortence irritable and that ain't never good. She knocked the milk bucket over twice with her long ole tail, and then she stepped right on my bad toe. She know better than all that. All this here excitement done upsot the whole barnyard...and me too."

"Vonion, I hope we don't have a fox or a bobcat hanging around out there. That's about all we need right now. I sympathize with you, but this is a difficult time for everybody. We'll make it through by the grace of God."

"Yes'um, we've seen worser times than these. We be all right, if'n you say so. Now if'n Mr. Will were here rat now, we could just depend on him to fix ever'thang."

"Well, he's not here...and he's not coming back! So just pray." Vonion and I had the same sentiments exactly. "Now, if you've finished with your chores, please help Ora Lee in the house. She's plum wore out this morning, and we haven't even started preparing dinner for everybody. I imagine some of the searchers will head this way about noontime. We'll certainly have to be hospitable and feed them."

"Ms. Bee, you knows I ain't no hand in the kitchen. I's'll just be in the way in there. Plus, Ms. Bess on the rampage this morning. When I brung the eggs and milk to the kitchen, she met me at the door and ordered me to take my boots off a'fore I come in. You knows good and well I ain't got time to unlace my brogans and pull'um off ever time I walks into the kitchen. Then I gots to put'um back on and tie'um up again when I goes back out. How a man gonna get any work done?"

I was actually quite amused but gave Vonion a firm look. My high position at the farm had certainly been uprooted the fateful day Bess set her baggage down here. "I'll talk to Bess about that. She's just wound up this morning. Vonion, offer your services, and if there's nothing for you to do, just get out of Ora Lee's way. But I'm sure Bess has a list of things for you to do."

"Yes'um, I'm sure she do. She always do," Vonion muttered reluctantly.

I headed to the dining room.

Mavis, with a freshly molded, seductive smile spread across her pretty face, was seated in one of the dining chairs placed against the wall. As if by chance (but I knew better), Mavis had chosen the only chair in the room where the sheriff had a bird's-eye view of her entire voluptuous body. With her long legs exposed under the hem of her skirt and several of her blouse buttons recently undone at just the right places, little was left to the sheriff's imagination. He was standing by the window, and his eyes were firmly planted on Mavis's shapely form.

Mavis casually tossed her long hair over one shoulder, ran her fingers through her silky locks, and protested, "Like I told you, Mr. Sheriff, I didn't know the man until yesterday, and we've hardly spoken ten words between each other since then." Mavis changed her position in the chair, crossed her well-proportioned legs and pulled at her skirt, exposing much more of her slim ankles and legs. The sheriff quickly averted his eyes but not quickly enough. He blushed. It was obvious the lovely Mavis was well-accomplished at getting a man's full attention.

"Now, Ms. Mavis, where do you come from and what is your maiden name?"

"I'm from Macon. Born and lived there ever since. McNeely, Mavis McNeely." Mavis seemed to be relaxing and smiled a bit as she suggestively maneuvered her long, willowy body into another position in the chair.

"What is your occupation?"

"Why, you know very well, Mr. Sheriff, I'm a married woman. I don't have to make a living any longer. My husband takes good care of me now."

She smugly smiled as if she had achieved her main purpose in life.

"What did you do fer a living before your marriage? I understand you and your husband have just recently married."

"I was a waitress at the Blue Bell Café and was very fortunate to have that job. Employment is hard to come by these days." She blinked her lovely brown eyes several times. Her every movement was self-choreographed and so obvious...to me, but to the sheriff...? I wasn't quite sure.

"And where did you meet your husband?"

"At the café. He ate there regularly." She seductively crossed her legs again, and this time her skirt shifted up just a little higher.

"And he's a student. Is that correct?" The sheriff, having no safe place to focus his attention, peered out the window.

"Yes, he is, but he'll soon be through with that dreary old law school. He plans to make a living as a big-time lawyer, and we'll make a fortune right off the bat." Mavis alluringly smiled again and adjusted her skirt up another inch or two. It was quite apparent to me she sought to gain the sheriff's admiration; after all, what better advantage could she have? "I'll have my own car and everything then."

"And I suppose you won't be workin' much longer."

"Oh, I've already quit that boring job. I'll never have to dirty my hands again in any ole café or noisy juke joint. Dickie wants me at home where he can pamper me fulltime. He's already talking to a maid service. Dickie and his family are already financially secure, but we'll have even more money when he starts working." Mavis seductively smiled again. I closed my eyes and swallowed, hardly believing what I was hearing or seeing.

"And where did you work prior to your job at the café?"

"Oh, I was desperate for a decent job back then, and the only thing I could find was at a hot night spot. I was a floor dancer. I, ah, danced with the gentlemen, waited on tables, sold cigarettes, checked coats. Really, anything they needed done, I did it." I could only imagine what else she did. "It was just a dive, really not a high-class joint. I was glad to get out of there." Mavis tried to appear pitiful this time and was clearly working on the sheriff's sympathy.

"Tell me about your family, Ms. Mavis."

"Well...I have my mama and an older sister, Maxine. Daddy died in the Big War." Mavis leaned over and displayed a bit of cleavage for the sheriff.

"Did you live in your mother's house before you married?"

"Yes...sir."

"And your sister, Maxine McNeely, is that right? Did she live there also?"

"That's her name, but, oh, no. She's lived out of town for some time now. I'm not sure exactly where. We hardly ever see her anymore."

"Do you know what kind of work she does?"

"Oh, um, I'm not real sure. She doesn't have a real vocation that I know of."

"Is she married?"

"No, she's not. I don't think so, anyway."

"And your mother. Is she employed?

"No, she hasn't been able to work in years. She gets a small pension from the government. You know, because of Daddy…"

"I see. Now, you claim you did not know Richard before yesterday. Is that accurate?"

"Yes. That's absolutely correct. I've never laid eyes on the man before." Mavis yawned as if she was becoming bored. "You don't have a smoke, do you, Mr. Sheriff?"

"Sorry, I don't, but we'll be through here in a minute. And how long have you known Dickie?"

"Oh, about two months. We had a whirlwind romance." Mavis seductively smiled at the sheriff. "Dickie fell madly in love with me almost immediately." Mavis yawned, stretched her long arms, and dramatically blinked her eyes several times.

"I see. Now tell me, have you ever been married before?"

"Oh, my goodness, no. What kind of girl do you think I am?" Mavis puckered her red lips and batted her heavy eyelashes at the sheriff. The sheriff, realizing he was the object of Mavis's flirtation, blushed again.

"And were you, uh, financially secure before you and Dickie married, Ms. Mavis?"

Mavis frowned and leaned forward, allowing her blouse to fall open. "I don't know what you're getting at, Mr. Sheriff, but I did not marry Dickie for money. He is a good catch, I do admit to that, but that's not why I married him. Dickie and I are very much in love with each other." She tossed her head back and smugly said, "We're going to have a wonderful future, that is, if his mean old mama will ever leave us alone."

"I'm sure you will, Ms. Mavis. Is there anything else you need to tell me while we're havin' this discussion? Anything at all about your past or about your marriage?"

"I'm sure there's nothing else I could tell you other than this situation is a total nightmare. And if you need to talk with me again, let's do it alone next time." Mavis gave me a quick glance. "I like to keep my private life private. I don't care to have everybody knowing my personal business."

"Er, I'm sure we've covered all the bases. You can be excused now, but please don't leave the farm unless I'm notified. Thank you."

"I told you I couldn't help you. I don't know anything about this dreadful business." The sheriff received one last come-hither glance before Mavis stood and marched out.

I quickly rose and closed the door. "Whew, you might have more than you can handle with Mavis, Sheriff."

"Oh, I can handle her. She's just puttin' on an act. She thinks she's a real good actress."

"I'm glad you recognize that. Sheriff, are we getting anywhere?"

"Maybe. Mavis interests me. She definitely married with the idea of a life on Easy Street. That luxurious lifestyle can only be accomplished with the use of Richard's money for the time bein' until her husband pinches the blood out of his first big client. I need to check out her story. Mavis might have been doin' more than just dancin' at that hot night spot."

"She definitely thinks you're a big pushover. She's obviously used to having her way with men. She thinks all she has to do is bat her eyes and cross her legs."

"You are the real observer of people, Ms. Bee. Now what do you think the chances are of gettin' any information out of your cousin Myrtle? She was here yesterday also, I believe."

"I'd say slim or none. Myrtle can't stay awake long enough for you to question her. But I'll get her if you think we can learn anything from her."

"No, Ms. Bee, don't worry about that right now. I'm think I'm gonna catch up with the search party and find out if they're on to anything yet. And then I've got some checkin' around to do. I know it's an imposition but, in the meantime, don't let any of your kin people leave the premises."

"I'll do my best, Sheriff. I assume you're planning on talking with a few people in Swainsville about Richard. See if he had any known problems or bad debts or anything like that. Check his bank account and see if he's withdrawn a large amount of money recently. And as bad as I hate to think it, there's always the possibility that Richard could have been having an affair. And what about Mavis? She might not have been totally truthful about her past. Could there be a connection between her and Richard?" I can absolutely never help myself. It's just my nature to give instructions to the sheriff.

"Just give me some time, Ms. Bee, to do some checkin' around. And I'd like to talk with Dickie as soon as I possibly can. Give me a call when he comes in. And, Ms. Bee, I don't need you to do all the sheriffin' this time. I can handle the situation."

I smiled sweetly as I stood on the porch, watching the sheriff's car leave the yard. Sheriff Ledbetter didn't really believe that I wasn't on the case, did he?

I pondered, will Dickie inform the sheriff about his last encounter with his father? I wasn't quite ready to give all my information to the sheriff yet...but soon. And where was Mavis's sister? Mavis seemed to be uncertain about her whereabouts. That was odd. Oh, and please, Richard, wherever you are, please come back. I don't know how long my hospitality can hold out.

CHAPTER TWELVE

Preparations for lunch filled the rest of the morning. A few of the searchers had begun to trickle into the yard, bringing with them their hungry hound dogs. We were prepared for the men, but we had absolutely never thought about hungry dogs. Ora Lee ordered Vonion to get the grease left from the fish fry, and she dropped hunks of corn bread down into the greasy pot to make a mush for the dogs. The dogs seemed satisfied with the vittles, but they continuously barked and pulled at their leashes, never relaxing any length of time.

Ora Lee reserved the other pan of corn bread for the humans. What was left of the barbecued goat and fish was heated and served along with the leftover vegetables, salads, and desserts. The food was washed down with plenty of sweet tea and some easily detected jugs of liquor and forbidden moonshine.

Vonion's job was to be hospitable and guard the tables against pesky insects and gnats. As each of the men came by and picked up a plate, Vonion invited him to help himself to whatever he wanted. As the last of the men sopped their plates and rubbed their full bellies, we knew we had done our duty.

The warm afternoon had lingered on. It had become a strong likelihood that the day would end without a shred of evidence about the whereabouts of Richard, or Eddie Pink, for that matter.

Edwina had weathered the biggest part of the day in her room and had only appeared to bring her empty lunch plate into the kitchen and to ask once in the afternoon about the search. She was depressed and withdrawn.

Mavis also stayed to herself in the front room most of the afternoon after her noonday meal was eaten alone at the dining table. Everything was almost too quiet on the home front.

After the dishes were put away and the scraps all gathered for the animals, Bess, Ora Lee, and I collapsed on the porch, swearing that this nightmare had to soon be over. There wasn't enough food in our larder to feed hungry men who tramped through the woods and along the creek banks another day.

Sheriff Ledbetter drove up later in the afternoon, looking about as forlorn as a man who had lost his dog. He kicked the bottom porch step in frustration before he uttered a word. "No sign of a dang thing. I got to believe Richard has done left these parts, and there's not one shred of evidence where he is now. He's a smart cookie, that's fer sure. I don't believe he's dead, or we'd have found a body somewhere out there. The only answer is he's found a way out of here right by himself...or with somebody's help. My guess is he's teamed up with Eddie Pink, and the two of them have walked off together. It makes sense. They've both just vanished, disappeared into thin air!" He waved his arms. "We ain't fount a thang, not a hide or a hair!" He kicked the step again, this time harder.

"What are you gonna do next, Sheriff?" Bess reluctantly called from the porch.

"Well, I need to reexamine Ms. Edwina, and I want to interview Dickie. Then I'm gonna go ahead and put out a missing person's bulletin. It's been time enough now since Richard's been gone almost twenty-four hours."

"Have you learned anything from the sources that you've contacted?" I asked as I walked over to the door. "By the way, we're alone here. You can talk freely. Edwina and Mavis are both out back. Edwina walked down to Ora Lee's house, and Mavis is walking in the orchard."

"Not much. Richard was in debt, but not that bad. His business had fell off some, but from what I could tell from his bank accounts, he was still solvent. I put in several calls to different individuals over in Swainsville, and nobody I talked to knew anything about an affair, but several people said they wouldn't have blamed him fer one. It seems Ms. Edwina is the one with the reputation. I couldn't find one person who spoke kindly of her. That really leads me to lean toward the conclusion that Richard decided to leave his overbearing wife and make a whole new life somewheres else. Maybe this is his dishonorable way of leavin' her."

"Will the men continue to search?" I asked hopefully.

"Yes'um. Since there's a manhunt going on fer Eddie Pink, we'll continue lookin' fer Richard, too. I hope you ladies are prepared to keep Ms. Edwina and her family fer a few more days. I know it's an imposition, but I need to keep them close by. And, Ms. Bee and Ms. Bess, I need you to watch their every move and listen to every word they say. The clues to finding Richard could be right here under our noses. Are y'all up to it?"

"You betcha we are. Remember you deputized us this morning. We're definitely on the case," I eagerly answered. Bess rolled her eyes.

"Deputy-ing, cooking, washing, ironing, nursing, entertaining, what else?" Bess sighed. "Sheriff, you better hurry up and find that man. We can't keep it up forever."

"I'll do my best. Remember, ladies, I'll do the sheriffin'. Y'all just do the snoopin'."

I nodded and Bess sighed.

In the cool of the late afternoon, Bess and I took a break from the routine of housework and wandered out to help Vonion in his garden. I was busy dipping water from an old, dented milking bucket onto young tomato plants that Vonion had started from seeds in tin cans that he had placed near the wood cooking stove in Ora Lee's kitchen. Bess was heeling the potato vines with extra dirt. The young potatoes would need plenty of soil around them as they grew and matured in the ground. Vonion's garden was thriving. It was his pride and joy, especially his watermelons. A garden takes lots of time and effort, and Vonion kept his garden weed free, fertilized, and watered. He hardly ever accepted our offer to help, but today was different. Vonion sensed that we needed to be out in the open afternoon air, away from the complications that Edwina and Mavis had brought into the house.

Dickie had not returned from the search during the day, and Bess and I were beginning to get a little concerned that something might have happened to detain him. I was leaning over a tomato plant with the dipper in my hand when I heard a loud scream coming from the direction of the porch. Bess dropped her hoe and ran toward the house with Vonion and me bringing up the rear. As we rounded the corner of the house, another shriek filled the air, along with the sound of breaking glass.

Two wild women were rolling around on the porch, the younger one with a fist balled and ready to knock the daylights out of the older one. The older one had a handful of long hair. Skirts were flying. The older one was holding her own, but it was obvious that the younger, thinner one was bound to win. Just as Bess opened the screen door, a left fist came down on a fat nose, and a sprinkling of blood splattered across the floor. The right fist reared back and was aimed toward the older one's fat cheek when Bess grabbed at it from behind and held on before it could do more damage. I grabbed the injured one and stumbled forward as I attempted to shield her from more hard hits. The older one was more powerful than I realized and pushed me back as she grabbed for another handful of hair.

"You little bitch," Edwina screamed. "You might think you can come in here and have my only child, but you've never had to deal with me. I'll never, ever give him up to the likes of a gold-digging hussy like you." Bess was sitting on top of Mavis by now, and an amazed Vonion was running around in circles. "I know about girls like you. When I get through with you, you'll wish you hadn't ever laid eyes on Dickie Perkins, much less married him." Edwina was pulling hair with the strength of a mother tiger. Mavis was able to dislodge Bess from her position and reached over to claw Edwina's arm and the hand that was holding onto a clump of her hair. Edwina twisted out of my hold and grabbed at Mavis's hand and bit down on her little finger. Mavis screamed in pain as Edwina took advantage and bit even harder. That's when Vonion jumped right in between the ladies (and I say that loosely) and started grabbing arms and legs. I didn't have any choice; I slapped Edwina across her face. Bess quickly sat down on top of Mavis again, and I jumped on top of Edwina while she was still in a daze. We finally had them trapped.

"Time out!" Bess screamed. "Get control of yourselves, ladies. Are you trying to kill each other?"

"Yes," they both yelled. Bess and I held on.

Mavis screamed, "You're impossible! If you think for one minute Dickie would choose YOU over ME, you are stupid. You might not have noticed, but I've got a big advantage over you. Dickie happens to love my sexy body! I've got him now, you big, fat, old woman." (Edwina had finally met her match.)

Dickie stormed in from somewhere, frantically hollering, "What's going on in here? Are y'all crazy or something? Mama, have you lost your ever-loving mind? Mavis, dear, are you hurt? Here, let me help you up."

Dickie carefully lifted Mavis from the pile of legs and arms. Vonion, nobly, but not necessarily gently, reached down and helped a battered and scarred Edwina to her feet as Bess and I slowly pulled ourselves up.

Tempers cooled down considerably after I insisted that our captives sit at opposite corners of the porch. Vonion paced back and forth between the two, ready to pounce if anybody made a sudden move. "Y'all's just amaze me. I ain't never seen notin' worser, sep'tin' when my baby brother tied two wet hens over Ma's clothesline and left 'um there to kill each other. "

"What's going on between the two of you?" I pleaded. "You're both supposed to be adults. I know this is an unpleasant situation, but, ladies, please act like ladies. We don't need this kind of drama right now with everything else that's going on around here."

"Well, she shouldn't have started it," Mavis replied, as she straightened her blouse. "That old woman told me to go home because she wasn't about to share Dickie with me. Who does she think she is, anyway? I'm the wife, and she's only the mother. Dickie's tired of her smothering him to pieces." Edwina glared at Mavis, and Mavis returned her glare.

Nursing her swelling nose with her handkerchief, Edwina didn't back down. "Listen, you little hussy. I've been Dickie's mother for twenty-five years, and I've taken good care of him. You come in here and think you can take over my son after all I've done for him? Well, you've got another think coming. I'll never turn him loose. Never!"

"Dickie," I quickly jumped in, hoping to change the subject, "did y'all find any trace of your father?" Edwina hadn't thought to ask.

"I'm afraid not. It's a total mystery. No sign of that Eddie Pink, either. Mama, I just don't know what to think."

"Oh, my Lord," Edwina whined. "What am I gonna do? Without your father, I don't have a penny. Everything we have is tied up in his business." Edwina was crying real tears now. "I don't know what I'll do without my Richard."

I wanted to scream, "Go home and get a life," but I didn't. I just sat tight, looking at my overturned porch table and Mama's McCoy vase, smashed to smithereens, lying on the floor in a puddle of water and broken daffodil stems. I was so tired and so ready for the entire Perkins family to just go somewhere else and leave us alone. Does that make me a bad person?

"Mama, I think we have to face reality. Daddy is gone, and I don't think he's coming back. He either left on his own accord or something dreadful happened to him. I just can't imagine where he is. Mama, do you think he wanted to leave you bad enough that he would just walk away?"

"I...I don't know," Edwina squalled. "He...he might have wanted to leave me...but I can't imagine Richard doing such a dreadful thing to me. He must be dead. That's all I can think of."

"What about you, Dickie? Do you know of any reason your father would leave? I know he was shocked that you married, but that wouldn't have caused him to walk away."

"I can't think of a thing that would make Daddy angry enough to leave. He and I had a good relationship; we never argued or disagreed with each other about anything." Boy, did a red flag go up in my mind.

"Well, something happened," Bess commented. "By the way, Dickie, the sheriff wants to talk with you as soon as possible. I'll see if I can get him on the telephone. In the meantime, I'm sure you're hungry. Mavis, will you please fix Dickie a plate while I call the sheriff?"

"What does he want to talk with me about? I can't think of a thing that would help him in an investigation," Dickie anxiously replied.

"Well, obviously the sheriff should be the judge of that," I answered a little too sharply.

The tension in the house was tight and getting tighter by the minute.

CHAPTER THIRTEEN

As soon as Bess walked away, I asked Dickie to encourage Edwina and Mavis to make amends with each other. He suggested they take a leisurely walk out in the late afternoon air. I knew more walking had to be the last thing on Dickie's mind after a long day of hiking through the woods searching for his father, but a truce was crucial to our sanity right now. "We do need to cool the atmosphere around here," he said, as he turned to open the screen door for the ladies. Oops! I didn't call Edwina and Mavis ladies again, did I? "It'll do Mama and Mavis good to walk off some of their hostility. Tell Cousin Bess we'll be back in shortly, and I'll eat as soon as we return."

I suggested (really ordered) Vonion to walk with them just in case Dickie needed a referee. Vonion hesitantly stood to leave, but not before giving me that look of his that would raise the dead from the grave. I had really begun to rely on Vonion much too much lately, and I was beginning to realize that he might head for the hills if I didn't let up on him soon or maybe later. As soon as the foursome rounded the corner of the house toward the pecan orchard, I headed for Edwina's room. I had not had an opportunity to go through Richard's personal things, and now was the perfect time. I'd better hurry.

The room was a total disaster. Edwina's oversized suitcase was lying wide open with her clothes jumbled inside as if a small child had been rummaging through the contents looking for a particular item. Pieces of unmentionables and a dressing gown were hanging over the sides of her luggage, and a couple of dresses were carelessly thrown over a straight chair. Her shoes were scattered across the floor, and her toiletries were strewn across the dresser. Pressed powder coated the top of the chest of drawers, and hairpins were scattered across the rumpled, crocheted scarf on the bedside table. Her opened clutch purse and a wrinkled handkerchief were carelessly thrown on Mama's rocking chair by the fireplace.

On the other hand, Richard's one small piece of luggage sat closed in the corner, as if he had not yet had the chance to open it. Hoping I had enough time to rummage through it, I threw the suitcase across the bed and quickly snapped open the clasps. It was extremely organized. His extra shirt was lying on top of underwear, and socks and a tie were neatly rolled and slid into the corner, along with a small cloth bag containing a tie clip and a pair of cuff links. Richard always had been a spiffy dresser.

That's when I realized Richard had to have been in the suitcase yesterday, sometime after their arrival. Lying under the cloth bag were his dark glasses, the ones he always wore in the bright sunshine and especially when he drove. I distinctly remembered him wearing them yesterday as he drove into the yard. A small scrap of paper was neatly tucked under the glasses and, you absolutely know it, I picked it up and read it. The scratchy pencil-written print on the paper had been written to resemble a child's handwriting. It read: "We can do it again. SOON." No signature. What on earth did that mean, and who was it from? I noted the paper looked strangely familiar to me. Where had I seen it before? I hastily folded the paper and placed it in my pocket; after all, Richard wasn't here to know whether the note had been removed or not. That's when I realized exactly where I had seen that paper—in my own home. Someone had to have removed the paper from Bess's fancy notepad and handed Richard the note after Edwina's and his arrival. Richard had hidden the note in his suitcase. How very odd.

I hastily peeked into the cloth pocket of the lining in the lid of the suitcase and discovered a set of keys, a fingernail file, a small plastic hair comb, a check stub, and a small black savings account book.

I really hated invading Richard's privacy, but right now my good detective skills had really kicked in.

Richard noted a balance of $10.49 in his checking account. Could that really be all the money Richard and Edwina had in their account? I could hardly believe it. Maybe that's why Edwina only sent $2.00 for expenses toward the weekend; they didn't have any money. I imagined Richard was relieved we never cashed that check.

The first check stub indicated a check had been written a week ago to the dry cleaners for $1.95. The second stub was for a check written four days ago as a loan payment to Kingsborough Finance Company for $36.75. Checking back further, I discovered the third and latest check stub. It indicated that Richard paid for gas at a service station. It was written for the amount of $2.34. Nothing unusual about any of that; he was probably gassing up for their trip here. The rest of the checks and check stubs were unused. The little black savings book clearly showed that Edwina and Richard were really down on their luck. Richard had started out the year with $265.35 in savings. Over the course of a few months that amount had decreased considerably. The savings account, showing several recent withdrawals, was now down to $39.14. Not much savings, if you asked me, and I know all about dwindling savings accounts.

I carefully tucked the contents back into place, closed the suitcase, and placed it back in the exact spot where I had found it. As I began to think about what I had learned, I moved Edwina's purse and handkerchief from the rocker to the dresser and sat down before closing my eyes to ponder.

Somebody had passed Richard a note, a note written on a piece of decorative notepaper. The tea-stained colored notepaper was embellished with pale green ivy encircling the center and was exactly like the ones in the pad that sat on the table beside our telephone. The note had to have been passed to Richard after he arrived at the house yesterday by someone with access to our home. I was absolutely sure of that.

Two heads are always better than one. I'd show the note to Bess immediately; maybe she could shed some light on the situation. I quickly looked around for any evidence that I had been in the room before placing the purse and handkerchief back into the chair seat and walking out to find Bess. Unfortunately, the strollers were walking up the steps as I hurried to the kitchen. I quickly changed my course and greeted them, feeling a smidgeon guilty about going through Richard's personal things. Not really.

A peace treaty must have been made from the looks of the trio. Dickie, looking dreadfully fatigued and haggard, placed his arms around each of the significant women in his life after they stepped into the porch. "Mother understands my situation a little better now, Cousin Bee. She says she can accept my and Mavis's marriage. She knows she doesn't have much choice in the matter, and she says she'll treat

Mavis with respect from now on. I think we got a lot of things settled. Now if we only knew where Daddy is."

"Dickie, why don't you go on ahead and eat, and Mavis, dear, why don't you accompany your husband into the kitchen. I know he would love to have your company. Edwina, I'm sure you're in need of rest after your taxing afternoon. Go on to your room and lie down awhile. It'll do you good."

"I am a bit weary, Cousin Bee. Rest will help and a little snack would be wonderful as well. Do you think I might have a ham and cheese sandwich and maybe a few of your homemade pickles? Just a little mustard on one side of the bread and mayonnaise on the other would be nice. Not too much, though. I have to watch my figure, you know. Oh, a piece of chocolate cake to top it off would be heavenly. And a cup of coffee would help settle my nerves...if you don't mind. I'll take it in my room on a bed tray. Oh, Cousin, you are such a life saver. I can't think of a place I had rather be right now than here, surrounded by my family, giving me comfort. If only my Richard were here."

"I'll get your food, Edwina," I replied behind gritted teeth. "Just go on to your room...and rest."

Bess and I didn't get a minute to ourselves until later that evening as we were preparing for bed. Everyone else was finally tucked away for a peaceful night, I hoped. Bess was ill as a hornet, and my nerves were frazzled as well. "Bess, I want you to get a good night's rest tonight. I've already asked Vonion to take Cousin Myrtle to the bus station in the morning, so we'll have one less person to feed after tomorrow. The sheriff surely won't mind if Myrtle leaves. She's totally unaware of what's going on around here anyway. I don't know how long the sheriff wants Edwina and the lovebirds to stay, but however long it is, we'll just have to deal with it. I put in a call to the sheriff a little while ago, and he said he'll be here first thing in the morning to question Dickie and Edwina again. The day will have to start fairly early tomorrow, but I'll get up and cook breakfast by myself. You need to lounge around in bed for a while in the morning and get some extra rest."

"Oh, Bee, that's so thoughtful of you. I'll feel guilty, but I might just take you up on it."

"Good. Bess, I found something this afternoon while I was rummaging through Richard's suitcase. I haven't had time to show it to you yet, but I think it's an important clue. Look at this." I handed the slip of paper to Bess.

"It makes no sense to me," Bess said, after examining the note. "It's my notepaper though. I ordered the notepads from a stationary company several months ago, and I've never seen any others just like them. That's why I liked them; they're a little nicer than what most folks have."

"They are, Bess. You do have wonderful taste. Anyway, somebody passed Richard this message, and it must have meant something to him."

"It is very odd," Bess answered. "But Bee, I'm just too tired to think about it right now. I feel as though I've aged twenty years in the last two days. I've got to get some sleep. I'm going straight to bed. And Bee, please go to the bathroom before you go to bed and don't get up five times during the night...and please don't snore or kick me."

"I could say the same thing to you, Bess, but I'm too considerate to hurt your feelings."

"Oh, brother!"

CHAPTER FOURTEEN

Morning's light had already broken through the horizon when I opened my eyes for the first time after an undisturbed night's rest. Bess had not moved a muscle all night long and neither had I. Being dead tired does have its benefits, and a good night's sleep is usually one of them. I quickly remembered I had mentioned to Bess last night that I would be in charge of breakfast this morning. What was I thinking? I was as overworked as she was, but I suppose I realized we were both in need of a break. Maybe tomorrow Bess would clear her conscience by volunteering to make breakfast.

I gently pushed the covers aside and eased out of the bed, trying not to disturb Bess. Padding over to the window, I pushed the curtains apart and sighed. Everything seemed as it should be out in the barnyard. How could anything as dreadful as a missing relative mar the simplicity of our farm life? I asked myself, as I assessed the day—more cooking, cleaning...and, oh, yes, pretending to enjoy the role of being a good hostess. Being cordial and pleasant was almost more than I could bear for three days in a row, I agonized, as I willed myself to face another busy day.

Clouds had rolled in during the night, making the morning's light dimmer than usual. Rain was sure to come from those overcast clouds, I thought to myself, just before noticing the first drop of rain fall and settle on a fence post right outside the window. A couple of geese that had flown in from the pond were waddling across the meadow near the house, squawking and alerting my senses to the other sounds of the morning. One of the barnyard roosters crowed loudly, and Hortence returned the greeting with her usual long moo-oo. A gentle breeze stirred the damp air, ruffling the chickens' feathers as they ventured under my window, continuously pecking and scratching.

The rain would be no help in the search. It would only mask the scent of a human and destroy evidence left behind. As the gentle rain gained strength, that old melancholy feeling that overtakes me from time to time carried me back to the days of Will's and my first years together as man and wife. We had sacrificed and worked hard but always labored side by side. Will had been my rock, and I had been his leaning post. Margaret had few sad memories of her growing up years because Will and

I had always shielded her from any worry or unpleasantness.

Margaret had left for Waynesville late yesterday afternoon after only a short stop by the house. Foy had been uncommonly ill most of the day, and she had stayed to help the new nurse with his constant need of care. Margaret said that Walter was treating his symptoms, but with Foy's already-crippled body, he was not really able to tell the extent of all his ailments. I really should stop by over there today, check on his condition, and maybe take a chocolate cake for his sweet tooth as a surprise.

Just as I had done hundreds and hundreds of times before, I grabbed my robe and headed out to the kitchen to start the coffee brewing and the grits boiling. I'd dress for the day later, after I turned the stove eye down under the grits pot. Left-over ham and sausage were already cooked, waiting for me to pop into the oven to heat a bit. Biscuits and syrup were always good on a rainy morning. I'd scramble eggs, and we'd have a breakfast fit for a king.

To my surprise Ora Lee came trudging into the kitchen just as I turned the stove on. "Thought you's could use some extry help in the kitchen this mornin'," Ora Lee said, as she reached into her bosom to remove her twisted rag. I knew exactly what was in the scrap of fabric after years and years of watching her unwrap her hidden cloth and take a swig from her medicine bottle or fill her cheek with her snuff. "Vonion in the barn already, but he shore a worn-out old man," Ora Lee said, after sipping her first taste of tonic for the day. "He walkin' mighty slow this here mornin'. The damp air done brung on his arthritis real bad. I done told that hardheaded old man not to volunteer fer notin' today, jest do what had to be done and let the rest lie. Hit'll still be here tomorree, waitin' to get done."

"I could say the same about you, Ora Lee. You're just as tired as the rest of us. Why, you've hardly set foot in your own home since the start of the weekend—just to sleep is all. Why don't you just sit on the porch and wait for me to call breakfast? I'll have it ready before you can count to five."

"No'um, I ain't gonna sit on no porch whilst there be work to git done. No ma'am, I ain't. I'll get started on the biscuits right now. Now where the buttermilk?" Ora Lee muttered to herself as she had always done. "I could a'swore we had a full pitcher. We had some yestidee. Hit were sitting right here on the top shelf of the icebox."

"Ora Lee, are you sure about that? You could be mistaken."

"No, I knows good and well I ain't mistaken, Missy. I know what I see, and I see'd buttermilk yestidee right in this here icebox. I ain't blind yet and I shore ain't senile, like some peoples 'round here claim I is."

"I imagine Dickie drank it during the night. We'll use sweet milk for the biscuits this morning instead of buttermilk. These city people we're feeding don't know sweet milk from buttermilk, and they'll eat anything we put in front of them. I just wish Dickie would quit sneaking around all night long looking for something to eat and drink. He must have a hollow leg that we can't fill up."

"Yes'um, he shore seem to."

"Ora Lee, I thought we had a few slices of ham left over last night. I don't see them anywhere," I said, as I began to plunder inside the refrigerator. "I reckon we didn't, but I could've sworn we did. I guess we'll have to make do with sausage."

"Seem like Dickie like ham, too."

The sheriff arrived just as Ora Lee and I were putting breakfast on the dining room table. Of course, I had no alternative but to ask him to sit down and eat breakfast along with the rest of us. I figured he had already eaten breakfast at the diner as he usually does every day, so I anticipated him declining the offer. He didn't decline; instead, he pulled out one of the eight chairs at the table, the very one I had recently and haphazardly repaired with glue and bailing twine, and deposited all of his considerably more than two hundred and fifty pounds on it with a heavy plop.

After letting my breath out in relief that Sheriff Ledbetter wasn't nursing a broken tailbone down on the floor, I picked up the small dinner bell that had sat on the sideboard for as long as I could remember and rang it just as Mama had always done to beckon stragglers to the table or to call Daddy in from the yard or lot. Soon the relatives, including

Edwina, all seemingly unaware that the food hadn't been magically placed on the table by an invisible fairy, began to trickle in. Distorted, drowsy expressions covered their pinched faces, and none had bothered to dress for the day, with the exception of Dickie.

"I didn't realize that guests had to get up with the chickens around here. It seems as if we're getting up earlier and earlier every day," Mavis complained, as she took her seat and quickly reached for a hot biscuit.

"We're country folks out here, Mavis. After seven in the morning, we feel as if we're burning daylight. There's lots to be done every day," I gently reminded her before asking Cousin Myrtle to say grace.

As sweet Cousin Myrtle stirred her hot coffee, she commented that she would be glad to stay on another day or so and help out with the mounting chores. "I don't have one reason to get back home since my neighbor's feeding Milton, my cat. Why don't you tell Vonion we'll postpone my trip to the bus station this morning?"

"Oh, no-o, Cousin Myrtle," I quickly and anxiously replied. "You're much too fragile for farm work or housework. I insist that you go on home and see about Milton. I'm sure he's grieving over you right now, and you know yourself that a grief-stricken cat won't eat a thing. He'll soon just shrivel up and die. Now I don't want to hear another word about you staying away from a heartbroken Milton another day." I knew I had laid it on a little thick, but I was desperate. Cousin Myrtle was a sweet and gentle soul, but she was, after all, one more mouth to feed and one more person to clean up after.

Sheriff Ledbetter seemed content as he blew into his hot coffee cup and then slurped noisily. Just as he picked up his fork and positioned it to dig into the huge mound of scrambled eggs on his plate, we heard the back door slam, shaking the entire house. An excited, wild-eyed Vonion, waving his arms to and fro, raced into the room, almost knocking over Mama's large Roseville plant stand sitting on the floor beside the dining room door. Breathing hard and fast, Vonion tried to catch his breath, but excitement had gotten the best of him. With the little bit of breath left in his overexcited body, he hollered, "In the well! Hit's a arm...and hit's down in the well!"

"Calm down, Vonion. Calm down. You're gonna have a heart attack," I cautioned, as I had done so many times in the past when Vonion was overly agitated. "What on earth are you talking about?"

Between deep breaths Vonion managed to get out a few more words. "I...I seen it... with my own two eyes. A arm...on the bucket...down...in the well!"

Sheriff Ledbetter dropped his fork, Edwina swooned, and Dickie jumped up so quickly that his chair overturned behind him.

Bess, tying her bathrobe around herself, walked in from the bedroom and quickly spotted the red mud on the floor brought in on Vonion's shoes.

"VONION!" Bess declared, raising her hands to her hips. "I've told you and I've told you not to come into this house with those muddy brogans on your feet. Now I don't care what the circumstances are, TAKE-OFF-YOUR-SHOES before you come into this house. Now go take those nasty shoes off before you mess up the floor any worse."

"Uh, yes'um! I will, uh...next time, but Ms. Bee, come on now...quick, and, oh, you too, Sheriff!" Vonion was dancing with excitement by now, and the mud was slinging from his boots in every direction. "Hit's down there, right under our noses...right there in the well! Come on and see fer yourself!"

Vonion beckoned us to follow him by flinging his arms in the direction of the back door and headed out with Dickie right behind. Reluctant to leave his breakfast behind, the sheriff gobbled a big bite of eggs and hurried behind Dickie's long strides.

Knowing the rain would be a wet nuisance, I rushed to the hall, grabbed my rain bonnet and slicker, and headed to the back door. Through the yard and down the lane I dashed in the rain, trying to avoid mud puddles as I hurried. In the distance I could see that Sheriff Ledbetter and Vonion had already made it to the well and were peering over the ledge into the deep hole. Dickie had lingered twenty or so yards behind and was hunched over, heaving and gagging. I hurried to comfort Dickie.

"It's him, I imagine!" the sheriff called out to us. "I can see an arm draped over the bucket down there. If there's an arm, there's bound to be a body attached to it."

"Oh, dear God," Dickie cried as his body collapsed to the ground. "Is it my daddy, Sheriff?"

"I ain't too sure 'bout notin' right at this minute," the sheriff called back, "but if'n I were a bettin' man, which I am, I'd bet the farm that it is your daddy. Ms. Bee, come on over if'n you've got the stomach fer it and take a gander."

I left Dickie, pitifully crying with his hands over his face, and walked toward the well. The childhood memory of Tom Wilson's daddy, Mr. T. B., pulling a colored man who had met his maker from our pond while fishing and drinking at the same time, suddenly came into my thoughts. Trapped beneath a log, the body had not completely surfaced when Mr. T.B. went into the water and pulled it out to the banks of the pond as the dead man's wife stood nearby, wailing and screaming. All those years and I still held on to the memory of that wet, limp body rising up in the water after Mr. T.B. untangled his lifeless body from underneath the log.

I quickly looked into the well, anticipating another gruesome sight. "It's an arm all right," I said and steadied myself against the wall of the well. "I imagine you're gonna need some help getting him out of that watery grave. I'll stand guard here while you find somebody. Tom Wilson's more than likely around his house right now. It's too wet to be in the field. I'm sure he'll help. But there's no need to hurry. The man's dead, and he's not gonna get any deader. You know, Sheriff, it could possibly be Eddie Pink down there, not Richard. We won't know 'til we bring the body up."

"I reckon you're right about that. Now, Ms. Bee, I'll be back as soon as I get some help and a grappling hook. Vonion and me'll get Dickie back in the house before I go to huntin' up Tom. Don't touch a thing 'round here 'til I get back, and I mean nothing. Do you understand what I'm a'saying?"

"Yes sir, I completely understand...I won't touch a thing."

As soon as the sheriff and Vonion walked away, I began my search. There, lying at the base of the well in a patch of ivy was a woman's hairpin. "Poison ivy!" Ignoring my instructions completely, I reached down and picked up a stick to fish the pin out of the bed of green, three-pointed leaves.

Why would a woman's hairpin be lying on the ground out here by the well, a pin not rusted or corroded from weather or time? I was sure it wasn't Ora Lee's. Her hair was always braided without the use of hairpins.

But whose?

CHAPTER FIFTEEN

Thinking about a dead body in the well was a little unnerving to say the least. Maybe just a little peek at the remains, I thought, as I cautiously moved closer to the well opening and quickly glanced down into the dark cavern. I knew in my heart it was Richard.

There it was...a wet, lifeless arm flung over the top of the bucket. An arm, I was sure, that was attached to a body that had been carelessly hurled to a watery grave. Was it possible Richard intended to kill himself by jumping into the well or had somebody helped him along to a premature death? And how long had the body been in the well? It could have possibly been in there several days. It was likely Vonion had not gone near the well all weekend since we had virtually hog-tied him and Ora Lee to the house for most of the last few days.

Oh dear, I selfishly thought, my well is polluted with a dead body floating around in the dark water! Vonion and Ora Lee will never drink another drop from "Old Reliable." How on earth could Richard have been so thoughtless as to die in Vonion and Ora Lee's well, their only source of water at their house? And was there any way to clean the water to Vonion's satisfaction? There was absolutely no way I could even think about having another well drilled on my limited budget. Oh, my goodness, I quickly thought, how completely selfish of me to be thinking about my budget at a time like this, but...of all the inconsiderations...first Edwina took over my entire house with her whining and boo-hooing and fainting, and now Richard had landed, dead as a doornail in my well, contaminating all the water. I wish I had never heard of the Perkins family. Bess and I should have never tried to get the family together. We should have gone on a vacation to the beach instead. We would be returning home about now, all rested and relaxed, maybe with a nice tan on our skin, and not a farmer's tan like I kept year round on my arms and neck. Instead, here I was out in the rain, guarding a dead body in my well, with inconsiderate relatives in my house eating my food, and I had no idea when they would ever leave. Oh! And my budget was stretched tighter than last year's girdle across my expanding backside.

The rain had begun to subside a bit, and the morning sun was trying to break through the low clouds. I was soaked to the skin and chilled to the bone as well. I had promised the sheriff that I'd wait right here at the well, and I meant to do it even if I had to stand in a hail storm.

I hugged my body with wet arms and gratefully watched Tom Wilson's pickup truck hurtle down the muddy lane, his tires splashing water from every mud puddle he wasn't able to avoid in his haste. The truck made a quick, jerky stop in Vonion's side yard, and Tom quickly jumped to the soggy ground.

"Bee," he called, as he sprinted around the corner of Vonion's house, "come on and get into the truck, and I'll run you back to the house. You're gonna be sick. The sheriff never should have asked you to stay out here in the rain. That inconsiderate man doesn't have a grain of sense in his big, fat head. I'll come back and wait for the sheriff."

"No, Tom," I steadfastly answered, "I'm gonna wait right here for the sheriff. I told him I would, and I mean to do it. Maybe when the body is brought up, we can figure out how Richard died, that is, if it really is Richard's body down there."

"Well, you're the one to judge all about that, that's for sure, but I still say you're gonna get sick standing out in this rainy mist. I wish you'd let me get you back to the house."

"I'm okay, Tom. It'll take more than a little rain water to make me sick. Hey, look!" I pointed up the lane. "There comes the sheriff now and...oh good, that's Mr. Lawson's hearse behind him."

The sheriff pulled his car clear around Tom Wilson's truck and into the backyard, then motioned for Mr. Lawson to pull up to the chinaberry tree near the well. "Bee," the sheriff called from his car, "we'll take over now. You can go on back to the house."

"I'm not going anywhere 'til you bring that body up."

"Suit yourself, but it's not gonna be a pretty sight," he called, as he opened his car door and spit the cigar stub from his mouth onto the ground. "Just stay out of the way. Uh, I say that respectfully, of course."

"Morning, Bee. Morning, Tom," Mr. Lawson called, as he tipped his wide-brimmed hat to us. He slammed the hearse door shut and walked around to the back of the long, black car.

I nodded back to Mr. Lawson, and Tom Wilson tipped his cap. "Morning," Tom answered. "We appreciate you coming out here this morning."

"Just part of the job," Mr. Lawson replied, as he opened the wide doors at the back of the hearse and began to rummage around.

The sheriff pulled a heavy hook and a large jumble of ropes from the trunk of his car, but didn't bother to close the lid. "Mr. Lawson, you got a tarp or something inside your car to wrap the remains in? It's gonna be a mess, I imagine. I just hope we get it out in one piece, but if'n it falls apart, be prepared to pick up all the pieces."

"I'm getting one now, Sheriff. I try to stay equipped for all kinds of emergencies."

"Ms. Bee, I 'spect it's best for you to get on to the house. I know you said you wanted to stay, but—"

"Just go on about your business and don't mind me, Sheriff. I've seen worse, I'm sure. I'm an old farm woman, you know. I've seen plenty of dead, bloated animals."

"Yes'um, if you say so, but if'n you start feeling faintified or somethin' like that, grab hold to somethin' before you fall."

I didn't think that remark deserved an answer.

The sheriff began fiddling with the tangled ropes. "That dim-witted Vernon didn't take the time to straighten out this mess the other day after we drug off that ole dead dog from behind the stores. I can't count on him to do nothin' right anymore," complained the irritated sheriff, as he studied the jumbled mess and began unraveling the long lengths of rope. After the maze was figured out and he had the ropes laid out in a circle on the ground, he clamped the large hook to the end of one of the ropes. "Just give me a little time, and I'll nab something down there. We'll know who we got pretty soon now," he said as he lowered the rope with the big hook over the side of the well.

Vonion and Roscoe came running from the direction of the barn just in time to hear Sheriff Ledbetter say he thought he might have hooked the arm. Vonion began gasping for breath as soon as he stepped into the yard and stumbled over to the chinaberry tree to use it as a leaning post. As soon as he had time to recover his limited breath, he began instructing the sheriff in his most authoritative tone of voice. "You'uns better pull easy now, Sheriff, that is unless you wants to have a big ole mess on yor hands. Just pull slowly and gently. I done pulled a many a dead cow out of the pond, and I knows what I's talkin' about. You's want me to do it fer you?"

"Naw, Vonion. I can do it." We suddenly heard a kerplunk. "Oh, dang nab it! I reckon it weren't hooked good. The whole thing done dropped back down. I'll give it another try."

Try again, he did. And again…and again. The disheartened sheriff looked completely defeated as he laid the rope down over the ledge of the well opening. "I'm just about ready to give up. Ain't no way to hook that there dead body."

"I'll go down, Sheriff, and hook it," Roscoe brightly replied, with pure determination in his voice. "You can lower me down with another rope, and I'll hook him some way to'nother. You got plenty of ropes there, it looks like."

"Oh, he's got the rope, but you sure you want to get into that deep hole, boy?" Tom Wilson cautioned Roscoe. "It's darker than the inside of a cat's belly down there. And you know full well there's a dead man's body floating around along with other things such as snakes and spiders."

"Yessiree, I can do it. I'll just pretend in my mind that I'm hanging onto a limb in a tree."

Sheriff Ledbetter handed one end of the other rope to Roscoe to tie around his middle. "Soon as we've lowered you into the water, tie the other dangling rope around the dead man, hook it securely, and we'll pull him on up."

Roscoe took off his brogans and said a speedy prayer before bravely climbing over the side of the well. Both the sheriff and Tom Wilson held on to the rope as they lowered Roscoe down into the dark hole. I knew Roscoe was afraid, but he never let on to any fear at all. As soon as Roscoe felt the cold water against his dark skin, we detected a verbal shiver rise from the well. "Give me a minute, Sheriff, and then pull."

"Try to wrap the rope around the man's arms and hook them together, boy," the sheriff called down. "It'll hold."

We tensely waited until we heard Roscoe call, "I got both arms tied to the rope and the rope hooked. Pull it on up, Sheriff. I can tread water fer another minute or two."

The sheriff and Tom began to pull hard on the heavy rope attached to the dead man. The rope soon became taut with the weight of the waterlogged body as it began to rise from the dark waters below the surface of the earth.

"You out of the way down there, boy?" the sheriff called down.

"I's over to the side. Now pull harder. Hit's a big man all right, and he's a mess."

Slowly, the sheriff and Tom Wilson pulled. "It's on its way up. We've caught a big one and it's heavy as lead!" the sheriff hollered. Suddenly, another kerplunk sound rose from the deep well, and the men fell backward to the ground, the heavy sheriff landing on top of Tom Wilson. "Dang nab it!" the sheriff cursed, as he maneuvered his heavy body off of Tom Wilson and stumbled, trying to get back on his feet.

"The rope done slipped off, Sheriff!" called Roscoe from below.

"We know that, boy!" the exasperated sheriff disparagingly hollered back. "This time twist the rope all the way around the man's middle. Hook it good; now you hear me, boy. Can you do that?"

"I'll try, but keep a tight hold on to me. I'm tiring out fast now." We could hear splashing water. "Send on down a little more rope, Sheriff." With every second now I was praying Roscoe's energy would hold out a little longer, and he would keep his nerve about him. The water had to be extremely cold, and I knew Roscoe couldn't stay in the frigid water much longer.

Roscoe finally called up. "Pull him up now, Sheriff! He ain't gonna fall. I tied him gooder this time."

The sheriff and Tom Wilson gripped the rope and began to tug a second time. The waterlogged body rose as the sheriff and Tom pulled with all their might again. Just as the limp body rose to the top of the well opening, Mr. Lawson reached over and grabbed it. The sheriff and Tom kept a tight grip to the rope as Mr. Lawson carefully rolled the heavy body over the ledge of the well. The three men gently placed the wet, bulky body onto the ground, and I moved in closer. There it was, lying on the ground in a puddle of water, the remains of my cousin Edwina's dearly departed husband. It was, indeed, the tangled, waterlogged, bloated body of the late Richard Perkins.

"Hey, pull me up!" called Roscoe from down in the well. "I ain't too friendly with this here turtle that's trying to nip at my nose."

The tired Sheriff smiled, and he and Vonion quickly and easily pulled a victorious, lightweight Roscoe up from the well. "Boy, you done real good," Vonion declared, as he patted his wet grandson on his back. "You done real good, and I's right proud of you." Roscoe grinned as he gloried in his grandfather's pride.

"It twern't notin'. I's glad I could help out the sit'ation."

"You did do real good, boy," the sheriff replied. "Most grown men wouldn't have even attempted what you just did."

Roscoe grinned wider this time, showing a full row of large white teeth.

Tom Wilson nodded his approval also before patting Roscoe on his back. "I knew you had it in you. You're a good boy—I mean, man."

The sheriff crouched down beside the remains of Richard's body. "Something really heavy caved that big neck slam in."

Mr. Lawson squatted down beside the sheriff. "The man's neck is surely broken. From what it looks like, something heavy and hard struck the back of that neck, and it's broke slam in two. Bad gash, too. I can't do my magic on this man's head if'n they want me to funeralize him. Can't be no open casket, that's for sure. You can only do so much, you know. Too much decay and swelling. Let's wrap him up, Sheriff."

"Oh, wait just a minute, men. Let's examine the body a little closer," I interrupted, breaking my silence. Carefully, and not so gracefully, I'm afraid, I bent over and I looked at what used to be the strong, robust figure of a man. The dangling neck had been broken by a heavy object that had struck from behind. A big gash ran between the back of the hairline and the top of the shoulder blades. There were other lacerations and scrapes on the body, but the broken neck had to have been what killed him. I cautiously ran my hand over the gash in the back of the neck and felt a large splinter puncture my finger.

I slowly pulled out a chunk of wood the size of a small toothpick that had been lodged under the pasty, grey skin. "This came from the murder weapon, men," I said, as I held the wood fragment up. "It looks like an oak splinter to me. Somebody must have hit Richard from behind. I think we can assume our murder weapon is a limb or a log from an oak tree. Richard was probably already dead when his body was thrown in the well. Check his pockets, Sheriff."

The sheriff fiddled about the body. "His wallet's still in his back pocket; a couple of dollars are tucked under a hidden flap, but no big money. He reached into one of the front pockets and pulled out two nickels and four dimes. Must have been a robbery. I'm sure Richard would have had some big money with him since he was traveling. My guess is Eddie Pink had everything to do with this. He's slippery. No telling where that boy is by now."

I wasn't so sure about a robbery. Richard might not have had much money in his wallet before his death because he didn't have money. And where was his lucky rabbit's foot?

"Why he have to throw him into my well is what I's want's to know," Vonion declared, as he stared down at the dead intruder to his well.

"We don't have any evidence that Eddie Pink did this. But somebody, and it could have been Eddie Pink, had to hide a dead body. That's why. Somebody killed Richard and threw him into your well to hide his body," I answered. "You've got your work cut out for you, Sheriff."

"Let's load him up, Mr. Lawson, and get him out of here," the sheriff replied. "Roscoe, if you don't mind helping again, let's wrap him up in this here tarp."

As Mr. Lawson pulled out of the yard with an extra passenger on board, Vonion declared, "What I gonna do fer water now? This here well is polluted and ain't fit fer human beings. What ARE we gonna do now? If'n Mr. Will was here right now, he know what to do."

I sadly answered, "Well, he's not here, Vonion, and he won't be coming back to give us any more answers. It's high time we started thinking for ourselves."

CHAPTER SIXTEEN

Trudging back to the house through the mud and muck, I kept thinking that an easier way out of this miserable situation would be to stand in front of a Nazi firing squad with guns aimed straight at me. No, I stubbornly thought to myself, that would be the coward's way out. Keeping harmony in the house while investigating Richard's premature death would be a big challenge, to say the least, but I was up to it.

After removing my wet, muddy shoes on the porch, I hesitantly opened the back door, only to hear loud, pitiful cries of grief coming from the other end of the house.

Ora Lee was standing at the kitchen sink rinsing the breakfast dishes as I sloshed in. "Child, get in this house, and get those wet clothes off'n yor back 'fore you catch yor death a'cold. I saved you a plate. Eggs won't be as good as they was a hour ago, but they's still eatable. You gonna need plenty of nourishment 'fore you goes in to see Ms. Edwina. You's hears all that wailin'. She been goin' strong since Mr. Dickie told her the turr-ble news. She really a mess...and her educated son, a mess, too. Ms. Bess in with her right now, but Ms. Bess don't seem to have the knack for sympathizing with them city folks."

I plopped down in the nearest kitchen chair, and water began to puddle about me on the floor. "She'll have to do for right now," I answered despairingly, as I squeezed water out of my hairdo, or maybe I should say, what used to be my hairdo. "Oh, Ora Lee, I just dread going in to see Edwina. Lord, please give me the strength."

"That pitiful little prayer you just sent up ain't gonna be nearly enough fer this here sit'ation we done gots ourselves into. You gots to get down on yor knees and plead to the good Lord fer his guidance this time."

"I will, Ora Lee...and thank you for reminding me."

"I's been remindin' you yor whole life, and I suppose I got's to keep remindin' you 'til you learn yor lessons."

"Yes'um."

"Missy, I knows you gots lot on yor mind right now with Mr. Richard and all, and I hates to add to yor worrying, but what's we gonna do 'bout that well? Ain't no way me and Vonion and Roscoe can drink that tainted water where a dead man been wallowin'. It ain't fitin' fer notin', not even washin' clothes. Why, I cans't even go near that well no more just thinkin' 'bout a dead man's body been floatin' round down in that hole. We's gonna have to figure something out real soon. Maybe we's can use them lard cans out there on the porch to haul water from yor well down to the house fer a spell."

"We'll figure it all out, Ora Lee, but right now, I'm mad as blue blazes that somebody didn't think any better of us than to throw a dead body in our well that we use for drinking water. Talk about being inconsiderate!" Water was dripping down my forehead and into my eyes by now. "Oh, Ora Lee, it was a dreadful sight, seeing what was left of poor Richard. His big ole body was shriveled up like a giant, dried-up, gray prune. Somebody wanted him dead, and the well was a real handy place to hide his body."

Ora Lee handed me the old, tattered bath towel we kept hanging by the kitchen door for wiping our hands. "And now we's the ones is got to suffer all the consequences," Ora Lee complained, as she stacked the last plate into the dish drain. "Oh-h, I's feels sorry for Ms. Edwina." Ora Lee sighed and sat down beside me before reaching into her bosom for her snuff. "Losing yor man is a terrible bad thang. You's knows 'bout that better'n me, I reckon. We's ain't got no choice but to deal with Ms. Edwina long as she be here, and that a fact." And as if that thought suddenly sunk in, Ora Lee quickly added, "And how longs you think that gonna be?"

"I don't know, Ora Lee. We've got to do what has to be done as long as it takes. You and Mama taught me that lesson long ago. We can't neglect our God-given duty; you know that better than me."

"You right, Missy. Yor mama and me, we taught you good. We'll get through it some way. It just that Ms. Edwina so-o demanding. She can't do notin' fer herself. She ask me to roll her stockings on her legs yestidy mornin'. I ain't never had to do that fer nobody, not even yor mama, and you know youself, I'd do anything fer her."

"Ora Lee, you are not a servant in this house, and don't even think about doing such personal things like that for Edwina. The very idea of her asking you to roll on her stockings! I'll straighten her out directly, you just watch me."

"Yes'um," Ora Lee answered, with the hint of a smug smile.

"I know it's hard on you, Ora Lee. It's hard on everybody. I'm sorry we have to depend on you so much for help."

"God'll give all of us the strength we need." Ora Lee reached out and tenderly patted my hand. "We just have to ask to receive it. It ain't that hard to understand."

I began to notice water running across the floor. "It's a good thing Bess isn't in here. She'd get me for bringing all this rain water into the house."

"And she be right, too. I'll get the mop 'fore she sees this mess. No need fer her to get any more riled up over a little rain water. Now get in there and get out'a them wet clothes. I'll set yor plate out and pour up some hot coffee fer you."

"Thank you, Ora Lee. I don't know what I'd ever do without you."

"You'll find out sooner or later, Missy. My time ain't so far off. I ain't gonna be 'round forever, and you knows that to be true."

"Don't talk about that right now, Ora Lee. I've got enough to worry with. You're gonna outlive the rest of us anyway...er, Ora Lee, you don't have any idea about what could have happened to poor Richard, do you?"

"Not nary one idea, but I 'spect you probably does by now."

Bess walked into my bedroom just as I was adjusting the belt to my housedress. My hair was still damp, and I had really not tried to do much with it. It just didn't seem too important to me right now. Before she had time to close the bedroom door, she started in. "All right, Bee Martin, you better get your thinking cap on and figure out who killed Richard." She closed the door and began to whisper. "We can't deal with this crazy family much longer. We've got to get them out of here before I absolutely lose all my religion." Bess was shaking with frustration.

"Is Edwina being difficult?" I softly asked Bess, as if I didn't already know.

Bess forgot to whisper this time. "Is Edwina being difficult? Is rain wet? Do frogs jump? You know good and well, she's being extremely difficult, and she's a raving maniac right now."

"I'm sorry." It seemed as if all I was doing lately was apologizing. "I'll go in to her as soon as I eat a little something."

Bess remembered to lower her voice back down to a whisper this time. "Well, I am sorry about Richard. It's just terrible. And what on earth is Queen Edwina gonna do without that man?"

"I don't really know, Bess."

"Well, whatever she does, she's got to do it someplace besides right here. Another day with Edwina will probably put me clear over the edge."

"Well, she won't be going anywhere in the next day or so; I can honestly tell you that. Sheriff Ledbetter says we have to keep her right here under our noses."

"Does that man have to know everything?"

"Well, he has to be able to find Edwina, and it is a fact that she can't go anywhere until this murder is solved, so you might as well put that in your pipe and smoke it."

"Well, I don't have to like it one bit."

"I don't like it, either, but that's the way it has to be right now. We've all endured worse. Remember that summer when Fred's mama came to your house with a broken leg for you to nurse her back to health. You had to wait on her hand and foot. You handled that pretty well, as I remember."

"Oh, yea, you just think I did. I came real close to breaking her other leg, but I knew she'd never go home with another injury." Bess dejectedly plopped down in the rocker. "I'm just not cut out to be a nursemaid. I have no patience at all with helpless people."

I could second that.

"You've got many strong points, Bess. Patience just happens to be one of your weaker ones."

"I guess so." That self-constructed pedestal was crumpling right out from under my older, self-reliant sister. "All right, let's hear it. I know you've got something going on in that brain of yours about Richard's untimely demise. You've picked up on something by now; I'm certain of that."

"Well, I've picked up on the fact that Richard is definitely dead, and he won't be coming back to life anytime soon. Somebody knocked the daylights clean out of him from behind with an oak limb or log, or maybe a board made out of oak wood. I know he had his lucky rabbit's foot in his pocket earlier, but it was missing from his pockets when he was brought up from the well. Remember, Bess, he had that rabbit's foot when we were riding with him up to Myrtle's house a couple of years back, and he swerved around to miss that dead dog in the road. We fell all over each other in the backseat. I think my neck was permanently injured in that maneuver."

"Oh, I do remember that, Bee. Edwina's hat flew out the window, and Richard had to stop the car and go back to find it. After he climbed back into the car with Edwina's ugly hat, I clearly remember him pulling his rabbit's foot out of his pocket and saying its lucky charm had kept him from hitting that humongous dead dog and wrecking the car. That rabbit's foot's magic most assuredly did not keep us from almost getting whiplash that day, though, after we slipped around all over that backseat. And it didn't help much in the hat department either."

I smiled as I remembered. "Edwina claimed her hat was crushed beyond repair, and she could never wear it again. She threw it back out of the window and told Richard that he'd just have to buy her a new one." We quietly chuckled, and it seemed to break the tension a bit. "Well, anyway, Richard was still carrying that rabbit's foot right up to last weekend, but I don't think it's been bringing him much good luck lately. Bess, I saw that rabbit's foot when Richard accidently dropped it, then picked it back up and put it back into his pocket after he ate dinner Saturday. Anyway, that lucky rabbit's foot wasn't in his pocket when he was pulled from the well this morning. But, Bess, I found something else peculiar down there. Growing right up against the side of the well is a small patch of poison ivy, and that's where I found this woman's hairpin." I pulled the hairpin out of my pocket and held it out for Bess to see. "Look at it. It's not rusted or corroded one bit. It looks like a brand new pin, right from the store. Don't you think? Now you know that if this pin had been in that ivy patch more than a few days, it would be tarnished some."

"I guess so, Bee."

"Have you been to the well in the last few days, Bess?"

Bess reached for the pin, examined it, and handed it back to me. "Bee, I've never even been to that well at all."

"Well, somebody lost this hairpin there, and I mean recently."

"I guess that could mean something, but we've had a bunch of company lately, Bee. The pin could belong to anybody who happened to have walked down around the well."

"It definitely means something. It means that a woman's been at that well recently. I don't know if she was there with Richard or not, but a woman has been at that well in the last few days."

"I guess so, but Bee, I keep thinking about what you told me about Dickie and his daddy having that heated argument out back of the house. Bee, you don't really suppose…"

"We can't rule anything out yet."

"I know that boy couldn't have killed his own daddy, for Pete's sake, so Bee, don't even think about such a thing. It's pretty obvious to me that Eddie Pink must have run into Richard out there and then set out to murder him to keep him from talking. That sorry sheriff of ours needs to find that Eddie

Pink right now and arrest him all over again, this time for murder. Then he'll have the killer, and Edwina can go back home, and we can get back to the life we had before you insisted on having a friends and family reunion. By the way, what are we going to feed that bunch of hungry people for dinner today? Most of the barbecue has already been eaten."

I thought for a second. "Egg salad. Get Ora Lee to boil some eggs."

"Ugh! I suppose it'll have to do. I'll slice some white bread and fry up a few potatoes to go along with it. Vonion can ring a couple of roosters' necks, and we'll have fried chicken for supper. We'll have rice and gravy, string beans, and biscuits along with the chicken. Bee, we're gonna soon run out of options for meals, so somebody better hurry up and figure out this whole situation. But I still say it was Eddie Pink that did the dirty deed."

I'd learned to humor Bess. "You're probably right, as usual."

I was finishing my late breakfast when the telephone rang. Two rings—one long, one short—that's us. I quickly gulped down the last of my coffee and rushed to the telephone in the hall. Nellie, our telephone operator, was really in all her glory. "Bee, my switchboard has been lit up like a Christmas tree all morning long. The news about that murder out at your place is a hot topic, and everybody wants to talk about it. I've been trying to give y'all a little privacy, and I keep telling everybody to call back later or, better yet, go out there this afternoon with a dish of food to help feed those hungry relatives. I do hope you appreciate all my Christian efforts."

"Oh, I do, Nellie. Just give us a little more time, and we'll take calls later in the day."

"Well, there's one call you can't put off. Mr. Lawson is on the line right now, and he wants to speak to either you or to Mrs. Edwina Perkins. Take your pick, but he says he's got to get through to one of you. He says Mr. Perkins can't lay out much longer. He's got to do something with the remains quickly. And I know what I'm talking about when I say he's absolutely right about that."

CHAPTER SEVENTEEN

The dark rain clouds of the morning had drifted clean away, leaving a pale gray afternoon sky. A blanket of sunlight fell across the fertile, damp earth and warmed the soil and air around us. The newly planted field of corn back of the house glistened as the rain water slowly soaked into the earth's surface, nourishing tender roots. The refreshing atmosphere outdoors did little to change the dreary, suffocating mood inside the house where despair and gloom seemed to rule with an iron fist.

The grieving, overwrought widow, and most assuredly our unwanted houseguest, was lying across the rumpled bed in the darkened bedroom. "I can't stand the light in my eyes," she complained, so I closed the curtains. "I feel a fever coming on," she whined, so I gave her two aspirins and laid a damp washcloth over her hot forehead. "The heat is just unbearable in this house," she grumbled, so I stood over her fanning her with last week's newspaper.

It was becoming quite apparent to me that Edwina had no intention of starting a conversation about the dreadful matters at hand but, instead, was uttering only commands and complaints. I was losing patience. A discussion about Richard's funeral and burial could not be put off much longer. Mr. Lawson would surely show up soon. His prompt arrival at the deceased's family's home was as predictable as his wilted, lifeless handshake and morbid undertaker demeanor. His dyed black hair would be slicked back from his face with too much Vitalis, a drooping, pink carnation would be pinned to his discolored white shirt, and a fake smile would be plastered across his round, pimpled face. A standard obituary form, ready to be filled in with every relative's name from third cousins twice removed for the last hundred years or so to all the special friends, would be clipped to a notebook clutched under his arm.

I laid the newspaper down and reached over to grasp Edwina's clammy hand. "Edwina, we have got to talk. Mr. Lawson will be here directly, and he's going to ask you what your desires are for Richard's funeral and burial. Have you thought about it at all?"

"Oh-h, my head hurts too bad to think, and I feel nauseated," Edwina whined and rolled over in the bed to face the wall. "Maybe we can put him off until tomorrow, Bee. I'll feel a little stronger by then. I just don't think I can bear to see anybody today."

"Edwina, no. I know it's hard on you, but you have to face the fact that a funeral has to be planned, and nobody can do that except you."

I walked around to the other side of the bed and looked straight into her red, swollen eyes. "Do you understand what I just said, Edwina? There's no getting around what has to be done."

Edwina's muffled answer came between several sniffles. "You'll just have to plan the funeral, Bee. I don't care anyway. Whatever you decide will be fine with me. Just make sure it's in the cool of the late afternoon." Through a couple of fake coughs and more sniffles, she added, as if she already had planned the whole affair in her mind, "Oh, Bee, I'd just love to have a small reception afterwards right here. You know, with a little refreshment to cool everybody off. Maybe you and Bess could serve little petit fours and that divine strawberry punch that Bess makes with the little strawberry pieces swimming all around in it." What was Edwina thinking? A funeral is not a social gathering. And where would we get strawberries this time of year?

"We'll get to that part later, Edwina, after we've discussed other more pressing issues with Mr. Lawson. There are bigger decisions to be made than what kind of refreshments we'll serve, and those decisions can be made only by you...or Dickie, and he says anything will be fine with him. Now what's the name of your preacher, and how can we get in touch with him?"

"My preacher? You can't be serious, Bee. He's so old and senile. He can hardly stand behind a podium for more than ten minutes without sitting down, and I know darn well the man couldn't walk out to a cemetery from the church and have a decent burial prayer in the humidity we've been having. He's pathetic. Why, he can't even remember doodle dust anymore. Last week he clean forgot the title of the sermon he was trying to preach, "The Holy Spirit and You," and started preaching on tithing right in the middle of the service. Most people in the congregation were already asleep and didn't even notice, but I certainly did. He'd probably forget Richard's name in the middle of the eulogy and call him Roger or Raymond, or something like that. Anyway, Richard hated our church. I had to beg him to go most of the time. The only reason he'd ever relent and go with me was to watch that woman exhibitionist we had for a piano player a while back bounce her backend up and down on that piano stool. She'd hike her dress up, and you could see everything she had, toes to tonsils. And I'd have to sit there in the congregation right beside him and endure him drooling all over his clean, white shirt every time she happened to grin our way. Not only was I embarrassed to death, but I was the one who had to wash and iron that shirt. I finally had to change our seating arrangement, and I'm quite sure every woman in the church knew the reason for the move."

"Oh, my goodness."

"It's all true, Bee. You just don't know the burdens I carry around. I try not to complain."

"I'm sure you never have, but—"

"Please, Cousin Bee, I want Richard's funeral over here in Jeffersonville at a dignified church. He's got to be buried with my people—you and Bess, in our cemetery plot."

"Why, Edwina, that's Will's family's cemetery plots, not your family's. There's no room in our section for more people. It's laid out just for Mama and Daddy and Bess and Fred and me and Will and our children. You should know that."

"We'll just have to squeeze in another grave, one for Richard and, oh yes, one for me too. Oh, and we'll have to reserve a place for Dickie, also. We won't worry about that floozy wife of his. She probably won't be around that long, anyway. Oh, it'll be easy, Bee; just ask Mr. Lawson. He can see about it. How much room will it take for a few more graves anyway? Richard's short. He won't need as much space as a big, six-foot-tall man."

"That is totally ridiculous, Edwina. Each grave is the exact same size. It doesn't matter how big somebody is. Now, that section in the cemetery is for Will's people. He graciously allowed it to be used for Mama and Daddy, and then when we realized we wouldn't have but one child, he sold the other grave plots to Fred and Bess for them and their

children. It's not a family section for everybody.
Surely Richard and you have a family cemetery near
your home. Where are Richard's parents buried
anyway?"

"Oh, I don't know, for goodness' sake,"
Edwina answered. I could tell she was getting
irritated. "At some little ole dinky country church
nobody ever heard of on a dusty, dirt road. It's
called Mount Holiness or Holy Mountain or
something like that. They don't have but about
fifteen members, and most of them are so old they're
almost dead. As a matter of fact, they lost a member
not so long ago. They handle snakes out there, and
during one of their revival meetings last summer, the
preacher got bit by a rattler and died right there in
the church." I gasped in disbelief. "They probably
haven't even been able to replace him. Not too many
preachers handle snakes anymore, I imagine."

"I guess not, but—"

"Listen to me, Bee. I can't put Richard back
there in the sticks with those backwoods snake
handlers. Why, I've actually seen, with my own two
eyes, goats gnawing on the tombstones in that
weedy, overgrown graveyard by the church.
Richard needs to be in a cemetery in town where the
graves are kept up and seen about. I want to be
buried right next to my Richard, and I'm certainly
not going to be buried out in the boondocks like
some ole country bumpkin along with those snake
handling people."

"I guess not, but Edwina, your mama and daddy are buried at Ebenezer. What's wrong with that? I think your daddy's people are there too. I think that would be a suitable choice."

"No! I can't stand the people at that church. They aren't anything but a bunch of holier-than-thou Primitive Baptists. They actually have foot washings out there, and I'm not about to wash anybody's smelly ole feet. I doubt they even wear shoes half the time. I insisted that we go to the revival one night a year or so ago, and the preacher commenced to washin' my feet. Why, I ended up having to kick the living daylights out of that man when his knotty old hands ventured off my foot and up my leg." Now I knew Edwina had to be exaggerating. "That preacher needs to find out where a foot ends and a leg begins, if you ask me, before somebody else kicks the tar right out of him. I hadn't really thought too much about it until right now, but some of those old country women probably like all that rubbing. I know the preacher loves doing it."

I couldn't help myself and laughed out loud. Edwina smiled but became deadly serious again. "They don't have a piano or screens in the windows, and I swear I actually saw a big rattrap set in the corner of the vestibule once. Why, I'd be embarrassed to death to take Richard's remains back to that dusty, old, backwoods church. Mr. Lawson wouldn't even be able to find that church, anyway, it's so far back off the main road."

"I'm sure he could, but why don't you want to use the undertaker in Swainsville? Mr. Lawson can transport Richard's remains over to him."

"No, I want Mr. Lawson to do the funeral, and I want Richard buried right here in Jeffersonville in a town cemetery where they mow the grass with a lawn mower, not a herd of stupid billy goats."

"If I'm not mistaken, you referred to us as country folks the other day, Edwina. Make up your mind if you consider us hicks from the sticks before you go any further."

"I really didn't mean that y'all are uncouth, country people, Bee. You're reading too much into what I said. I'm proud to call Jefferson County my home."

"You were brought up here, and that is a fact."

"Sometimes I say things that I just don't really mean, Bee. I'm cursed that way. I'm sorry if I hurt your feelings."

"There's no harm done, but listen to me good, Edwina. You'll have to inquire with Mr. Lawson about other sections in the cemetery if you really intend to bury Richard here. You can't use Will's and my plot. There's no more room in our section of the cemetery, and that settles that. My suggestion to you is that you buy one of those plots over by the woods in the far corner and start your own family section. I imagine some of those plots are still available, but I'm not really sure about that. I just don't understand why you don't want to go back to your hometown and bury Richard among your friends and family over there."

"I just don't. Now that's settled, and I can't think about this anymore. My head hurts and I have to go to the bathroom. All I can really think about right now is WHY my Richard is dead. He might have jumped into that well, for all I know. Maybe he just wanted to end it all with one big splash." Edwina burst out in an avalanche of more tears. "I've never known of anybody dying in a well, of all the undignified places. He probably jumped into that well just to hurt me and embarrass me in front of my family; I just know he did. It would be just like him to do something like that. I could just die myself!" More tears and louder wailing.

"Listen to me, Edwina. Richard did not just jump into that well. Somebody hit him over the head with a limb or a two-by-four or something like that and threw him in there. He did not commit suicide, and you can get that silly notion right out of your thick skull right this minute."

"Well, why in blue blazes would someone want to do such a terrible thing to my poor Richard? He never hurt anyone, not even a flea, except maybe me."

"I don't know, Edwina, but I'm giving it a whole lot of thought. Maybe you can help me—"

"Oh, no-o, Bee! I can't think about that right now!" Edwina jumped off the bed and ran toward the bathroom just as I heard a car door slam out in the yard. That had to be Mr. Lawson. The poor man

didn't have a clue about what he was getting himself
into this time.   If he did, he would turn that car
around and head for the hills.

I smiled as I formed a picture in my mind—
Edwina spying a large dead rat caught in that big ole
rattrap at that backwoods church as she and Richard
walked in.

CHAPTER EIGHTEEN

It was Sheriff Ledbetter out in the yard, not Mr. Lawson. I made it out to the screen door just in time to watch the sheriff kick one of the worn front tires on his car and to hear him spout adjectives that were clearly not meant for the female gender's ears to hear. Actually, I'd heard those same words a few times in the past from Vonion...and maybe a few times from Will.

Just as I called out a greeting to the sheriff, Vonion walked from around the corner of the house, shaking his head from side to side. He seemed more aggravated than usual. "What's the matter now, Vonion?" I called, as I reached the bottom of the steps. "Please don't tell me the hogs are out in the corn field again. I don't have time to chase those greedy pigs all afternoon."

"No'um, hit ain't that this time. I'm just so flusterated. Hit jest ain't no way to keep them skittish animals content no more. I's just had to jump out uv the hog pen to keep from bein' attacked by Big Mable. Soon as I landed on the udder side uv the pen, Hortence tried to kick the livin' daylights right out'a me. Something bad disterbin' the peace out there. Maybe they know's we havin' trouble out here in the people's world. I just don't know any more."

"That ole possum's probably been sneaking around back of the barn, and he's more than likely sucking eggs again too, Vonion. Have you seen any signs of that?"

"No'um, not lately, but layin' is off pretty bad. Most likely the moon ain't just right, and, them animals, they knows them thangs better'n us humans does. I jest wish they would settle down some 'for Hortence kicks me way into next year. She aimin' to be replaced permently if she don't quit actin' up."

"Now, Vonion, you know you could never replace Hortence. No other cow would ever be able to learn your language."

"I 'spect you right, but the onliest bad thang about that is...Hortence, she know it too." We all chuckled. "Oh, uh, I found somethin' in the dirt back there." Vonion reached into his pocket and brought out Richard's lucky rabbit's foot. "Ms. Bee, looky here. This here was layin' in the dust back toward the barn. Who you 'spect could have lost it?"

I reached out as Vonion offered it over to me. I knew exactly where it had come from, without a doubt. "I don't know, Vonion. One of our guests might have dropped it over the weekend. I'll hold on to it. Maybe somebody'll ask about it." I casually dropped it into my dress pocket.

The sheriff didn't seem particularly interested in a rabbit's foot being found out by the barn, and I still wasn't prepared to tell all that I knew about Richard's last hours. I saw no need for speculation about Dickie's part in Richard's death until there was more evidence that Dickie knew more than he was letting on.

Bess called out to Vonion from the porch just as the sheriff motioned for me to come over to the shade of the oak tree for a private word. A disheartened Vonion looked toward me in his pleading, helpless way, but I knew Bess meant business, and I nodded for him to go on in.

"She clearly don't know nothin' 'bout the slaves being freed in the Civil War," Vonion muttered, as he shuffled back into Bess's prisoner of war camp. "She probably want me to hang unmentionables out on the clothesline to dry, but I ain't doin' no personal work fer no female."

"You don't have to do anything like that," I called out to Vonion as the sheriff and I headed toward the coolness of the shade tree. "If Bess asks you to do anything personal, just tell her I said you are needed in the barn."

"Yes'um, I do that, but that woman always catches on to me when I tells a tale."

As soon as Vonion was out of earshot, I immediately asked the sheriff, "Have you got anything on Eddie Pink yet?"

"No'um, we thought we had a lead an hour or two ago, but it turned out to be something else entirely. Ms. Mildred called into the station to tell me that her clothesline was robbed again this morning, and she could have sworn she saw a mysterious man standing around on the street corner outside of her house earlier in the day. I figured it possibly could have been Eddie Pink trying to get some getaway clothes, but just to be on the safe side, I decided to call her previous clothesline thief, Mrs. Ricketson, on the telephone and ask her to come into the station for questioning."

"Did you get her to come in peacefully, Sheriff?"

"Oh, she came in as peaceful as an angel, all dressed up in a green dress with big, purple flowers, very similar to one of the dresses Ms. Mildred described as being stolen from her clothesline. I quizzed her about where her dress came from, and she asked me if I liked the color. I said I did, and I'd like to buy one just like it for my mama, that is, if it came in larger sizes. She was flattered, and said she bought it from the Sears and Roebuck catalog, and Earnest Lee Black had delivered the package in the mail a few days earlier. She said it also came in red with big yellow flowers, and she thought those colors would be more attractive on Mama since she had a darker complexion. She said she wasn't real sure if it came in real large sizes, but she could check for me. Anyway, when I suggested that she might have been mistaken about where the dress actually came from, and could she have possibly removed Ms. Mildred's clothes from her clothesline, uh...accidently, of course, she accused me of being 'way out of line.'"

"Oh, dear. Did you ever get a confession out of her?"

"Only after I informed her that I positively knew where her new dress came from, and it wasn't from the Sears and Roebuck catalog, and Ms. Mildred was on the warpath. I told her that if she didn't confess to clothesline thievery, I'd have to turn her over to Judge B. N. Paradise, and he'd probably give her twenty years to life in the state penitentiary for thievery. She finally admitted that she was trying to be of help to Ms. Mildred and took her clothes off the line before they got soaked from the shower of rain. She claimed that she intended to iron and fold them as a special favor to Ms. Mildred, and she had just not had the time to finish the chore."

"Oh my. What are you going to do about Mrs. Ricketson and her, uh...clothesline problem?"

"I haven't really decided yet. Ms. Mildred said to throw the book at her and keep her in jail for awhile, but I ain't gonna go that route. I might fine her a few dollars and make her clean the office a time or two, though. Ms. Mildred ain't gonna be too happy about that. She says she wants justice, but I ain't gonna arrest Mrs. Ricketson. You know as well as I do the poor woman has a sickness, and she can't help herself. She'll have to do more than clothesline thieving fer me to put her away. Anyway, I learn't it weren't Eddie Pink doing the stealing."

"You know, Sheriff, that slippery man could be anywhere by now."

"You're right about that. I'm beginning to believe he's done skedaddled clear outa these parts. But, Ms. Bee, I do have something pretty interesting to tell you. You remember I asked Mavis, Dickie's bride, about the whereabouts of her older sister, Maxine."

"Oh, yes, I remember. She was pretty vague about it."

"When I called Carl Cottonwood, the sheriff in Emory County, on the telephone and asked if Richard's behavior or activities had changed any lately, he said, 'Oh, yes.' According to the sheriff, a young lady named Maxine has become a fixture over at the Buttercup, a little restaurant in Swainsville, of all places. The sheriff said this Maxine has been cuddling up with some of the businessmen that come in to eat, and she's been particularly interested in no other than—guess who—the late Richard Perkins."

"Well, I'll be doggone."

"It seems, according to Sheriff Cottonwood, that old Richard's been carryin' on pretty hot and heavy with Maxine. I asked the sheriff to do a little more checkin', and he called back with her last name and a good description of Maxine. Her last name is McNeely, and she's a dead ringer for none other than Mavis McNeely. Evidently, Maxine's been in Swainsville for about nine months now, and she got a job as a waitress right off the bat. Anyway, Richard's been spendin' money on her like there's not gonna be a tomorrow, and now he's pretty well spent out. That's what his banker tells me. You see, Ms. Bee, I got all kinds of sources. The banker said that Richard had come into some serious money a few months ago, and he's been spreadin' it around, mostly on Maxine, you know, really livin' it up."

"Could that be a coincidence, Sheriff? Maxine, living it up with Richard, while Richard's own son was courting and then marrying Mavis, Maxine's younger sister?"

"Naw, it ain't no coincidence at all. Mavis probably started workin' on Dickie after Maxine told her that Richard had a son in Macon who might have some big money. Mavis, more than likely, got pretty nervous after she unexpectedly met Richard here at your farm for the first time and figured that the man might put two and two together and figure out that she and her sister was up to somethin'. Richard might have figured out the whole scheme before he got the ax, or the two-by-four, or whatever it were that kilt him."

"So, Sheriff, you think that it's possible that Mavis could have wanted to keep Richard permanently quiet after she realized that Richard might have noticed a resemblance between herself and Maxine? Richard and Mavis could have had a conversation earlier in the day and planned a rendezvous out there somewhere in the night. Mavis might have figured that she had to nip the whole situation in the bud right off the bat before Richard had a chance to blow her cover."

"All that is totally speculation, Ms. Bee, but it is a strong possibility."

"Yes, it is, Sheriff. It definitely gives us something to go on, anyway."

"Oh, yea. And the fact that Richard's banker is absolutely sure that Richard has squandered a whole lot of money lately, and he has no idea where Richard's money windfall came from is really interestin', too."

"The money's gone, but unfortunately, so is poor Richard. But we might just be getting somewhere now. It seems that it's a strong possibility that there was somebody else out there in the night besides Eddie Pink who needed to keep Richard permanently quiet. The suspect list just got longer."

"Well, I thought the information would give you somethin' to think about, Ms. Bee." The sheriff hitched his belt up and pulled at his suspenders. "Let's keep all this to ourselves, but this could be our big break."

"Right."

"Oh, Ms. Bee, I've been thinking Mama would look real good in that red dress from Sears and Roebuck. I'd like to surprise her with it. I ain't got no catalog, and I ain't never done no orderin'. You think you could fix up an order fer me? Red dress with big, yellow flowers, size twenty-eight. Mama's a little on the heavy side, you know."

"Why, I'd be glad to. Give me a few days to get the order written, and you can pick it up from me and then mail it off yourself. I 'spect your mama would look real nice in that dress." Dear Lord, forgive me for fibbing...again. "That's real nice of you, Sheriff."

"It ain't notin'. Ms. Bee, I got to hit the road. We'll talk again soon, but in the meantime, keep your eyes and ears wide open."

"Yes sir."

This surely did give me something to think about—another motive to keep Richard quiet. But was Mavis strong enough to throw a man as big as Richard into a well without an accomplice? And was it possible that Eddie Pink helped a frantic Mavis push Richard into the well before he took off to parts unknown? Could it have been Mavis's hairpin lying in the poison ivy beside the well?

Little did Mavis—or Maxine, for that matter—know that Richard's and Dickie's money train had wrecked. And where had Richard's sudden wealth come from?

All these thoughts were spinning around in my head as I walked back into the house just in time to hear the telephone ring—one long, one short—that's us.

CHAPTER NINETEEN

The predictable Mr. Lawson, unpredictably, called on the telephone to say that it would be the next day before he could possibly come out to make arrangements for the body. He coughed into the telephone and explained between several loud sniffs that he had developed a bad head cold from being out in the elements and was slightly under the weather. I absolutely knew that Nellie, his next door neighbor and our chatty telephone operator, would be on the warpath about a dead body lying around any longer than necessary. I told the ailing Mr. Lawson we understood, and we'd be waiting for him around ten o'clock the next morning. Really, it was probably a good thing since Edwina would have more time to get herself together. The few extra hours would also give me more time to investigate the crime before we laid Richard in his final resting place (wherever that happened to be).

Mr. Lawson had been very apologetic that he wasn't up to speed today. Of course, my main concern was leaving poor Richard above ground much longer, but Mr. Lawson assured me that he had the body lying in a bed of ice. I shivered as I thought of that. The reality was, first Richard was hit over the head with a heavy piece of wood. Secondly, he was dumped into a well of cold, dark water. Thirdly, he was lying on a bed of ice like two hundred and fifty pounds of ocean mullets being brought into town in the back of Cleo's rolling store, ready to be bought by every homemaker within smelling distance of his truck. Fourthly and finally, his final resting place would be a sealed wooden box with six feet of dirt thrown over the top of it. A cement slab would seal the whole thing up. How undignified the whole process was. I wouldn't tell Edwina about the ice unless she questioned me. She was in a world of her own making and probably wouldn't even think about Richard lying up there in that funeral home with Nellie right out the window in the next house, catching whiffs of the dearly departed as the wind changed directions.

The day progressed much as I would have thought. Edwina clung to her bed, and Dickie and Mavis rode off in Dickie's car, explaining that they needed time to themselves and would return late in the afternoon. Vonion returned to his chores and the peacefulness of his garden, and Ora Lee, soon tired from all the extra work, headed down the lane for home with a pail of fresh water clutched in her hand and a dozen eggs and a slab of bacon in her cloth knapsack draped over her old, worn shoulders.

Bess and I managed to put together a noon meal for Edwina and ourselves, cleaned the kitchen from top to bottom, and scoured the bathrooms before we collapsed in the porch rockers for a little relaxation before time to start supper. Bess was soon peacefully dozing, but my mind was too busy whirling with the events of the last few days for me to relax.

I knew there was a time and a place for everything, but why on earth had our home been the place for another murder? Bloodshed was no stranger to our home. Last year Bess and I had been attacked by a deranged killer right here on the porch because of our meddling...oh, I mean investigating. This whole messy murder business was too close for comfort as far as I was concerned.

There had to be more evidence; all I had to do was recognize it. Maybe if I closed my eyes for a spell, my mind would relax and I'd be able to think clearer.

The afternoon light had faded to pale gray when I opened my eyes and noticed that Bess's rocking chair was empty and still. I could hear pots and pans rattling in the kitchen, and I knew that Bess was busy preparing our next meal. From the musky smell in the air, I knew that beef liver was frying in hot lard. I was hungry.

The evening meal gave us a time of togetherness but not a casual ease. Edwina had relaxed somewhat, but Dickie and Mavis both seemed reserved and distant toward Edwina, Bess and me, and, I noticed, even each other. I easily detected a wedge of discontentment developing between the newlyweds. The restless couple ate quietly before closing the front room door to unwanted intruders.

Now that Cousin Myrtle had returned home, Bess and I could each have our bedrooms back to ourselves. Edwina moved into the guest room, and I returned to my private sanctuary. As night fell about us, we welcomed our time to ourselves and a good night's rest. I willed myself not to think about Edwina and her mounting problems as I rolled over in my own bed and lost myself in dreams of the sweeter times of my youth and early marriage.

Morning came and with it more chores. Bess was out on the back porch loading the washing machine, and I was busy sweeping up the last crumbs from the dining room floor. I paused and listened to Ora Lee's melodious voice drift in from outside. She was singing one of her old spirituals while she meticulously manicured the dirt in the front yard with one of her brooms she had fashioned from dried dog fennels.

A car door slammed, and a masculine voice interrupted Ora Lee's sweet serenade. "Morning, ma'am." The singing abruptly stopped, and I heard a tap at the screen door. I hurried out and nervously greeted Mr. Lawson.

Mr. Lawson asked, between sneezes, to see the grieving widow. I directed him into the front sitting room. Following close behind, not wanting to miss a single word between the heartbroken widow and him, I discovered a reinvigorated Edwina sitting on the edge of our settee, her head held high and her back straight as an arrow, as if she were on her queenly throne. She was wearing a dress from which Ora Lee had pressed away the traveling wrinkles, and the shoes on her feet had been polished by Vonion. She was displaying an arrogance that only Queen Edwina could exhibit, even in the most difficult of times. She was definitely ready and able to give Mr. Lawson a run for his money…literally.

Mr. Lawson walked across the room and extended a limp hand toward Edwina. "Ms. Edwina, my condolences to you. Lawson's Funeral Parlor is here to assist you in your time of heartbreak and grief." I knew that puny handshake was just part of the act. I was braced and ready for the inevitable clash. It had not been determined as of yet who would become the biblical David and who would become Goliath, but we were definitely dealing with two forceful personalities.

Edwina nodded and primly patted her eyes with her freshly laundered (by none other than me) handkerchief. "Ms. Bee indicated to me that it's your desire for me to conduct your late husband's funeral and burial. I would be honored to be of any assistance to you. Your wish is my command."

"Thank you, Mr. Lawson. I do hope that you can conduct a dignified service. Richard was a distinguished man, even though the method of his untimely death was totally beneath his character. Only the best will do for my Richard."

"Oh...yes. I completely understand. I would assume you're interested in our premium package. That particular package defines the elegance and grace that you demonstrate, dear lady." Mr. Lawson relaxed a bit, and I tensed up. At this point I'm quite certain Mr. Lawson began to see dollar signs floating around the room. "The premium package is complete with a beautiful, carved, mahogany coffin, lined in pale blue taffeta, a blanket of fresh white carnations, a service fit for a king right here in Jeffersonville at the church of your choice, and burial in the church cemetery. We provide a beautifully written obituary for the local newspaper, a tent over the grave site, chairs and fans at the cemetery for the mourners, and last, but not least, music by one of our local, gifted vocalists."

"Since we're not residents of Jeffersonville, would you also send the obituary over to our newspaper in Swainsville? I'm sure it would be of great interest over there," Edwina said.

"Certainly, ma'am. I'm not sure the notice will be printed in any newspaper before the actual funeral, but I will send it on to the papers as soon as we make the arrangements."

"Good. And when do you think you can be ready for a service?"

"I can have everything ready in a matter of a couple of days. I do need a suit, shirt, and tie for the beloved to wear. There are a few more details concerning the dignified service you desire that we need to iron out now, if you are up to it, dear lady."

"I will attempt to muster up the strength." Edwina wiped a fake tear from her eye and sighed. "Would you care for a glass of wine before we continue, sir?" Oh, dear Lord, Edwina thinks I keep wine. Mama had been a teetotaler, and Will and I had never had an ounce of liquor in this house. I don't even have wine glasses.

"Oh, no thank you, dear lady. Very kind of you to offer. Now, I'll need a list of pallbearers, the name of your minister and, of course, we need to discuss where the final resting place of the deceased will be." Thank goodness he declined the offer of wine.

"I prefer the Jeffersonville Baptist Church and their preacher. I want Richard buried in one of the sections over by the woods in the church cemetery. I'm sure there's an available site over there that's not occupied. Oh, and I want to buy a whole section, if possible."

"I'm sure that can be arranged, madam. There are a few sections still available at this time, I believe. I'll make all the arrangements."

The meeting went off without a hitch until Mr. Lawson rose to his feet to leave. "Oh, by the way, Mrs. Perkins, the premium package is quite the way to go, but I do need a small deposit before I proceed any further. The total for the package is one hundred and thirty-seven dollars, plus the cost of the grave plots. I believe they're twenty-five dollars apiece. I'll need at least fifty dollars in advance, you know, for my initial expenses."

"Get Richard's checkbook, Bee, if you don't mind. That won't be a problem at all, Mr. Lawson."

My heart missed a beat as I stumbled to my feet. "Edwina, dear, I'm sure Mr. Lawson would wait until tomorrow for the deposit. You can have the bank wire the money. Would that be a huge problem, Mr. Lawson?"

"Er, I suppose I could wait until tomorrow, but I'll need it first thing in the morning. I'll have to pay the grave digger up front, you know."

"Of course, Mr. Lawson," I mumbled.

"Now, ladies, please send a complete list of the pallbearers, the preacher's name, and the songs you desire to be sung at the funeral to me by five o'clock today. Oh, and I'll need the suit for the deceased by then also. I'll be at the funeral home waiting."

"Thank you, sir," Edwina said, as she raised her hand to the man as if she expected him to bow down and kiss it. "I'm sure all can be worked out nicely."

I showed Mr. Lawson to the door and headed for the kitchen to find Bess.

Bess was chopping pickles for chicken salad sandwiches as I walked in. "We've got to talk."

"We sure do, and it's got to be with Dickie. The leftover liver I saved for Vonion has disappeared. One of the pecan pies is gone, and somebody drank at least a quart of milk last night. Our secret eater has struck again."

"Maybe our secret eater is Edwina or Mavis. Or maybe they all have a party every night after we go to bed and eat again. I don't see how Dickie could eat so much after the supper I witnessed him wolf down last night."

"I don't know, but it's got to stop. I feel as though I'm feeding an army. We're going broke trying to feed this family...and whoever it is that's sneaking around in the night."

"Oh, you don't know the half of it, Bess. We're in deeper trouble. Edwina's got to give Mr. Lawson fifty dollars in the morning. Now, somebody's got to go in there and tell her she doesn't have fifty dollars in their checking account. I hope they've got a big, fat savings account somewhere we don't know about."

"Surely they do. Go tell her to call the bank and get the money transferred. It's gonna be simple."

I handed Edwina the telephone for her to make the call to her banker. She never hesitated, but seemed confident that all would go as planned. She was to ask the manager of the bank to wire one hundred and eighty-seven dollars to the Jeffersonville Bank and Trust Company, and one of us would pick the money up there first thing in the morning. Edwina boasted that Richard had an insurance policy also, and Dickie could pick up the policy papers when he returned to their home later in the day to pick up Richard's best suit. It would have been so much simpler if they had just gone home to make all these arrangements and had the funeral in their own church, but no-o... Edwina said she'd tell Dickie to bring her best black dress, her black Sunday shoes and matching purse, and her lavender hat with the tiny blue flowers.

So far, so good, I thought as I stood over to the side watching Edwina tell Nellie to call the bank over in Swainsville.

I soon witnessed the blood run clear out of Edwina's face before she swooned, closed her eyes, and slammed the telephone down. "I've been robbed by that low-down, sticky-fingered, money-sucking crook at that bank! He said we didn't have that much money in his thieving bank, and I know good and well we have plenty of money! Richard always had money in his pockets, and he could always write a check for everything we needed. I'm gonna call the law on that greedy crook, and he'll be in jail by nightfall if I have anything to do with it!" Edwina gasped as if she was about to have a heart attack and fell backwards.

"Bee, call that fat, stupid sheriff of yours and tell him to hurry over to the Swainsville Farmers and

Merchant Bank and demand my money....No, don't do that, I'll go over to that bank myself and straighten that robbing manager out!" Edwina suddenly rose to her feet and grabbed me by the arm. "Come on, Bee, you can go with me! I'll need somebody to back me up when I give that scoundrel a piece of my mind or maybe my right jab or my left hook!"

"Oh, no, we're not going to that bank! Call that sheriff over there in Emory County. What's his name? Sheriff Cottonwood or something like that. He can check on things for you."

"You mean Sheriff Carl Cottonwood? He's nothing but a conniving crook himself. Oh, Bee, what am I gonna do? That idiot banker says I'm completely wiped out!"

"I don't know, but hurry and call Mr. Lawson before he orders that mahogany coffin, and tell him you've decided against the premier package. Tell him Richard looks better in whatever color the cheapest package comes in, and tell him to hold the carnations, too. We've got plenty of yard flowers that will do nicely."

CHAPTER TWENTY

The funeral went off without a hitch, even though Richard was buried in an oak coffin and surrounded by daffodils and wildflowers. There weren't many people at the service to notice Edwina's embarrassment. Only a few of our good friends and relatives and a handful of Edwina and Richard's friends and family from Swainsville attended. Even though the funeral and burial was the cheapest package Mr. Lawson had to offer, Bess and I each ended up donating one hundred dollars to the cause. Of course, that didn't come close to covering the cost of the small reception Bess and I hosted after the funeral and all the other little expenses, such as Edwina's trip to Thelma's Cut and Curl beauty parlor to have her hair retouched before the service, a new pair of nylon stockings for Edwina from Pearly's Department Store, and all the long distance telephone calls made to bankers and insurance men by a devastated Edwina.

Bess and I would have to cut back on all our living expenses for the next ten years at least, and it's hard to cut back after you've already cut back. Edwina confidently assured us that as soon as Dickie got his first big case, we'd be first in line to recover all our money. I'm not holding my breath for that to happen. We're so deep in the hole right now that Dickie would have to work overtime for twenty or more years to recover half the money Bess and I have spent on the Perkins family. Of course, I'm exaggerating a bit, but...so far we've had a well polluted that no humans would ever want to drink from again, and an expensive, new well would have to be dug to replace it. We've literally been eaten out of house and home, and we've paid for an entire funeral, four grave plots, and a reception.

We had even paid extra to have Airy Glover sing "I'll Fly Away" during the service. "I'll Fly Away" was her trademark song, and after you'd heard her sing it a few times, you'd wish she would fly far away, and you'd never have to hear her sing it again. She couldn't carry a tune in a bucket, and her voice cracked so badly that it made you want to grit your teeth, but she was the best we could do in a pinch.

A devastated Edwina had been told by Richard's banker and his insurance home office manager that she was completely broke. Richard had recently cashed in all his life insurance policies, and their only asset was the house. Thank goodness, it was paid for, but their car had a newly placed lien against it. Edwina didn't drive anyway, so I imagine she could do without a means of transportation since her house was in the middle of town and in walking distance of most everything.

Mavis showed signs of real discontent, but she had not left her loving husband's side yet. She knew she couldn't. Sheriff Ledbetter had informed the whole crew that nobody could leave the county until he had time to further investigate the brutal murder. It seemed as if Bess and I were stuck with the whole bunch of freeloaders. I was really under duress to come up with a lead fairly soon before Bess and I had to start using our meager savings to feed the mourning family, or even worse, mortgage my farm. I'm sure Will and Daddy would both turn over in their graves if I ever resorted to such a thing.

Our food burglary continued, but Bess said we had to just ignore it. Dickie had a big appetite, he loved to eat at night, and that's all there was to it. Edwina had recovered somewhat and now was actually helping around the house a bit, that is, if you consider swatting flies or setting a table once in a while for a meal. Dickie tried to stay out of everybody's way, and Mavis continually fussed and fumed about the inconvenience of being stuck out in the middle of nowhere with nothing to do.

By this time I had taken several opportunities to revisit the well. I had also walked the woods behind it many times, searching for a broken oak limb or board that could have been used as a weapon. I believed that I had found it—an oak limb, caked with mud and a smidgeon of dried blood, lying among overgrown weeds and grass in a ditch that divided a group of young pecan trees from a straggly section of pine trees. In my way of reasoning, the limb had to have been carelessly thrown over into the ditch as the murderer fled the well through the woods and headed for the highway that ran across the front corner of Foy Jackson's place, a good half mile away. No good fingerprints would ever be found on the log since it appeared that the murderer had wiped it with dirt and mud before throwing it into the bushes.

The idea that Dickie could have angrily struck his father from behind with a heavy weapon seemed to be a remote possibility to me. I realized that Dickie was enraged that night, but was he capable of killing his own father? If he had followed his father behind the house that night and perhaps on into the woods, where did the deadly encounter occur? He would have had to walk several hundred yards into the woods to find the small oak limb where it had fallen from the tree. After the fatal run-in with his father, he would have had to drag the heavy body to the well, throw it over the side, walk off in the opposite direction of our home, throw the limb in the ditch, and then walk back to the house. All that seemed to be a whole lot of wasted effort on Dickie's part to me. Chances were strongly against his having the presence of mind to make all those decisions in an anxious state of mind since I'm quite sure he would be a novice to the act of homicide. He was definitely still on my suspect list as well as the seductive Mavis.

Mavis wanted lots of money, and she knew how to go about getting it. She married for it, and now she might have thought she'd have to murder for it. After all, Richard stood in the way of Dickie's immediate inheritance. Actually, there wasn't any inheritance at all, but Mavis wasn't aware of that at the time of Richard's murder. Maxine, her conniving sister, had probably led her to believe that Dickie's father was filthy rich. Dickie had been squandering money given to him by his father on Mavis as if the deep well would never run dry. Since Richard had not quite come to the end of his financial rope, Maxine was still under the impression that she had met her rich sugar daddy. A greedy Mavis was willing to nip all her sister's good fortune in the bud and grab the bundle of cash while the getting was good.

And then there was Eddie Pink, a desperate young man running from the law. Maybe an encounter occurred between Eddie Pink and Richard somewhere back of the house or in the woods. Perhaps Eddie Pink ran into Richard and, realizing he couldn't leave a witness behind, savagely beat him to death with the oak limb. He then hid the distorted body in the watery grave where he figured it wouldn't be quickly found. No talkative witness would be left behind, and he had a better opportunity for a clean getaway. If that's the case, Eddie was long gone...or was he? Eddie Pink was definitely on the list of suspects.

And then there was always the unlikely possibility that Eddie Pink or Dickie assisted a desperate Mavis in murdering Richard. Eddie Pink would have fled afterwards and disappeared into the night to travel out of the county and probably out of the state of Georgia. Where was the connection and...was there a connection?

Oh...perhaps a loan shark had followed Richard here to our farm and done him in right here under our noses when Richard wasn't able to come up with the next payment. I know...I'm getting carried away now, but...you never know.

Richard was a desperate man, and desperate men act desperately. Was Richard Perkins capable of committing suicide? Now that was a strong possibility, but I really didn't think so. How could we account for the bruises to his head and neck if he jumped into the well of his own free will and then drowned? I knew if Sheriff Ledbetter or I didn't come up with some good explanation soon, the sheriff would explain the whole thing away as a reckless act of suicide just so it would appear that he had solved the crime. He does have his pride, you know.

All I needed was a little more time to ponder this thing out and a little more information.

I had one strong hunch that needed to be explored before heading back to the house. I hurried toward the barn and stopped a few feet away, attempting to catch my limited breath. Praying to God that I'd remain calm, I slowly walked up to the heavy barn door and pushed against it to release the latch. Twisting the wooden door handle just as I had done for years and years in the past, I felt the tension mounting up inside myself. The old barn door groaned loudly as I pulled it slightly open, enough for me to peer inside. A shaft of sunlight angled perfectly into a growing sphere in the dark atmosphere as I opened the door wider. Floating about in the heavy, thick air was a blanket of dust particles disturbed only by a few enormous horseflies swarming about. My nostrils soon filled with the pungent, musky odor of the present occupants as well of those that had inhabited the barn in past times.

Hortence was standing in her stall, contentedly chewing her cud as if she didn't have a care in the world. We still kept old Ned in the stall next to Hortence. Ned was the last of the mules that had worked our land for Daddy and Will over the years. Blind and feeble now, Ned wasn't any good for anything except for us to pet and to keep Hortence company, but we kept him on anyway out of love and devotion to all God's creatures. Vonion continued to feed and exercise him daily, knowing the end was near for our beloved, old workmate.

As I entered the dark interior, I was reminded of the years of my childhood, playing about in the hayloft overhead. It always filled me with delight when Daddy packed the upstairs cavern full with the new hay of the season, giving me a new and fresh playland to tumble about in or to hide in from Ora Lee or Mama when chores were waiting. Vonion still stored our hay in the loft, but now it was tied together in bales that Tom Wilson supplied to us after he cut the hay out in the meadow.

I closed the heavy door behind myself, shutting out the bright sunlight, and stood in silence, waiting to hear any unusual sound. When none came, I walked farther into the darkness and waited again as my eyes grew accustomed to the dimness, where only small holes and cracks in the walls allowed small beams of sunlight into the large space. In the faded darkness I spied an enormous pack rat scampering across the dirt floor, causing me to hold my breath and stiffen my back. Soon it was gone and silence filled the air again. I continued to wait, but, for what? I really wasn't sure.

My squeaking voice interrupted the silence, and I startled myself when I called out, "Eddie Pink. I know you're in here, so you might as well show yourself." I braced myself for an answer.

CHAPTER TWENTY-ONE

No answer. This was a foolish idea. I repeated, "I know you're in here, Eddie Pink. I'm not going anywhere 'til you show yourself. I'm not here to judge you. I just want to talk with you. Come on out."

No answer. Was I wrong?

"I remember you as a child, Eddie. Sweet and innocent, with not much guidance from your parents. You needed a haircut and a coat back then. I wish I had followed up on you. It's the grown people that usually are to blame when a child goes in the wrong direction. I will not turn you in to the sheriff if you can convince me that you didn't have anything to do with the death of my cousin's husband. If you're guilty of that crime, stay put, and I'll leave you to your running, but you'll never have anything but misery and torment for the rest of your life. You'll always be looking over your shoulder. Is that how you want to live, on the run like a wild animal? You'll lose your home place and all your possessions. Now, I know you don't want a life where there's no peaceful rest."

Still no answer. I must be crazy for even thinking Eddie was hiding in the barn.

"Why are you running in the first place, Eddie? The sheriff told me you didn't have much more time left on your prison sentence. Surely you had a good reason for running from your work detail."

I heard a faint rustle. Oh, my stars! My hunch had paid off! He was here! My body began to stiffen with apprehension. I knew it! I just knew it!

"You're in here. I'm sure of it now. I'm sitting on the milking stool, and I don't have a place to go. I've got all the time in the world." The pesky flies weren't going anywhere either. One in particular had circled my head four or five times before making a dive landing on my forehead. I swatted at it but missed.

"You're not gonna turn me in?" It was almost a whisper.

"No, I just want to talk with you. You can run away after we talk if you've got a mind to. I'm not gonna stop you or tell anybody that I've talked with you. That's a promise and I don't break my promises." My hunch had paid off! I sat stiffly, agonizing that each breath might be my last; after all, if Eddie had killed one time, he'd probably kill again. And I could be the next victim.

I had taken a big gamble coming into the barn by myself. Tense and terrified that I might be murdered right here on the milking stool, I sat and waited. My nerves felt as if they were compressed springs, ready to explode at any second. I was braced for a knife in the back or a rope around my neck. Or maybe Eddie would hit me over the head with a big rock or a two-by-four. I quickly decided the fastest way to die would be my first choice.

Several minutes passed. I continued to sit...and sit. As time slowly churned by, a calmness and an assurance that I was safe overcame me. I was beginning to feel fairly relaxed even though an escaped convict was just a few feet away.

I first noticed two scruffy boots and then a couple of pants legs dangling from the loft. The body of a skinny young man dressed in a faded gray convict suit soon dropped from the ceiling onto a pile of fertilizer bags stacked on the barn floor. After a hard landing, Eddie Pink raised his head. Eyes full of torment and fright as well as embarrassment stared at me, and I stared back in amazement that my hunch had actually paid off. I sensed immediately that I was as safe as a newborn baby in its mother's loving arms.

"You shore you ain't aimin' to turn me in?" he asked again, as if he couldn't believe my words. "You ain't just sayin' it to make me come out'a hidin', is you?"

"I'm not gonna turn you in and you're not gonna hurt me. Isn't that right? We're just gonna talk because we have an understanding."

"Yes ma'am, if'n you say it to be."

"Have you been getting enough to eat, Eddie? It is Eddie Pink, isn't it? If you're hungry, I'll fetch you something right now. There's leftover chicken in the kitchen."

"That chicken does sound mighty good, but I'm not famished yet. I'm sorry 'bout all the food I been takin' from the house. I guess I would a' starved by now without it. Y'all some good cooks."

"It's all right about the food."

"I am truly sorry, and I plan to pay you back fer every mouthful. That is soon as I get some work."

"That's not necessary. God's word tells us to feed hungry strangers and the less fortunate. I've never turned anybody away from my table, and I'm not going to start now."

"My ma had to turn everbody away. She'd tell tramps to git and don't ever come back, if'n they come up to the door. My pa would've beat her good if'n she ever give a mouthful of food away. Sometimes I'd take a chance and sneak out the door with a hunk of corn bread or a hoecake fer a hobo after Ma sent him off, but I'd make certain Pa didn't know notin' 'bout it. Ma were scared all the time that Pa'd lose his temper and kill her 'bout somethin' she ain't done quite right."

"It's been hard times, and your pa wanted to protect his family from starving, I 'spect."

"Yes'um."

"How'd you get on the chain gang, Eddie? It is Eddie Pink, isn't it?"

Eddie sat up and gradually slid closer toward me but stayed on top of the fertilizer sacks. His tattered uniform was several sizes too large and hung on his small frame as if it were hanging from a peg on the wall. A splotchy, graying beard and deep-set eyes covered his gaunt face. Even in this questionable situation, I would have loved to dunk him into a tub of hot water, scrub him down with a wire brush from the top of his head to the tip of his toes, and then whack several inches from his straggly mop of wiry hair.

I recognized him, even after all this time and in his present condition. I especially remembered his eyes. Set in his head like tiny, shining pebbles, they had a longing and loneliness about them. I quickly detected the sweetness and gentleness that I distinctly remembered in his youth.

"Yes'um, it's Eddie Pink. The law caught up with me on the road early in the mornin' 'bout five or five thirty after a load of hogs was stole from Mr. Maynard Meeks over in Burt County during the night. I was comin' home in my old truck from that direction, and the sheriff pulled me over. I didn't have no hogs in my truck, but my truck smelled like hogs. The sheriff claimed I had already sold them and was comin' home after a night of thievin'. I didn't steal them hogs, and I didn't know nothin' 'bout no hogs being stole. My truck smelled like hogs 'cause I raised hogs and hauled them to the stock market from time to time. Them law men didn't believe not nary a word I said, and I didn't have no alibi."

"Why didn't you have an alibi, Eddie? Most folks are at home in bed at that time of morning."

Eddie dropped his head. "I can't really say."

"I will believe you, Eddie. Maybe I can help you."

"Naw. Nobody can help me now. It's way too late fer that."

"Try me. I'm not the police or a sheriff. Just tell me the truth. If you weren't stealing hogs in the middle of the night, what were you doing out on that road?"

"I'd, uh, been out a'visitin'." Eddie continued to lower his head to avoid my eyes.

"Visiting in the middle of the n—? Oh, you mean you had a girlfriend and had stayed late at her place. Is that it?"

"Uh...not really a girlfriend, but it were kind'a like that."

"Eddie, be honest with me. Tell me what you couldn't tell the sheriff. Where had you been? If you had been with a girl, she could have backed up your story, and it would have all been over long ago."

"Uh, Mrs. Martin, it is Mrs. Martin, isn't it? You don't really understand..."

"Call me Ms. Bee like everybody else does, and I'm still listening."

"Well, er, you see, Ms. Bee, that girl couldn't tell nobody nothin' 'cause she were dead. She were kilt right after I left her place that night...uh, I mean fer the first time. I didn't stay long, just long enough to talk with her fer a few minutes. Hit weren't my night to be with her, you see, and when I got to her place, she turn't me down flat. We didn't ever git down to business, but she told me to come back later on. She said she might work me in then. She got a knock at the front door, and I pretended to leave after she said she had to get the door 'cause she had a bigger fish to fry. I didn't rightly know what she meant by that, but I left the house by the back door. I had parked down the road a piece, but I decided to wait in the bushes 'round at the back of the house 'cause I figured that if I give her a little time, we could finish our visit. That weren't to happen."

"Go on, Eddie." I leaned in closer, not wanting to miss a word.

"I didn't see the man go in, but I did see him come out. I went up to the back door after he left out, and I knocked again, but she didn't come to the door. I thought that were strange so I eased through the back door, hopin' maybe me and her could finish our visit, but I soon spotted her dead body lyin' in a bunch of blood. I felt fer a pulse, but hit were like I had figured; she were already dead. Hit put real fear in me, so I skedaddled out of there like a scared rabbit and never once looked back. I made it to my truck and left town in a hurry. I were real fearful and real tired, too. I had coon hunted most all the night before and picked cotton all day fer a neighbor man. I pulled over beside the road to close my eyes a minute, and I guess I fell plum asleep. Just as I were pullin' back to the road, I saw the lights from the sheriff car. I kept goin', but the law catched up with me."

"Go on."

"I feared they was stoppin' me fer the murder, so when the deputy said somethin' 'bout hogs being stole, I were partly relieved. You see, Ms. Bee, if'n I'd told where I had really been, I'd have been arrested fer murder, not thievin'. I weren't up to no good, that's fer sure, but I ain't no murderer. Stealin' hogs ain't half as bad as murderin' somebody, so I figured I'd take the wrap fer the hogs."

"Eddie Pink. You're telling me that you were hiding behind the house while that prostitute was brutally murdered."

"Yes'um, I suppose I am. I were there the same night she died, and hit were the same night the hogs were stole off'n Mr. Meeks. Ain't that all a coincidence?"

"Eddie, was the girl's name Dixie?" My mind was spinning in anticipation as I waited for the answer.

"Yes'um, hit shore were. Did you know her?"

"No, I didn't know her, but I've heard about her and her murder." Right here in my barn was a witness to the murder Bess and I had investigated last year. The killer had finally been revealed to us, but not before Bess and I had been assaulted and almost killed ourselves by the murderer.

"So, Eddie, you took the wrap for hog thieving to keep from being associated with a murder, a murder you probably would have been charged for."

"Yes'um. I ain't proud of it, but hit's the honest to God truth. I didn't steal no hogs, and I didn't murder nobody. By the time I learnt that Dixie's killer had been fount out, I was already in the pokey, serving my nine months fer hog stealin'. Sometimes hit's just better to keep yor mouth shut 'bout everthang, and I figured this were one of them."

Bess called from the porch.

I had fibbed to Eddie. I did have somewhere else to be. Bess and I were to run into town for a few groceries. I had told Bess that I needed a few minutes to think and wanted to stroll through the orchard to clear my head before we left for town. She said to take all the time I needed, but I'd better come up with a lead to this crime real soon before our pantry shelves were completely empty. She was ready to go into town. I decided to answer her but to put her off.

"Eddie, I'm going to step over to the barn door and answer my sister. You can watch me from here. I'm going to tell her to go on into town without me. I'll be right back. Don't move a muscle."

"Yes'um."

I walked over to the barn door and opened it wide enough to walk through. I stood right outside the door where Eddie could see me. Knowing Eddie's eyes had followed me and was watching every move I made, I called, "Bess, I'm right here. Go on into town without me. I've found a few holes in a few of Vonion's croaker sacks, and I'm repairing them before they get any bigger." Boy, was that a fib, but maybe Bess would fall for it.

"Bee, you can't be serious. You don't even have a needle and thread out there. You just don't want to go, do you? Stay home and I'll go right by myself. I don't know why you hate to go to the store."

"Thank you, Bess. I'll start the vacuuming as soon as I go in. Check with Ora Lee before you leave about her snuff. She's probably out by now. Oh, and remember to get chocolate squares. We have to get a cake over to Foy tomorrow at the latest. We promised, you know."

"I remember that we promised a cake before we knew we'd be feeding the entire Perkins family for days on end."

"A promise is a promise, Sister." I eased the door closed and returned to my seat. I could feel Eddie tense again.

"I'm not going back on my word and tell, Eddie. I'm your friend, not your enemy."

"Yes'um, hit's beginning to sink in...Hit's just that I ain't never had too many friends that I could really count on…'cept my dog, Tick. He was my best friend 'til he died. Got bit by a big rattler and there weren't notin' I could do fer him but watch him suffer and die."

"I'm sorry. It's awfully hard to lose our pets. Sometimes it's more painful than when a human dies we're close to."

"Yes'um."

"Eddie, how can you prove you were at Dixie's house? Was your name in a book or a ledger or something like that? You know, like you had an appointment."

"Well, there might have been a name in a ledger, but hit weren't my name. I never give Dixie my real name. I doubt she really cared what my name was, so's I just made up one, and hit weren't in that ledger fer that night. My needs were unexpected, and I didn't have no appointment. I were just takin' a chance Dixie was free, but she weren't." Then Eddie gave a little, fake laugh. "Dixie weren't never free, but she were reasonable."

I smiled too. "Oh, Eddie, if you had only stayed home that night, you wouldn't be living in my barn right now."

"Yes'um, and I've done learnt my lesson, but hit's way too late."

"Why did you run away from your work detail? Your time in jail was coming to an end."

"Two months. That's about all, Ms. Bee. I ain't proud of what I did, but hit had to be done. Fat Man, that's what we called the guard. He were beatin' Lizard—that's my buddy—with the butt end of his rifle fer being lazy out there on detail. Lizard ain't lazy; he's sick. He's got some kind of cancer, and he ain't able to do the work no more. I just couldn't stand there and watch Fat Man beat him no more. I grabbed fer the rifle and threw it back at Fat Man and told the others to stay put. After I realized what I did, I ran fast as a hound dog after a possum. I knew what I did was wrong, but I couldn't stop myself. I was movin' so fast I didn't think to turn around and take my punishment. Fount that little house out back there down the lane and crawled under. I jest don't know what to do now. Hit's way too late to go back and make amends. I just hope Lizard is all right. He was mighty sick, and there ain't no doctorin' in jail."

My heart was breaking for this young man and for Lizard. There are many injustices in this world and not enough people to rectify them. I promised myself right then and there to do everything in my power to help Eddie and Lizard, too.

"I want you to stay put, Eddie. Don't go anywhere. I'm going to check all this out and clear your name. I promise you, Eddie. If it takes every breath in my body, I'm gonna clear your name."

"Thank you, ma'am. I shore could use a friend 'bout now...Oh, Ms. Bee, there's somethin' else you might be interested in. I thunk I seen a murder the other night. You know anythang 'bout somebody throwin' a man into the well back of your house?"

You could have knocked me over with a feather, but I quickly recovered from the shock.

"Eddie, there was a dead man found in that well. It was my cousin's husband, Richard Perkins. We've been searching frantically for some clue as to what really happened."

"I seen the whole thang the day I escaped. I had fount a good hidin' place under that old shack back there and hid up close to the chimney foundation. I figured the dogs wouldn't sniff me out, what with all the other strong odors under there. Anyway, I had just about fell asleep when I heard a noise like pantin' or heavy breathin' or somethang like that. I inched closer to the edge of the house and saw a big man with a great big belly drag another big man over to the well and ease him over the ledge. Hit were hard to lift that heavy body, but the man finally got hit over the edge. Soon as the body fell into the well, the man took off and run back into the woods...as fast as a big man can run, that is. Hit all happened real quick like." Finally some real evidence!

"What did the big man look like? Was he tall or short? Anything you can remember, tell me. We've been looking for the murderer ever since we found Richard's body."

"Well, um, he were fat, I can say that. Big chested, but not firm. Had on overalls and a floppy, wide-brimmed hat. I couldn't see much skin, but he were white, not colored. Strong as a mule, but sluggish."

"That gives me something to go on. Is there anything else you can remember? Did you hear him say anything?"

"No'um. Not nary a word. Just pantin' like he were tired and out of breath. Soon as I saw what happened, I crawled back to the chimney and stayed there 'til right before daybreak. I run to this here barn whil'st hit were still dark, and I been in the loft ever since. I figured y'all was lookin fer the murderer and me when I heard all the commotion out in the yard. I were pure nervous 'bout them dogs. I been a' sleepin' and a' daydreamin' ever since. Ms. Bee, I been right scared that hit were gonna be me they suspected of murderin' that man. I promise I ain't had notin' to do with any of it. I didn't even know that man."

"I'm convinced of that, Eddie."

"Yes'um, but what you gonna do 'bout me?"

"Nothing, right now. Stay put and let me think about what you've told me. Just stay in the loft a little longer. Do you want me to bring you a book or a magazine to read?"

"No'um, I can't read words. I 'spect I'll be gettin' hungry, though."

"I'll put your food inside the barn door tonight right after dark. Don't come back into the house. It's too dangerous. I'll bring breakfast in the morning as soon as Vonion is out of the way."

Eddie hung his head and said, "Ms. Bee...uh...Ms. Bee, I'm really countin' on you."

"I know you are and don't worry; we'll work it all out...And Eddie, I'm really counting on you too."

CHAPTER TWENTY-TWO

"B arn's on fire!! Barn's on fire!! Somebody call the fire de-part-ment! Hurry!" Vonion frantically hollered as I was finishing up the last of the breakfast dishes the next morning. "Barn's a'blazing!"

Vonion's panic quickly ended my daydream about the good ole days—the days before the reunion and the murder. As the dreaded words reached the kitchen, I threw my drying towel down to race out the back door. I quickly saw flames steadily crawling up the side of the barn and heard the crackle and pop of a hot fire. Suddenly, Hortence and Ned plunged from under the burning embers of their stalls and galloped through the open gate of the corral for safety. Bringing up the rear was Eddie Pink, excitedly waving his arms in the air as the animals raced ahead. Eddie grabbed the water hose lying on the ground and began dowsing the fire as I frantically ran toward the dangerous blaze. With a sloshing bucket of water in each hand, Vonion suddenly appeared from the opposite side of the barn. The strangers ran right smack into each other as each attempted to extinguish the fire. Even in my haste to reach the barn, I witnessed the whole encounter—Vonion's obvious and total surprise at seeing an unknown person in a baggy convict suit dousing flames, and Eddie's sudden fear that Vonion might start hollering that an escaped convict was in the burning barn.

My old legs couldn't have carried me any faster. I swiftly reached the barn and grabbed a croaker sack from the pile by the door, ran over to the hog trough, drenched the sack with water, and ran back toward the barn to beat the flames as they steadily made their way up the side of the barn.

The three of us worked feverishly as the flames began to crawl over the side of the wall onto the roof. Eddie threw the hose toward me and grabbed the sacks from my hands. His youthful strength was amazing. With each beat, one after another, he tirelessly toiled as I continued to douse the growing flames with water from the hose. Vonion never stopped running back and forth from the trough to the barn long enough to question our young companion. Obviously, fear and adrenalin were motivating him as he steadily moved faster than a man half his age.

As fast as the flames had grown, they quickly began to weaken. Eddie unrelentingly drenched his bags again and again with the water from the hose and continued to beat the dying embers. Vonion stomped the last of the flames around the base of the barn wall as I squirted water across the side of the barn's charred surface.

Relief and exhaustion soon overtook me as the adrenalin left my body. Thankfully, the animals were safe, and the barn was spared by the quick response of my two heroes, Eddie and Vonion. How quickly the catastrophe had started; one minute the barn and animals were safe and sound, and the next, all was going up in flames.

Bent over in exhaustion, Vonion gasped between deep, long breaths. "A little water's all's I need and I's'll be fine." I handed the water hose over and waited for him to question where our heroic stranger had come from and who in tarnation he was. Vonion glanced over at Eddie with the quizzical expression he always uses when he doesn't quite understand everything. After several gulps, Vonion handed the hose to Eddie who gratefully took a few swallows and began to rinse his face with the cool well water. "I's shore glad you was here today, stranger. We couldn't 'a doused this blaze without you."

I knew the time had come to explain our visitor. I took a deep breath and plunged ahead. "Vonion, I'd like you to meet Eddie Pink. Eddie is an escaped prisoner who is presently residing in our barn," and I quickly added, "but he is an innocent man."

Vonion answered in a skeptical tone, "Ever man that ever been in the jailhouse say he an innocent man, but I'm glad of his presence today." Vonion reached out to shake Eddie's hand. "What you were in the pokey fer?"

"Vonion, I'll answer for our friend. He was charged with stealing hogs over in Burt County. He's explained the whole thing to me, and I'm totally convinced that he is innocent. I plan to clear his name. He's been living in our barn for several days, and I intend for him to stay there until we can get this whole thing straightened out one way or the other. Now are you with me on this, or am I gonna have to fight you tooth and nail about it?"

"You askin' me to help harbor a convicted man? Ms. Bee, you know we's could be put in the cell right next to this here criminal if'n the law gets wind a' what we is doin'. No sir'ee bobtail, I ain't gonna have notin' to do with all this. I'm gonna walk away right now, and you best better disappear from these here parts right now, Mr. Eddie, or whatever your real name is."

Eddie's troubled face fell, and his shoulders began to slump as he realized his troubles were far from over. "I'm sorry fer all the trouble, Vonion, and I'll be moving on now. Ms. Bee, thank you fer all you've done fer me." Eddie turned as if he was considering which way to run.

"Oh, no, you aren't going anywhere. You're gonna stay right here." I reached out to grab Eddie's calloused hand. "Running isn't the answer for you, and you know it. Vonion, let me explain all the circumstances."

Vonion nodded, but I knew he'd have a hard time seeing things exactly as they really were. After the long story unfolded, he hesitated and shook his head. "Ms. Bee, you done got me in trouble with the law a time or two before, and now you's tryin' to do it again." He looked directly toward Eddie. "If'n the law want to know anythang 'bout where you is, Ms. Bee gonna tells them Vonion don't know notin' 'bout notin'. The law is the law, and I ain't plannin' on going to no chain gang in my old age 'cause of some young squirt that sweet-talk Ms. Bee. No sir'ee, I ain't...and you can put that in yor pipe and smoke it. My deacon board at church would have me run clear out'a Georgia if'n they ever caught wind of what y'alls proposin' fer me to get involved in. Now, I'm gonna go see 'bout Hortence and Ned, and when I comes back, you best better be gone, young man. You hear me?"

"You not gonna turn me in, Vonion?" Eddie unbelievingly asked.

"I's a' gonna walk right out'a here likes I ain't never seen you, and then I'm gonna get some materials up to fix this here side of the barn; that's 'xactly what I'm a'gonna do."

Relief flooded my mind. Thank goodness I didn't have to carry on a fight and a feud with

Vonion now with everything else on my mind. "Vonion, before you go, what do you figure started this blaze?"

"I think I know," Eddie sheepishly answered. "Hit were a cigarette butt."

Vonion stepped back. "A cigarette butt? Did you throw one down? Ain't nobody else 'round here but me, and I's know's I ain't been so careless as to start no fire."

"Hit were that young man that's been hangin' 'round here, the one y'all call Dickie. He threw it a little too close to the side of the barn in a pile of dry hay. I seen him do it. Soon as he saw the hay was on fire, he tried to stomp hit out, but when he saw hit were more than he could handle, he took off runnin' toward the woods like a scalded dog. That's when I jumped down and tried to stomp it out. I soon speculated hit were no use, so I ran fer the hose. Y'all knows the rest. Hit were Dickie that started the blaze."

"Eddie, you mean to tell me that young scalawag ran away after the fire got out of control? Of all the cowardly things to do! He left the animals in the barn to perish! He could have at least opened the gate for them to escape! I just can't believe anybody would be so cruel."

"There that scalawag comes now, Ms. Bee. He's a'walkin' out of the woods. I better get back to my hidin'."

I can only report to my readers that my blood pressure went sky high at the sight of Dickie. Anger, rage, sadness, and most of all...murder filled my mind and heart. "Hurry, Eddie, get back in the loft, and Vonion, you better stop me if I start to sock Dickie into next year. I've never been so angry with anybody in my entire life."

"Calm down, Ms. Bee. Violence never helped nary a thing. Think what Mr. Will would do in this here sit'ation...uh...I 'spect Mr. Will would punch the livin' daylights out 'a Dickie; that what he would do. If'n anybody gonna knock his block off, hit gonna be me."

"Here he comes. Let's see if we can get the truth out of him for once in his life, that is, if the truth is in his lawyerly vocabulary."

Eddie skedaddled into the loft just as our culprit sprinted for us. "What happened to the barn, Cousin Bee?" Dickie called from a few yards out in a fake questioning tone of voice.

Vonion quickly answered, "A fire! Can't you tell, boy? You know anything 'bout it?"

Dickie turned every shade of green before he stammered, "No. I've been gone quite a while. Everything was fine when I left."

"Don't you smoke cigarettes, Dickie?" I accusingly asked, hoping my anger wouldn't become too apparent before Dickie began to deny our accusations. "Do you think you could have accidently dropped a lit cigarette butt on the ground before you left for your walk?"

"Oh, no-o ma'am. I never—"

"Don't deny it, Dickie! We have an eyewitness that said you left the barn as it began to blaze up. How could you have been so careless and then so cowardly and uncaring as to leave the barn with defenseless animals locked inside? Don't answer me! Just get out of my sight! Leave right now and don't ever come back...and take your wife with you! Go by the sheriff's office and tell him why you're leaving and where you're going! Now go, before I call the sheriff to come out here to arrest you for arson!"

"But, Cou-sin Bee, I—"

"Don't Cou-sin Bee me ever again! Now go before I really lose my temper! Spare your mother the truth about her darling son. She has enough to deal with without knowing her son is a coward, a murderer at heart, and a liar!"

"I am not a murderer!"

"If our precious animals had perished in the fire, you absolutely would have been one."

Dickie glared at Vonion. "I'll get you for snitchin' if it's the last thing on earth I do. You know you set that fire, nigger, not me. You can pretend all you want, but the sheriff will believe me over a colored man any day of the week!" Dickie kicked the side of the smutty barn and angrily strode off toward the house.

His accusations toward Vonion put the icing on the cake. It would have been hard to hold Vonion back if he had attempted to strike Dickie. And I don't know that I would have. But now we absolutely knew the truth. A coward's way out is to lie his way out.

Edwina's precious Dickie and Mavis left the farm that day without another word to us. At least one good thing came from his disgraceful actions. Only one more Perkins family member remained.

CHAPTER TWENTY-THREE

With heavy steps and a much heavier heart I closed the porch screen door behind me, carrying the pungent odor of the smut along. Edwina strolled out as I began to unbutton my sooty, soiled dress. Carrying a coffee cup and still attired in her flannel bathrobe and with pin curls in her hair, she had not even thought of dressing for the busy day or helping with the chores.

"Oh, Bee, I hate to be the one to bear the dreadful news, but poor Dickie had to leave unexpectedly." Edwina seemed to suddenly notice my dirty, disheveled condition and scolded me with an air of disapproval. "Where on earth have you been? You look as if you've been fighting a fire, and you smell like a filthy smoke stack." Evidently, she knew nothing about a fire and was totally in the dark about why Dickie had actually left.

"Edwina, we've had a fire at the barn. You didn't smell anything, for goodness' sake? Where have you been all morning?" My response might have been a bit snappy.

"Why, I was napping until Dickie woke me and told me he had been called back to Macon for an important job interview. He and Mavis left a few minutes ago and were going to stop by the sheriff's office and fill Sheriff Ledbetter in on his plans before he leaves town. You don't think the poor boy will have any trouble with that overbearing sheriff, do you, Bee? That uncouth, bungling sheriff better not give my boy any trouble, or he'll have me to deal with, and he doesn't want what I can dish out." I was sure Sheriff Ledbetter would be shaking in his boots, and if he didn't give Dickie his permission, he'd have me to deal with, too. "Dickie's probably going to be offered an important position, and he has to be interviewed by the prospective firm immediately." Then as an afterthought, Edwina inquired, "Where was the fire anyway?"

"At the barn. Vonion and I finally got it under control. Listen, Edwina, I'd like to stand here and gab with you all day, but I've absolutely got to bathe. This soot and smoke is making me purely nauseous, and I don't want the smoke odor in the house any worse than it already is. Why don't you start a little dinner, and I'll be in the kitchen directly. Heat up the leftover turnip greens and fry a little cornbread. There's cold meat loaf in the refrigerator.

We'll make do with that. And listen out for Bess. She'll be in from town soon."

"Oh, Bee, you know I don't know my way around your kitchen. Can't we eat a little later today?"

"Oh, no, we cannot," I answered a little too forcefully. "You can find your way around that kitchen. Go on now and get dinner started. It'll be good for you to have something constructive to do with your time for a change. I'll be out of the bathroom shortly, and I'm famished."

"Oh, all right, but I thought now that Richard has passed away my days in a kitchen were finally over. You know how I hate to lean over a hot stove."

"You like to eat, don't you? If you eat, you have to cook. That's a new rule around here." I could be as stubborn as Edwina, and as mad as I was right now, it's a real wonder I didn't throw her out of the house along with her ungrateful son, lock, stock, and girdle. I was suddenly bound and determined that Queen Edwina was going to start carrying her weight around here, and if she didn't like it, she knew which door to open.

As I stood by the bathtub, wrapping my damp body in a towel and watching the sooty, dark water slowly drain from the bathtub, leaving a black ring, I could feel my frustration growing. My feelings of despair were as raw as my scrubbed, tender skin. I felt as if my whole world had been completely turned wrong side out. My privacy had been invaded, my bank account drained, my home turned into a hotel for ungrateful people, my barn burned, and my animals frightened to death. Also, Vonion, as overworked as he already was, now had the task of repairing the barn. On top of all that, my mind was spinning with all the new evidence I had recently discovered concerning Richard's murder.

Eddie Pink was the key. He was an eyewitness to Richard's body being heaved over the side of the well. All I had to do now was to put the puzzle pieces together. But how? I knew I had to keep my wits about me even with the storm of resentment building deep inside. The answer was somewhere, probably right under my nose.

"Bee, how on earth did the barn catch fire?" Bess called from the porch, as she anxiously dashed into the house a little later that morning. "I leave home to go to town, and all hell breaks out around here!"

Edwina was standing over the stove, and I was placing the silverware on the table for dinner as Bess hurried into the kitchen with two grocery sacks in her arms. She set the sacks on the counter and impatiently waited for my hesitant answer. Trying to completely avoid the question in front of Edwina, I quickly replied, "I hope you didn't forget the chocolate squares. We have a cake to bake, you know."

"The barn, Bee, for goodness' sake. How'd the fire start? I didn't forget the chocolate. You've reminded me at least ten times."

"Oh yes, I guess I have," I sheepishly replied. "Now don't get overexcited. We're really not sure how the barn caught fire. It's out now, that's the important part. How'd you find out about the fire, anyway?"

"Everybody in town knows about the fire, Bee! Everybody knew it before I did!" Bess indignantly replied. "Vonion came into town to buy a few pieces of lumber to replace the burned-out boards in the barn and told everybody in the hardware store about the fire and how the two of you practically risked life and limb fighting the blaze. Bee, you know how news flies around that town. Mildred overheard Vonion telling about the fire while she was in the hardware store, probably purchasing more rat poison for all those field mice that keep invading her not-so-clean house."

"Bess, please, keep to the story."

"Well, it's true, and you know it. She never cleans her kitchen properly, and the mice can have a picnic in there anytime they want to, which is practically all the time."

"Okay, now Bess, go on."

"Well, Mildred's next stop was the grocery store, and as soon as she could find somebody who would listen, she was blabbing the news all over the store. I actually overheard her telling Old Man Peterson about the fire while I was trying to avoid his roving eyes. I was hiding behind a cured ham that was hanging from the rafters when I saw Mildred smile in the direction of Old Man Peterson, and his worn-out old eyes lit up like a Christmas tree. He returned her smile with that toothy grin of his. You know, you've seen it before. And we thought we were the only targets of Old Man Peterson's advances. I hope you aren't too disappointed to find out that he flirts with the entire population of women in Jeffersontown, Bee."

"Go on, Bess, and stick to the subject...And I am not disappointed. It's a free country after all. Old Man Peterson can flirt with whoever he has a mind to, and if he wants to flirt with Mildred, of all people, it just shows he'll flirt with anybody with a skirt on."

"She didn't have on a skirt; she was wearing those ghastly pants of hers, and they make her backend look like two watermelons in a sack."

"Bess, please."

"That's really all. I paid for my groceries and hurried home."

"Well, everything is all right around here, now that the fire is out, that is."

"It's a real wonder you and Vonion were able to put the fire out without any help. You know yourself that neither of you are spring chickens anymore...Are you all right, Bee? You look a little red and flustered. And what on earth happened to the color in your hair?"

"Thank you for finally asking," I answered facetiously. "I'm all right. I had to wash all the color out of my hair to get the smoke smell out, and I practically had to scrape my skin off the bone."

"Where was Dickie all this time? He might have been some help."

"Oh, he was down the lane taking a walk. He made it back to the house just as we were putting out the last burning embers. Now let's eat and think about the cake you're gonna bake this afternoon."

"I'm gonna bake. I thought you were gonna bake it."

"I'm gonna help Vonion repair the barn while you bake the cake. You know I'd rather be outside and you'd rather be inside. Now that settles that. And, anyway, your cakes are always better than mine." Flattery always gets to Bess.

"You're just saying that to make me want to bake the darn cake. Even if it is true, your cakes are delicious compared to Vera's dry cakes." Bess stopped short. "Bee, you've only put three places to the table. You know there are five of us. What's wrong with you? Did that fire affect your brain as well as your attitude?"

Edwina suddenly jumped right into the conversation and informed Bess that her precious son had been called away for an important job interview, and I just let her talk...and talk. Later in the day there would be a time when I could fill Bess in with the real truth about the fire.

"I'm gonna fix an extra plate to take to the barn," I announced when Edwina slowed down long enough to catch her breath. I reached for a slotted spoon to dip up turnip greens. "Vonion probably hasn't taken the time to go home and eat, and I'm sure he's practically famished by now." After piling meat loaf, turnip greens, and cornbread onto one of our old, chipped plates we kept for just such purposes, I hurried out the back door with the loaded plate before Bess had time to scold me for sending so much food. "Don't wait for me to eat," I called back. "Y'all go ahead. I'll be back in directly." I knew that Eddie Pink was probably famished by now, and I wanted to keep the young man satisfied.

The building materials were already unloaded from the truck on to the barn floor, but neither Vonion nor Eddie were in sight. I called, "Eddie, I've got your dinner. I'm gonna leave it on the bucket. Hope you like turnip greens. I know you like meat loaf. I'll be back in a while to help Vonion. Now remember, stay out of sight."

I heard a soft, "Yes'um. Thank you, ma'am."

"How long can I keep the boy hidden?" I asked myself as I closed the heavy barn door behind me. I muttered the answer out loud to no one except myself, "As long as necessary."

The afternoon was busy, prying and pulling damaged boards, measuring the new boards, and replacing the burned ones. Eddie ventured down from the loft and was a great help, especially with the sawing. The fruit of our labor was evident and satisfying. A little odd looking and a bit crooked in places, our project was soon completed. Vonion and Eddie piled all the burned boards into the bed of the pickup truck to be hauled off to the woods, and I put away the tools. Vonion headed home in the truck, and I hurried to the kitchen to find something for Eddie's supper.

Bess had finished the cake and left it in the middle of the table as if it was a centerpiece for all to behold, but she was nowhere to be seen. I quickly ran my finger around the base of the cake and popped the tasty chocolate icing into my mouth. Bess would never notice, I said to myself as I repeated the action. I hastily made two meat loaf sandwiches, wrapped them in a dish towel, and scurried back to the barn. After placing them on the feed bucket, and without a word, I closed the barn door, leaving our tired prisoner to himself. I hoped a good night's sleep was in order for him...and for me.

Subconsciously, something stirred within me as I lingered outside the barn door, sending me down the lane to Vonion's well, the scene of the crime. I was idly gazing into the deep water when it suddenly occurred to me there was something here I had missed earlier. The bucket was still hanging from the rope, the sweet aroma of the water continued to drift up from the deep, underground spring, and the poison ivy was still hovering around the base of the well, daring me to come closer and touch it. My inner senses were awakened, allowing me to be totally engrossed in my surroundings when it suddenly hit me.

How could I have missed it? Right in front of my eyes was another bit of evidence. A single strand of light brown hair, almost invisible to the eye and a close match in color to the faded, heavy rope, was loosely connected to the woven cord. I gently pulled the strand from the weave and examined it. Approximately eight inches in length, the strand was fine, much like my wispy hair.

I gently threaded the crucial bit of evidence around my finger. Certainly, it was not one of Vonion's or Roscoe's wiry hairs. It was much longer than Sheriff Ledbetter's or Mr. Lawson's, and not a match at all for Richard's darker strands.

My detective skills obviously were lacking, I admonished myself. I had simply overlooked the hair before. Eddie should examine this important piece of evidence; maybe it would prompt him to remember something more. With the afternoon sun slowly fading, I headed for the barn.

Eddie did not answer my gentle call after the heavy barn door closed behind me. The sandwiches were gone. The only sound disturbing the quiet in the musky air was Hortence rustling around in her stall and a soft snore coming from the direction of the loft.

Obviously, my prisoner was satisfied for the time being. Whatever it took, I had to keep my one and only eyewitness contented and close at hand.

CHAPTER TWENTY-FOUR

Bess and I were on our way over to Foy's with the chocolate cake Bess had baked the day before. We had encouraged Edwina to come along, but she declined. She insisted that it wasn't proper for her to be out in public, especially to visit a single man, for at least a month after Richard's funeral. Bess had told Edwina if she wore a black dress and a black hat she could go anywhere she wanted to. I thought they were both going a bit overboard and told them that I had not even worn a black dress to church the week after Will's funeral. Bess said that she distinctly remembered that particular day. Everyone in the church had stared a hole right through me the whole service, and several of our closest friends had mentioned to her that I had been inappropriately dressed. I couldn't have cared less.

"Don't let that cake slide out of your hands, Bee. Hold it tight, for goodness' sake. You remember what happened last year when we were on our way to the church for homecoming. You let the cake slide right off the plate into the foot of the car."

"Well, if you hadn't slammed on the brakes, the cake would have been fine."

"If I hadn't slammed on the brakes, as I remember it, we would have run into the rear end of Vera and Tillman's car. Tillman is really the one to blame. Everybody knows not to stop right in the middle of the highway when a car is following close behind."

"We might as well say it was all Vera's fault. She's the one who hollered at Tillman to stop the car and turn around in the middle of the road for her to go back home to change shoes. Why anybody would get into the car to go to church with their bedroom shoes on in the first place is beyond me," I replied, as I gripped the cake plate a little tighter.

"She was just rushed, trying to get her food ready for church, and I'm sure Tillman was yelling at her to hurry. Those bedroom shoes probably would have looked better than those beige pumps Vera wears to church all the time, anyway. You know, the ones with the feathers sticking out across the top. Vera looks like she's walking around with a chicken perched on top of each foot."

"I thought they were sort of attractive. I've seen worse."

"And what about those purple, size ten boats that Mabel Rooks used to wear? Now those were some ugly shoes."

Bess and I had a good laugh before I mentioned the bright green shoes that Bess had cherished, that is until she lost them, one at a time.

"Listen, we're here. Now don't drop the cake, Bee. And when I give you the eye, it's time to get up and go. I've got some cleaning to do this afternoon, and I don't want to wait too late to get started. And don't get too close to Foy. Remember how he pinches."

"If he pinches me again, I'm gonna...oh, I don't know what I'm gonna do. You know we've got to remember to be cordial to Foy. If Margaret and Walter have children, Foy will become the grandfather of MY grandchildren, and I don't want any family tensions."

"Well, he better keep his hands to himself today, Bee, if he knows what's good for himself."

"And act nice to Hilda, too. I'm sure she puts up with a lot from old Foy. Besides that, Margaret says that it's hard to find good nurses these days. They had a time with Foy until they finally found Hilda. So far, they don't have any complaints about her other than she smokes. I guess you can't have everything rolled up in one person."

Bess slowly pulled into the rut-filled yard and parked the car beside an overgrown hedge. It was evident that nobody did much yard work. The place had once been attractive years earlier before Foy had become crippled, but was neglected now. Pine cones and small limbs were scattered across the untrimmed, patchy grass, and the house hadn't seen a drop of paint in many a year. I stepped out of the car and gloomily looked around before carefully stepping over a branch that had fallen from a half-dead pear tree. "Just think, Bess, Margaret might have to live over here after she and Walter marry."

"This place is disgraceful," Bess complained, as she dodged a low limb from the same pear tree. "We're gonna have to get Vonion and come over here and fix this place up before the wedding. We can't have Margaret living here like this."

"I don't really think Walter will expect Margaret to live here with his father, Bess. He'll probably build them a nice brick house in town near the hospital, but she needs to get that straight before she marries Walter."

"That man is so good-looking; I'd live in a cave with him."

"I doubt that. Maybe if it had electric lights and indoor plumbing, you might. I know you better than you know yourself."

I held the cake, and Bess knocked on the rusty screen door to the front porch. As we were waiting, we noticed the hacking sound of someone chopping wood out back. Following the noise, we discovered Nurse Hilda Hawkins, dressed in old overalls and a flannel shirt, slinging an ax around as if it was as light as a fishing pole. Her strength was amazing for any female, much less a middle-aged, overweight woman. We stopped at the corner of the house and stood in silence and in awe as, one stroke after another, she sliced into the fat lighter stump with the strength of a youthful lumberjack.

"Good morning, Hilda," I called out after she had flung the ax aside and was stooped over to gather the wood splinters. I handed the cake to Bess, and we walked over. "We're here on a social call. I hope you can spare a few minutes from your chores and visit with us a while. Bess made a chocolate cake for Foy, and I'm sure he'll share it with all of us."

Hilda smiled. "That's downright neighborly of you ladies. I'll take the fat lighter on into the porch and make coffee. Foy will just love having a little company. I'm not dressed for entertaining—"

"You look fine," I interrupted with a lie. "You should see the way we dress around the house." I didn't look toward Bess, knowing she would have a negative reaction to that comment.

Hilda threw the wood splinters into a large wooden box and opened the back door to the house. "Y'all go on into the front room. You'll find Foy sitting by the fireplace. The hard winter's gone, but Foy still can't seem to keep warm. I'll be in with the cake as soon as I can get washed up and make coffee."

Bess placed the cake on the kitchen table.

"Bess, go on in and visit with Foy. I'll help Hilda with the coffee." Bess nodded and disappeared through the door into the front room. I glanced around the antiquated kitchen and made mental notes of ways to brighten it up. Oh, please, dear Lord, help Walter find a suitable home for my daughter before they marry.

"The plates for the cake are in the cabinet over there against the wall. Why don't you get them out, and I'll hand you the knife. Silverware is in the drawer under the plates. This is a real treat for us. Foy loves sweets and so do I. I made a bread pudding yesterday, but it was so dry we couldn't eat it. I ended up throwing it out to the dog."

Hilda walked over to the sink and rolled her sleeves. She quickly reached up to readjust one of the hairpins that was stuck in the knot of wispy, brown hair at the nape of her neck. I immediately noticed two red, inflamed streaks across her left wrist.

POISON IVY! I would know it anywhere!

My world suddenly stood still as I realized what I was seeing. I grabbed the corner of the cabinet to keep from falling to the floor. Everything fit together like a jigsaw puzzle. Overalls covering a large body, hairpins, wispy, dull brown hair, poison ivy. Oh, dear Lord, this has to be Richard's killer, right here in the kitchen with me...and she's reaching for a knife!

Hilda Hawkins murdered Richard. I was as sure of it as I was sure he was dead. Calm down, I told myself. Act natural. And how can I get Bess out'a here without Hilda realizing I know she's a murderer?

Hilda turned to face me and I smiled. (A little too artificially, I'm afraid.) "I'll have the coffee ready in a minute. Here's the knife. Go ahead and cut the cake if you don't mind, and take it on into the front room. I'm sure Foy's chomping at the bit for some of that delicious chocolate cake."

I reached out for the knife, and it accidently fell from my shaking hand to the floor. "Oh, I'm so clumsy."

"It's okay. I'll rinse it off. Are you all right, Ms. Bee? You look a little flustered."

My acting skills are so limited. "I'm a little tired, that's all. We've had a lot going on lately, but I'm fine. Now, where did you say the plates are?"

"In that cabinet over there and the silverware, right there in the drawer." Hilda pointed toward the cabinet.

I reached for the plates. My hands were shaking so badly by then I wasn't sure I'd be able to slice the cake. Hilda busied herself with the coffee, and I nervously began my chore. With four uneven slices cut and placed on plates, I reached for the four napkins Hilda had laid on the counter for me. "I'll be right back for the other two plates," I said to Hilda, as I picked up two plates.

Bess and Foy were looking at a photograph book when I walked in. "Look, Bee. Here's a picture of Walter when he was a baby. He was such a cutie-pie," Bess said, as I laid the cake plates on the table. I glanced toward the book and gave Bess a frown and "the look."

Bess misunderstood my look and shrugged her shoulders. "Are you all right, Bee?"

"I'm fine. Walter was a precious child and such a sweet baby. And just look at those chubby cheeks." I gave Bess another look and silently mouthed the words, "Hilda-is-the-killer." Bess looked confused. I mouthed the worded again, "Hilda-is-the-killer."

She's going to fall to pieces, I frantically thought. "Don't-fall-apart," I sternly mouthed and walked out to get the other plates.

Hilda followed me back into the front room, carrying the coffeepot and cups on a metal tray. I could immediately tell that Bess had not completely regained her composure since her eyes were nervously shifting back and forth, and her hands were trembling. Neither of us is a very good actress, I'm afraid.

"Now who wants cream and sugar?" Hilda asked, as she began to pour and handed Bess the first cup. With an unsteady hand Bess reached for the cup. "Are you all right, Ms. Bess?"

"Uh, yes. I'm just a little nervous that, uh, you...you, uh...won't like the cake."

Bess is a terrible liar, too. I wasn't quite sure Bess understood my words completely, but she definitely knew something was wrong with the situation.

Foy took his first big bite of cake and beamed in Bess's direction. "You don't have to worry about this cake, Bess. It's the most delicious cake I've tasted since this past weekend. I swear you can whip up the best cakes in the world."

Bess didn't look relieved at all. I glanced at her and mouthed, "I'm-sure-she's-the-killer!" As soon as she understood my silent words, she began coughing, spraying her first mouthful of coffee across the room. I hurried over and patted her on her back until she could regain her composure. Hilda seemed a bit confused but continued pouring.

"I'm fine now. Bee, stop hitting me, for pity's sake. The coffee just went down the wrong way." I gave Bess a stern look before asking Foy if he was enjoying the nice weather.

"I ain't really noticed the weather too much lately. My only pleasure these days is watchin' Walter go in and out of the house. That boy's so busy, he don't have no time fer me. I'm just glad he's stayin' here 'til he finds a good house fer himself and Margaret. Sittin' in this here chair ain't much of a life. Thank goodness I got Hildy here with me." He glanced toward Hilda and gave her a weak smile as he reached for his coffee.

After more strained chit-chat and a few swallows of Hilda's strong coffee, I glanced at Bess. "We'd better get going, Sister. We've got chores to do, and I'm sure Foy needs his rest."

"Oh, yes," Bess answered and quickly raised her cup for a last swallow. "It's been real nice, Foy and, uh, Hilda. I'm sure Cousin Edwina has sent out another search party for us by now."

"Speaking of a search party," Hilda suddenly asked, "what's the latest on the sheriff's investigation? We haven't heard a word about anything over here."

Bess coughed again and her cup tilted, spilling the last few drops of coffee in her lap. "We don't know a thing!" Bess dramatically answered, as if she had been in a fog for the last few days. Hilda gave her a curious, sideways glance.

Trying to dispel Hilda's skeptical look, I said, "We're still very much in the dark, also. Our sheriff isn't the sharpest, you know, and he must not have much evidence to go on. Why, he might not ever solve this thing. Bess, we've imposed on these nice folks long enough."

"Oh, er, yes, that's right. We need to be on our way."

"Hilda, don't worry about the cake plate. I'll pick it up later," I said, as we headed to the door. "Now, Foy, get out in the fresh air and watch the red birds."

Hilda wheeled Foy out to the porch behind us. We waved from the yard, and Foy called, "Come back soon, and I like brownies as good as I like chocolate cake."

CHAPTER TWENTY-FIVE

She knows we know; I'm sure of it, Bess," I whispered, right after I slammed the car door.

"How do you know she knows?" Bess asked in that skeptical tone of hers I've heard so many times in the past.

"Just trust me. She killed Richard, and she knows we know."

"You know you talk in circles half the time. She doesn't seem like a murderer to me; maybe a little on the masculine side and sloppy, but she's nice. You know yourself that you go off on tangents all the time, and you made me so nervous in there."

"I don't know the reason she killed Richard yet, but there's got to be one. Remember that note we found in Richard's things. Nurse Hilda, if she really is a nurse, sent that note. She lured Richard out into the night, killed him, and threw his dead body into Vonion's well, the same well that Vonion and Ora Lee vow they'll never drink another drop of water from. Boy, that makes me so mad. She just h-a-d to throw him into Vonion's well, and his dead body polluted the water."

Bess revved the car. "You can be so dramatic. And I think you're hallucinating again."

"I am not hallucinating, and I haven't told you everything I know. Just trust me. You don't know all the facts yet. Now get this car going, and let's get on the road before we get the heavy end of that ax."

Bess's body tensed as she gripped the steering wheel tighter and revved the car motor again.

"Listen, Bess, as soon as we get down the road a piece, let's hide the car in the woods and sneak back through the woods to the house on foot. We can hide behind the barn and watch what's going on. You know Hilda might try to make a fast getaway, and we are totally responsible for Foy's safety as of right now."

"Bee, that's two more of your crazy ideas. We're not responsible for Foy, and I'm definitely not going to ruin my shoes and stockings hiking through those woods. All we need to do is to get to the sheriff's office and let him do his official work."

"And let Hilda get away while we ride into town? Not on your life. We've got to stake the house out. We don't have time to fool around with that sheriff. He probably wouldn't believe us, anyway."

"Bee, I've got work to do at the house, and I don't have time for all your little spy games. I'm going home right now...like it or lump it."

"If we go home now, the murderer will probably never be caught, and Edwina will never, ever, leave our house. Have you thought about that, Miss Smarty Pants?"

"Oh, Bee, I don't know how I let you talk me into another one of your harebrained schemes. You've got me out here endangering my life again, and I don't have but one life. I know I'll never live to see my grandsons grow up."

"You will so. Bess, just think about the good side of all this. I didn't have to drag you all the way over the county line to investigate a crime this time. We're doing it right at home. Think how much more convenient it is."

"And you think that's a good thing! And what about my shoes? Who's gonna pay for them after I ruin them walking through that...that jungle over there?"

Bess anxiously put the gear in reverse. In her nervous condition, she never looked backward and never saw the large pine branch that had fallen to the ground. One big jolt later and we knew the car had straddled the dead tree limb lying in the yard. After several attempts to pull forward and backwards, we realized the car was definitely stuck.

"Bess, didn't you notice that limb, for goodness' sake?" I asked in an aggravated tone.

"No, I didn't, and I'll bet you didn't, either." Bess answered in that same tone of voice.

"Well, I'm not the one driving. I just don't know how you can be so unobservant. Mercy me!" I anxiously looked toward the house. "The old battle-ax hasn't come out yet? She's probably in there right now thanking her lucky stars our car is trapped over this limb. She can make a clean getaway now, and we can't follow her," I grumbled as my frustration grew.

Suddenly, Hilda stuck her head out of the screen door and called, "Are y'all stuck on that old tree limb? I meant to try to move that big ole thing last week but never got around to it. Foy said it was too big for me to handle by myself, and he'd get Tom Wilson over with the tractor. I guess we've waited too late."

"We do seem to be stuck, but don't, er, worry about it," I called back through the opened window of the car. "We're gonna walk home and get Vonion to bring the mule over to pull the limb out from under the car. We'll be back in a little while." Hilda nodded and closed the door.

"Under normal circumstances most people would have offered to take us home, Bess. Now you see something is really wrong."

"Let's get out'a here before Hilda gets the ax."

I nodded as I hurriedly slammed my car door behind me.

We had made it to the road on foot and were completely out of sight of the house when I grabbed Bess. "We're not going home yet. We're gonna circle back through the woods to the back of the barn and stake the house out. I'd bet the farm that Hilda's gonna try to make a fast getaway."

"What on earth can we do about it if she does? We don't even have a car."

"I don't know, but it's our sworn duty to protect Foy from that murderer. We'll think of something."

"Sworn duty? You must be kidding. I've never sworn to anything so ridiculous in my entire life."

"Have you already forgotten that you and I have been deputized by Sheriff Ledbetter? That's an oath that we swore to in front of God. Now it's too late to get out of our sworn duty. I can't believe that you took it so lightly."

"Bee, I was just pretending to be deputized. I don't want to be a deputy or any kind of law person."

"Listen, Bess, I'm not gonna argue with you about it now. Start walking."

"I'm tearing my stockings, and I don't have but one more pair," Bess complained as we entered the woods. "I think I'll just turn toward the house and call the sheriff from there. You can risk your life if you want to, Bee, but I'm not. Even if Hilda is Richard's killer, which I'm not totally convinced she really is, she probably doesn't really know we know.

I think you're overreacting to the whole situation. Come on, Bee, let's head back to the house." Bess grabbed me by the arm and started pulling me back toward the road.

"No, we're not going to leave poor, defenseless Foy with that murderer. She might decide to do him in, too. Now come on. I'll buy you a new pair of stockings the next time we go to town."

"There'll probably never be a next time, and besides, you don't have the money."

I pulled my arm back and stopped Bess dead in her tracks. "Listen, Bess, this isn't the best time to tell you all I know, but it seems to be the right time." I proceeded to tell Bess everything I had learned about Richard's murder and all about Eddie Pink. I told Bess that I didn't know why Hilda had murdered Richard, but I positively knew she had done the dirty deed.

Bess's eyes grew bigger and bigger the longer I talked. Within a few minutes Bess knew the whole story, and it was an ugly one. With no time to waste, I began pulling a reluctant Bess through the woods. Stepping high over fallen logs and foliage, dodging vines and low-hanging limbs, we trudged on. Bess let out a weak scream as a rabbit crossed our path, but it soon disappeared into the deep undergrowth. The bright sunshine faded into strips of dusty light as we hiked deeper and deeper under the wide canopies of large oak and poplar trees.

I cautiously plodded ahead as Bess cowered behind. I realized we'd have to cross the waterlogged ditch that divided my property from Foy's. There was no going around it if we were to reach Foy's house. I knew stagnant, bug-infested water always accumulated in the bottom of the ditch even during a drought. I quickly learned that the ditch wasn't to be our worst problem as I heard the distant barking of Foy's old hound dog, Blue. I knew the dog, and I knew he didn't like visitors. Our only chance of getting close to Foy's house was to keep him quiet. We stopped dead in our tracks as the yelping bark of Blue came closer and closer. As luck would have it, two more rabbits appeared from underneath the brush and hopped away with old Blue in hot pursuit. Bess and I scurried on, reached the ditch, removed our shoes, waded through the soupy water, and stopped only long enough to put our shoes back on.

I hurried on through the dense trees with Bess lagging several yards behind me. I heard her fall just as I opened my mouth to warn her that a gnarled root was growing above the soggy floor of the woods between us. I attempted to help her up, but all I did was make matters worse. We both fell this time, me on top of Bess. Bess pushed at me, and I struggled to roll off. Bess's left elbow caught me in the chest, and the pain from my fall was forgotten as the agony of a new pain overtook me. I fell backward, dazed, and with a face full of mud. Bess pulled herself to a sitting position and leaned against an oak tree. As I lay on the ground, I quickly realized the pain I was enduring right now was not to be as bad as the wrath Bess was about to dish out to me. Amazingly, she didn't utter a word as she ungracefully stood up. After regaining her balance, she reached out and pulled me to my feet. An odd time to bond, but sisterly love can overcome most obstacles.

The woods soon began to thin and eventually gave way to a deserted hog pen. We scrambled over the crumbling fence and scurried for Foy's barn as fast as one determined old woman could drag a reluctant old woman.

We ran under the slope of the rusted tin-roofed lean-to attached to the side of the sagging barn. After catching my breath, I crept forward under the dusty lean-to until I could see the back side of the house. Bess lingered behind, cowering against the side of the gray barn. The ax was still lying on the ground in the backyard. Nurse Hilda's car was still parked at the front side of the house under a large oak tree, and Foy's old pickup truck was still jacked up beside it, waiting for the left front flat tire to be patched or replaced. The dog was gone, still chasing rabbits, I supposed, and all was quiet. Smoke continued to curl from the chimney as I motioned Bess to sit down in a rusty yard chair that had been left in the dust under the lean-to. Without a word spoken between us, I continued to stare at the house.

Maybe I had overreacted, I began to think as the seconds became minutes, but I continued my surveillance. With no movement about the house, I backed toward Bess who now seemed more aggravated than frightened. She was sitting on the edge of the rickety yard chair examining her torn stockings.

"I told you Hilda wasn't going anywhere. I'd bet you my last nickel they're in there right now sitting by the fireplace eating another piece of my cake. Now let's go home. I've had enough of this snooping game for one day. Can't we walk home on the road like any civilized person with a grain of sense would do? I'm not putting my foot in that disgusting, nasty water in that ditch again. There's no telling what kind of worm will soon be growing between our toes. We could even become permanently crippled from some mysterious germ floating around in that nasty water."

"We're not going anywhere yet. Let's give it a little bit longer. Just rest for a while, and I'll stay on lookout...Hey, Bess, I'm gonna make a run for the house. I can get a good look into the front room through that window by the chimney. Maybe I can find out what's going on."

"No-o, Bee. Stay here. I'm scared, and if you leave me, I'll be scared-er."

"I'll just be gone a minute, I promise. Now be quiet and stay out of sight."

Before changing my mind like a coward, I quickly ran toward the house and pressed my back against the side of the warm chimney. From there I could peer into the front room through the low window that was situated next to it. Foy was sleeping soundly in his wheelchair, and there was no sign of Nurse Hilda about the room. I kept my position for a few more minutes until I heard the back screen door slam. Hilda must be leaving the house! And she's between Bess and me. Bess is probably scared out of her wits. I cautiously peeped around the side of the house and watched and listened as Hilda mumbled something about two nosy old women and a senile old man while she removed a large, faded pair of overalls, a flannel shirt, and two pair of women's flared underpants from the clothesline. Why, she's talking about Bess and me...and poor ole Foy!

Hilda hurried back into the house, slamming the screen door behind her. I turned to look toward Bess. Bess's heaving body was pressed against the side of the barn as if she were single-handedly holding up the entire structure.

Turning my attention back to the window, I watched Hilda walk back into the front room. Circumstances seemed to have changed dramatically. With her hat pulled down across her wide forehead, a large traveling satchel in one hand and a small handgun in the other, she walked over to a sleeping Foy and pressed the gun against the back of his neck. In sleepy confusion, he opened his heavy eyes as he felt the cold barrel of the gun on his skin and then heard Hilda's stern words. I couldn't make out what she was saying, but it seemed to be a sharp command. As soon as she had Foy's full attention, she dropped the gun into her satchel. Foy shied away from Hilda as she roughly picked him up from the wheelchair and carried him toward the front door. She kicked it open and walked out, carrying her terrified prisoner in her strong arms.

My first reaction was to try to wrestle her to the ground, but I knew she was much too powerful for me...plus, she was the one with the gun. As I began to think what I could possibly do to stop her, I heard the car door slam. Then I heard the other car door slam and the sound of the engine as it was cranked.

Fighting fear and panic, I raced around the side of the house as the car roared up the lane just as Earnest Lee Black turned off the main road in his little black mail car to deliver Foy's mail for the day. In her haste to get away, Hilda probably never saw the dark car as it chugged around the tree-lined corner of Foy's property. Hilda never slowed until the impact of a head-on collision brought her to a dead stop.

CHAPTER TWENTY-SIX

Steam and water from both vehicles began to rise above the collision. After my initial shock, I realized somebody might be hurt, and I rushed over to Earnest Lee's twisted car first. He seemed dazed and confused but was able to crawl out of the opened front window by himself. I reached out and grabbed Earnest Lee's spindly body to break the fall before he hit the ground beside his car. After giving him time to recover, I pushed him along ahead of me as I hurried to the passenger side of Hilda's dark sedan. Foy sat with his head lying against the back of the seat, unconscious. A deep, jagged gash ran from above his hairline all the way across his forehead to his swollen eye. Luckily, Earnest Lee was able to open the bent, caved-in car door. Earnest Lee pulled Foy from the car with strength and stamina I had no idea he possessed and gently laid him in the tall grass and weeds beside the dirt lane. Earnest Lee quickly ran back to the car where I was waiting for help with the other passenger. Hilda's limp body was leaning forward against the steering wheel. Earnest Lee attempted to turn the car door handle without any luck. "Just leave her be," I quickly commanded. "Hurry up to Foy's house and call for an ambulance on the telephone. I'll stay here until help arrives."

"Okay, but get back from the car in case of fire," Earnest Lee ordered, before he turned to head up the lane.

I nodded as Hilda's big head reared backward, as if she had suddenly awoke from a deep sleep. She quickly raised the gun to the opened window and pointed it straight at Earnest Lee. "You're not going anywhere, dude. Don't move or I'll put a bullet right between your eyes."

Earnest Lee froze. All the arrogance and conceit Earnest Lee so haughtily displayed most of the time seemed to be swallowed up by a swift dose of shock. The brim of his U.S. Mail cap began flopping as he stood trembling...and looking down the barrel of the pistol in Hilda's shaky hand.

That's when I noticed Bess cowering behind the broken boards of the wooden fence that was slowly rotting beside the road. I gave her the eye before she hastily dropped down among the thorns and prickly cockleburs.

"Where's that nervous sister of yours?" Hilda demanded, as she waved the gun toward me.

"Oh, she, uh, went on home to get Vonion. They'll be back soon with the mule. I decided to stay and watch the house. I figured you'd try to make a fast getaway."

"So you think you know something about me, do you? You don't know nothing, old woman!" Hilda yelled in frustration.

"I know a good deal more than you think I do!" I shouted back in disgust. "I know you murdered Richard Perkins and threw his dead body into the well back of Vonion's house... and...and I'm not the only one who knows. There's an eyewitness to your vicious act; so don't think you can kill me and nobody'll know what you did. You'll never get away."

Hilda jiggled the door handle and the jammed latch clicked. Holding the gun directly at Earnest Lee and then quickly back at me, she pushed the twisted door open and eased her battered body out of the steaming car. "Now move," she demanded and waved the gun toward the house. "Get the old man," she sternly commanded, as she aimed the gun back toward Earnest Lee, "and bring him with us." Earnest Lee, still teetering between a nervous breakdown and total collapse, somehow heaved a now-conscious Foy over his shoulder like a sack of potatoes and started for the house. I followed behind. Holding the weapon tight, Hilda brought up the rear, noticeably limping in pain.

Hoping Bess would follow us to the house, I did exactly as Hilda demanded. Hilda will have to kill us to make a clean getaway, I anxiously thought, as we slowly plodded toward the house. She had killed before, and I knew she wouldn't think twice about killing again. I wanted Hilda to admit she was a murderer before witnesses, witnesses that would live to tell about it. Our only hope was Bess. (Oh, what a pitiful thought.) Maybe I could make Hilda confess before Bess made her move or before Hilda used the gun on all of us.

From the expression on her pinched face, I knew Hilda was in a great deal of pain as she limped a step or two behind us, dragging her leg. Maybe her leg was broken.

As soon as we made it to the house, Earnest Lee placed Foy's crippled body on the cot that was kept on the porch for Foy lie on and enjoy the fresh air. Hilda waved the gun for Earnest Lee and me to stand against the inside wall of the porch, and then she took a hard plunge into the nearest rocker.

"Now, don't move a muscle. If I see one twitch from either of you, I'll shoot both of you graveyard dead. I just need a minute to think."

I opened my mouth to speak, and Hilda raised the gun toward my head. "Shut up. I don't like a lot of talk."

Hilda grimaced in pain as she continued to aim the gun toward Earnest and me. Several seconds passed and she never wavered or blinked an eye. She seemed to be deep in thought, probably trying to figure out what her next move would be. "I need a car," she finally said, as if she was talking to herself.

"I've got a car," I anxiously replied. Hilda's finger moved to the trigger of the gun...the gun aimed straight at my head.

"I said don't talk. You must don't understand plain English."

I nodded.

Hilda hesitated, then said, "You said your dumb sister had gone home. Call her on the telephone. Tell her to bring your car over here. If you say one wrong word, old Foy will be the first to die." Hilda waved the gun toward Foy. "Tell her to bring the car up to the porch, leave the key in the ignition, get out of the car, and walk slowly over here to the porch. One little hitch and I'll blow Foy's head off. Now walk slowly into the house and pick up the telephone on the table by the front window. I'll be listening to every word you say, so don't try to be a hero. Waving the gun toward Earnest Lee, she ordered, "You—move over by Foy." Then aiming the gun back toward me, she said, "Oh, and tell that stupid sister of yours not to run over any more dead limbs in the yard."

I slowly walked through the opened front door and over to the telephone. After picking up the telephone receiver, I said, "Nellie, ring my house please."

"Oh, Bee. I've been wanting to talk to you about your cousin, Edwina. Do you have a minute or two right now?"

"Nellie, I really don't have—"

Nellie interrupted. "She's been making a lot of long distance calls lately from your telephone, and I know you can't afford all those charges. Why, just this afternoon she's already called her son three times, begging him to come back for a visit. Then she called her banker and blessed him out. You know, she can use some pretty bad language when she's upset. Then she called Thelma to get a hair appointment. She said her hair was terribly brittle from all the dust in the air out at your place. Have you ever heard that dust could make your hair brittle? I've heard a lot of stupid things in my years as a telephone operator, but that just takes the cake. Anyway, you've got to do something about her use of the telephone before you absolutely go broke. I doubt very seriously she'll be able to help you pay the bill that's mounting higher and higher every day. Oh, and Mr. Lawson's been trying to get a hold of you. I think he wants to know what to have engraved on Edwina's husband's headstone, and Edwina must be avoiding having a conversation with him. Did y'all ever find out anything about who murdered Edwina's husband, the poor man? Why, I've been trembling in fear that the murderer would strike again. You know I'm here right by myself at night and—"

"Listen, Nellie, just ring my house if you don't mind. I need to speak to Bess."

"I'll try, but I heard Edwina tell her son that you and Bess were out visiting and had left her home all alone at the house to fend for herself." I heard Nellie ring my house number. Two rings— one long and one short, and then...again. "Sorry, Bee, but there's no answer at your house. I told you..."

I clinched the telephone and spoke. "Hey, Bess. I need you to do something very important for me."

Nellie interrupted and said, "Bee, are you all right? Bess isn't on the telephone. Who are you talking to?"

"That's right, Bess. Bring my car over to Foy's house right now. It's a real emergency. I need a ride home. Now do as I ask as fast as you can. I'm waiting."

Nellie answered, "Bee, are you out of your mind? You're talking to me, not Bess. Bess isn't even on the line."

"That's right, Bess. Bring my car to Foy's...right now. I'll be waiting."

"I think you are absolutely out of your mind, Bee. Do you know you're not talking to Bess?"

"I know. Now bring my car on over as quickly as you can. I'm ready to go home."

"Bee, is this some sort of signal or something?"

"YES! Yes, it definitely is!" I laid the receiver down and prayed Nellie would report my strange behavior to the sheriff, and he would come quickly.

"She'll be here soon," I said to Hilda, as I walked back to the porch.

"She better be or there's gonna be several dead corpses bloodying up this here porch." Hilda waved the gun again.

"Please, don't kill us, Hilda. After you get my car, there's no way we can follow you. We don't have any other transportation. Jerk the telephone out of the wall before you leave, and you'll have a big head start."

"Shut up."

"Uh, Hilda, you're really a smart woman," I said, trying to butter her up. "Nobody would have ever figured you to be a murderer. We didn't even know you knew Richard. If it hadn't have been for that eyewitness, I wouldn't have ever figured it out."

"I don't believe there was an eyewitness. You're lying through your dentures."

"I most assuredly don't have dentures! And there was an eyewitness. Listen, Hilda, you might as well tell me why you murdered Richard. Was he your lover and he betrayed you?" Surely she'd want to contradict that and tell me the truth.

"Are you out of your cotton-picking mind? I wouldn't have had that worn-out weasel if he was stretched out on a silver platter with an apple in his mouth. That crazy wife of his deserved every bit of him. He was just a business acquaintance, nothing else to me, except a turncoat and a snitch. I had to keep him permanently quiet."

"So you killed him to keep him from talking."

"Yea, I couldn't take no chances. If he hadn't of showed up at that stupid family reunion of yours, he'd still be alive. That weasel was going to turn me in at his own expense. He was guilty too. The ignoramus! Nobody turns on me and lives to tell it!" Hilda stomped her foot on the floor and grimaced in pain.

"Why, you are so clever. I never would have figured you to be such a prosperous businesswoman. What kind of business are you in?"

"The kind that you ain't gonna find out about. Now where's that sister of yours? She should be here by now."

"She probably couldn't find the keys, but she'll be here directly."

"She better be, or I'm gonna get trigger-happy real soon."

Earnest Lee cowered, Foy cringed, and I plotted my next move with or without the sheriff.

CHAPTER TWENTY-SEVEN

The seconds turned into minutes, and the minutes began to add up. Surely Bess is going to make a move soon, I desperately thought, as Hilda continued to wince with pain. But, where the dickens is she? Hilda will surely recognize my bluff soon. And did Nellie get my strange message and maybe, just maybe, notify the sheriff?

"There's the car," Earnest Lee excitedly called out. "And there's Bess in the car. You can make your getaway now!"

"The CAR! Where...How!" Oh, my gosh! It was my car! How in the world did Bess get the car? She was supposed to be hiding nearby.

"I plan to make a fast getaway right now, and I'm gonna take YOU with me." Hilda waved the gun at me. "And if I even think somebody's following me, I'm gonna shoot you, dead as a doornail, and ask questions later. Do you understand me, or do I need to make myself clearer?" Hilda shot at the front room window, and glass shattered across the floor. She definitely had my attention.

The car stopped in the yard and the driver got out. It wasn't Bess...It was Nellie!

"That's not your sister," Hilda said, as Nellie walked up to the porch.

Nellie didn't notice the gun at first glance and called from the yard, "Hey, Bee. Oh, uh, hey to you, too, Foy, and uh, Earnest Lee, and, oh, Hilda, I believe. Y'all havin' a party or something? Ready to go, Bee? I've got to get back to the house before everybody in the county is annoyed at me for leaving my station."

"What happened to Bess?" Hilda called, and waved the gun toward Nellie. I anxiously waited for her answer.

Nellie immediately focused on the gun in Hilda's hand and fearfully cowered, stumbling on the front door stoop. "Uh, don't shoot me. Oh, please don't shoot." Nellie quickly regained her balance and raised her arms in total surrender.

"I said, what happened to Bess? You can't understand good English or somethin'?"

"She was...uh, sick, and, uh... she couldn't make it. She asked me to bring the car over to get Bee. Bess is really...uh, sick with, uh...the gout. She said she might even have to go to the doctor."

"Get on the porch or you'll be the first to die, and ain't no doctor can help you then," Hilda snapped as she waved the gun in Nellie's direction, and Nellie jumped straight up.

"I...I really need to be going. I'll just wait in the...car."

"Get in here...now!" Hilda exploded. "Are the keys in the car?"

"Y...es. Y...es, they're in there."

"They better be. If they're not in there, I shoot you first, Nell or Nellie, or whatever your name is and ask questions later. Now get over there by Earnest Lee and Foy. NOW!"

Nellie scurried across the porch. "Are you gonna kill us? Oh, Bee, what have you gotten me into? I'm not ready to die!"

Hilda glared at me and grimaced as she waved the gun toward the backyard. "Go out to the barn and get all of the rope hanging on the peg right inside the door. Bring it back and start tying everybody up." I hesitated, and Hilda fired the gun at my feet. "Now!" Nellie gasped, then fainted dead away, right on top of a trembling Earnest Lee.

"Let's go," Hilda demanded, after the last knot was tied, and I had pulled the telephone cord from the wall. "We've wasted enough time. And I'm warning every one of you, if I even think somebody's following us, I'll shoot Bee's brains out. Now I mean business!" Hilda shot another front room window out and more glass shattered.

Hilda's left leg was visibly swollen by now, and I noticed a large bruise had popped up across her forehead. "You drive," she demanded, as I

287

walked and she limped toward the car. I had already figured that she was incapable of driving with her fractured, swollen leg and would need a driver. We slid into the car, and she continued to grip the gun. I remained her target.

"Which way?" I asked, as I nervously cranked the car.

Hilda's pain seemed to have increased. Her eyes were glazed over, and she was sweating profusely. "Don't you want me to get you to a doctor?" I asked in my sympathetic tone of voice. "Foy's son is a doctor. Why don't you let me take you to him?"

"No! Now start driving toward Swainsville. I've got a friend over there who can help me. She knows somethin' 'bout doctorin'."

I felt a tug on my dress tail by the car door. At first I thought there might be a roach or a wasp in the car. I looked down to brush off the invading creature and touched a human hand. I gasped and quickly looked around and saw that the hand was connected to a body, and the body was none other than...Bess's, stretched flat in the foot of the backseat. I quickly looked away. "What in the blue blazes is wrong?" asked Hilda as she waved the gun unsteadily toward me. "You see a ghost?"

"No ghost," I hastily replied, "just a reflection off the back window."

"Well, calm down and let's get this car on the road." Hilda winced in more pain.

Keep her attention on the road, I thought, as I drove out of the yard and began to formulate a plan in my head.

"I know a shortcut over to Swainsville, Hilda. It'll save time and nobody will ever suspect us to be on that road. I can get you there a lot quicker if you'll let me make a left turn up ahead."

"Go ahead, but if you think you can trick me, you'd better think again. Just remember the gun's pointed straight at your head, and I ain't afraid to use it."

"How could I ever forget?" I answered. Bess knew there was no shortcut to Swainsville, and she surely would catch on to my plan, I thought, as I turned the car onto the country road. I began shifting the gears and gave the car more gas as we rode along under the dancing shadows of the giant, ancient oak trees that lined the road. As we passed through the dark tunnel of foliage, I was steadily building my courage and taking deeper breaths. I leveled the car off at a fast thirty miles an hour as the countryside suddenly changed drastically, and large green fields sprung up on both sides of the rutted, hard-packed dirt road.

The gun was still pointed directly at my head. Maybe, just maybe, my plan would work. I needed Bess to know exactly where we were.

"You know, Hilda, we might see a wild turkey or a covey of quail along the way in the fields around here. There's lots of wildlife." I nodded toward a field to our left as a squirrel raced across the road, narrowly escaping our tires. "My daddy and my late husband used to hunt over in that field over there." Surely Bess knew where we were now and could guess what I was up to. The road had been deemed completely impassible after the heavy rains of last winter, and everyone around knew better than to take a chance and travel it — everybody, that is, except Hilda. (I hoped.)

We had cruised a mile or so onward when the car began to shimmy from side to side, but I maintained the speed at thirty miles an hour. The slight vibration turned into a rattling shake as the front wheels of the car began to spring up and down. The road became choppier, but we continued to bounce along, and with each bounce, Hilda's gun waved higher and then lower. A few more hundred yards or so down the road, the washboard surface of the road dipped deeper. I quickly slammed hard on the brakes as we hit, dead center, an enormous wash in the road.

The car pitched forward into the hole and stopped abruptly. Bess reared up from behind with a heavy glass cake plate in her hands and hurled it right at the gun in Hilda's hand before losing her balance and falling hard against Hilda's shoulders and head. The gun flew out of Hilda's hand, and Bess managed to grab Hilda from behind, holding on for dear life as I grabbed Hilda's trusty weapon.

Lucky for us, I had absentmindedly left Mama's Fostoria cake plate on the backseat of the car after the last church social. Now even Bess would have to agree; sometimes my lack of order actually paid off.

CHAPTER TWENTY-EIGHT

A ll's well that ends well, somebody once said, but unfortunately all had not ended well this time. Richard was dead and buried, and his sins were well-known to everyone. Richard's memory was tarnished and Edwina was crushed. She had been forced to crawl down from her ivory tower and face the bitter music that her husband had been a criminal and she was dead broke. Richard had been deceased for over four months, but we were still in shock that he could have gone so far astray.

It had all come out at a quick hearing soon after Hilda's arrest, and Hilda denied nothing. In her account of her previous crime, she proudly revealed Richard as an accomplice. Richard had been hard-pressed for cash for quite a while when Hilda came to Swainsville as a nursemaid to one of Richard's insurance clients. Before her employer passed away, Hilda bought a large life insurance policy on his life from Richard's company. Richard's company paid the bogus claim after Hilda's employer died a little prematurely. After becoming suspicious that Hilda could have possibly had something to do with the untimely death, Richard privately accused Hilda of helping nature take its course by poisoning him and then collecting big dividends. Hilda was trapped into coming clean to Richard after he suggested that they split the loot, and he'd stay quiet in return. All was well for a while. Richard had more money than he had ever had before, and Hilda left town, richer but not satisfied. She was on to her next victim. She put a small ad in our local newspaper for nursemaid duties and was hired by Walter Jackson to become his father's nurse and companion.

After Richard and Hilda accidently met up at our family reunion, Hilda knew Richard would quickly figure out she was up to her dirty tricks again. She wrote a quick note to Richard hoping she could entice him to become her accomplice one more time with the lure of more quick money keeping him quiet once again. She had already begun to slowly poison Foy and was helping herself to any ready money she could filter from his checking account at the bank and to anything valuable she could lift around the house. She was sitting on ready to take out an insurance policy on his life, this time with another company. Richard was on his way to a meeting with the scheming Hilda in the woods the night I overheard his argument with Dickie. Hilda testified that Richard's conscience would not allow him to go along with her deadly plan, and he threatened to turn her in to the law before she could do any more damage to Foy. Hilda did not deny that she reacted violently and took Richard's life to keep him permanently quiet.

After our investigation and Hilda's hearing had concluded, Edwina left our home to return to her house in Swainsville. Dickie and Mavis's marriage was annulled after Dickie learned the truth about his conniving wife and her equally deceitful sister. Maxine, Mavis's money-loving, home-breaking, waitress sister living in Swainsville, had previously become the object of Richard's affection and a luxury Richard had never been financially able to have before his tainted money bonanza. Maxine had been very receptive to Richard's advances and all the ill-gotten money he had squandered on her, as well as expensive clothes and jewelry. Maxine figured Mavis could tolerate Richard's son, Dickie, for a piece of the action also. Maxine had fingered Richard as being a rich old bird and had encouraged Mavis to quickly get into the Perkins family one way or another to reap fast, financial rewards. Mavis concocted the whole marriage scheme to filter as much money from Richard through Dickie as she possibly could in a short amount of time. It would have saved a lot of time and heartbreak if Maxine and Mavis had only known Richard was fast becoming broke.

Dickie didn't press charges against Mavis, citing that he had been taught a valuable lesson, and he would remain single for the duration of his life. His plan was to return to his childhood home and care for his brokenhearted mother as he set up a small law practice in Swainsville. We were happy that at long last Edwina had her loving son where she wanted him, right under her little finger. We're still waiting for that first installment check to cover the cost of Richard's funeral and those four grave plots Edwina splurged on.

Ora Lee had been mortified that young lovers destined to be divorced had tarnished our home's good reputation. She was absolutely sure God was fed up with the sins of man and that the end of time was upon us.

I had helped Eddie Pink with his appeal to Judge B.N. Paradise. After he came clean about his whereabouts the night of the hog thieving, the judge declared Eddie had acted foolishly and he upheld Eddie's sentence. The incident with the prison guard was another matter. The judge encouraged Eddie to swear in court about the abuse to Lizard he had witnessed. Eddie, as well as several other prisoners, took the stand in a hearing and testified about the atrocities and willful violence against inmates. Thankfully, Eddie was not punished for escaping.

After encouragement from Bess and me, Eddie started coming regularly to the house for tutoring. Bess began teaching him to read, and I started working with him on his numbers. He told us last week that he had stopped by to visit with Eve Waters on his way over to our place.

There's nothing immoral about that situation. Several months ago Eve was informed by the Georgia State Patrol that her deserting husband had been killed in a car wreck over near Savannah, leaving her a grieving widow.

Lizard's cancer spread rapidly, and he died in jail. After a nudge or two from me, Walter began to volunteer his time and medical services to the county prison population. I'm really proud of my future son-in-law. "Good things can come from bad situations," I always say.

Another sad footnote: Foy Jackson passed away soon after his entanglement with his so-called nurse, Hilda Hawkins. Walter can't seem to talk much about it yet; I suppose it's too painful for him. He said the old home place has too many bad memories now, and he decided to sell the property and build a brand new brick house in town near the hospital. Although he and Margaret haven't set a wedding date, he's building the house with a big family in mind.

Bess said she'll never risk her life again, no matter what the circumstances. Actually, Bess had thrown caution completely to the wind the day of Hilda's attempted escape. She had endangered her own life when she crawled into the backseat of my car after she flagged Nellie down on the road to Foy's house. Bess didn't level with Nellie about my fake telephone call she had overheard from outside the window of Foy's house luring Nellie to pick up my car and hurry over to Foy's, but told Nellie she wanted to surprise me by hiding in the backseat of the car. (I can't believe Nellie fell for that, but she went along.) I was so grateful for Bess's heroic actions. If it hadn't been for Bess hiding in the backseat and then hurling that cake plate, I'd probably be history now, and Hilda would have gone on to greener pastures. As it is, Hilda is now serving a life sentence in the state penitentiary for women, with no chance of parole.

By the way, Mama's Fostoria cake plate wasn't damaged when Bess threw it at Hilda's gun. We've now given it a place of honor on the sideboard between Mama's Nippon vase and Bess's dearly departed mother-in-law's cut glass lemonade pitcher.

Bess has been slightly disgruntled about our business's future ever since our last big case involving Hilda Hawkins and Foy Jackson. She decided that we should take a vote as to whether to continue our not-so-lucrative business, The B and B Investigative Services. Earlier, we had taken a reluctant Vonion in as a silent partner, but I decided not to allow him to vote, knowing full well he would have voted to terminate all future business. Bess and I cast the only two votes. As you probably have already figured, it was a tie—one vote to continue business and one vote to retire permanently. Since I was the founding member, I decided that my vote should count fifty-one percent and Bess's, forty-nine.

Of course, Bess was appalled with the outcome of the vote and complained that I had railroaded the whole voting process...but...thankfully, we're still in business!

Since our vote, I've encouraged Bess to become our one and only major stockholder. We needed a little money in our business kitty to pay for extra shoes and stockings and other items that are necessary for us to remain the good detectives that we have become. And she actually fell for it and contributed twenty dollars!

It's been over four months since we investigated Richard's murder, and business has almost trickled to a complete stop; however, thanks to Mrs. Ricketson's sticky fingers we have solved one small case since then. Thelma hired us to figure out who the low-down thief was who was stealing the fingernail polish from her display case in the Cut and Curl. It really didn't require much deductive thinking. It was none other than the illustrious Mrs. Ricketson up to her old tricks again.

Bess and I made up a flimsy excuse about wanting to get Mrs. Ricketson's late mother's cucumber pickle recipe, and we went calling on her. As Bess and I were chatting in the living room with Mrs. Ricketson about the exact proportions of sugar, salt, vinegar, and spices to mix for the pickle brine, I asked to be excused to go to the bathroom. Of course, that was the perfect opportunity to case the rest of Mrs. Ricketson's house. I easily found a large stash of Fire Engine Red, Flaming Flamingo Maroon,

Hot Pink Passion, and Tango-Mango Orange fingernail polish neatly lined on a shelf in her bathroom closet.

Thelma was so outraged with our findings that she hastily decided to prosecute Mrs. Ricketson, but eventually relented. Thelma unwaveringly told Mrs. Ricketson that if she caught her lifting one more item from her shop, she was gonna put a big ad in *The Reporter and Farmer* newspaper telling everyone in town about Mrs. Ricketson's illegal activities. How embarrassing for Mrs. Ricketson! I wish Mrs. Ricketson would learn her lesson, once and for all, but I imagine she won't. That is, not until Mr. Lawson plants her permanently in the ground under six feet of dirt and a heavy slab of concrete. And then there's always the off chance that she might lift some artificial flowers or a cardboard fan or two from the funeral home on her way out to the cemetery.

Of course, Bess and I would accept no monetary compensation from Thelma for our time and energy spent solving her mystery. Thelma suggested that she reward us by giving us both the works: coloring, permanent waves, trims, whatever we desired. We were thrilled! What a treat! I've decided that I want a whole new look.

Now, do I prefer ash blond or ravishing red?

The summer days had become long and hot. The butterbeans in the garden needed picking, our roses needed pruning, and the ironing was mounting up. The daylily bed could have used a good weeding, and the cucumbers were waiting to be pickled. (We were leaning toward using Mrs. Ricketson's late mother's recipe.) To top it all off, it was Bess's and my turn to place yard flowers in the church sanctuary this coming Sunday. There was so much to be done and not enough hours in the day to get it all done.

Bess and I were worn-out from the morning's activities and had decided to take a quick, five minute break from our chores. "And only five minutes," Bess had said in her most authoritative voice. It was early afternoon, and we were relaxing on the front porch, deciding which task we should tackle next. I sighed deeply, as Bess handed me a glass of her freshly squeezed lemonade.

"Why don't we wait to pick the butterbeans until later this afternoon after it cools down?" I unenthusiastically said, after my first long swig of lemonade. "Ora Lee said she'd help shell them in the morning. But I suppose we really do need to start washing the canning jars in a few minutes." I held the frosty glass of lemonade against my forehead. "It is so-o hot today. I just don't know where all my energy escaped to. Oh, I do dread bending over those butterbean bushes."

"It's got to be done," Bess half-heartedly answered, as she reached for the Lawson Funeral Home fan on the table between us. "Maybe Vonion will help us if we ask him nicely."

"I doubt that. You know he thinks picking butterbeans is beneath his dignity and, anyway, he's busy digging the last of the potatoes."

The telephone in the hall rang, two rings—one long, one short. "That's us, Bess. Just sit tight and I'll answer it." I wearily stood and walked into the hall.

A few minutes later, I raced back to the porch with my heart beating wildly, my dress tail flying, and the car keys clutched in my sweaty hand. "Bess, that was Vernon. Sheriff Ledbetter's waiting for us down at the river behind Earl's place, and he needs our help with another BIG case! Earl found a dead body in the river lodged against a log with what looks to be a bullet hole in its back. The sheriff told Vernon that the victim looks familiar, but he's not really sure who it is. Now hurry up! You can drink your lemonade in the car. We've got to go, and there's not a minute to waste!"

"But what about the butterbeans?" Bess quickly asked.

"Are you gonna let a few butterbeans come between us and the crime world?" I excitedly asked as I grabbed Bess's arm and pulled her down the porch steps.